RETRIBUTION

To my neighbors,
Carita & John Christiansen
1/30/17
Enjoy!

RETRIBUTION

A Story
of
Domestic Abuse

GERALD BULLOCK

ISBN: Softcover   978-1-4836-2612-3
             Ebook   978-1-4836-2613-0

Rev. date: 07/18/2013

To order additional copies of this book, contact:
Xlibris LLC
1-888-795-4274
www.Xlibris.com
Orders@Xlibris.com
128559

*To Brenda, who was able to escape her abuser
and flee to the freedom of a faraway state*

*And to Janet, who could not escape her abuser in life
but finally found freedom in death*

And to all their sisters

They'll take your soul if you let them ...
Oh, yeah, but don't you ...
Let them!

—James Taylor, "You've Got a Friend"

TABLE OF CONTENTS

PROLOGUE

SHE BARELY REMEMBERED HER MOTHER

She barely remembered her mother, being a mere babe when they were separated. She didn't even know if her mother was dead or alive. But she didn't really miss her. It's hard to miss someone when you were separated from her at such an early age that you don't even remember her.

Her mother didn't exactly take her to the woods and drop her off. She was just there, and then she was gone. The little one didn't even realize that her mother was gone, until later. She looked for her and got turned around in the woods and then just crawled into a tree hollow and sat, as if in a trance. She didn't know how to get food or water and now had no example to follow. She must learn on her own or starve to death. After a rough and hungry start, she finally learned to get by, barely, on whatever she could find or catch.

She had only been in the woods for about a week when the big storm came. At first the sky darkened as the clouds gathered. Then it began to rain, and the drops got larger and larger and fell harder and harder. She climbed a tree to escape from the rising ground water and hid in the crook of a large tree that had been badly damaged by a previous lightning bolt. At the height of the rainstorm, the lightning started and then the winds. The tree she had climbed swayed in the winds, almost hurling her to the ground several times.

The damaged tree limb continued to sway in an ever-widening arc with the increasing winds. Finally, with a large gust, the damaged tree limb passed its point of no return and came crashing to the ground. The little one was thrown to the ground but still wasn't safe. A broken branch fell on one of her legs, pinning her to the ground. She might have drowned in the cold rain water, but luckily she fell in an area of ground that was slightly higher, and the water had not pooled there yet. She was trapped there throughout the rest of the storm, unable to free her damaged leg from the large branch. Finally, after hours of working and seeing the leg move just a little at a time, she was able to get her injured leg free. Afterward, it had finally healed but was grotesquely twisted and useless. Now getting food was even more difficult and more dangerous.

She was at the mercy not only of the weather but also the predators who inhabit the woods. Not being trained in the ways of the wild, her imagination made every shadow and every noise feel threatening, whether or not harm was intended. At first, she simply ran the opposite direction whenever she heard a noise or saw a shadow across her path.

But finally she found a limb large enough for her to sit on comfortably, where she not only hid from her enemies but also became the predator of even smaller creatures. She rapidly learned the law of the wild, at least the law of survival. In the woods, everyone is both predator and prey. Every being is somebody's prey, but every being is also somebody's predator. Every creature is prey to those larger and stronger, but every creature is also predator to those smaller and weaker.

Then one day the big person came to the forest. She sat on a log and looked at something strange that she held in her hands. Every few minutes she turned a sheet of the thing, seeming to look forward to each portion the same as the last. The little one had never seen a book before and found it curious. She found it odd that such a thing held the big person's attention so completely when there were all the sounds and colors of the forest, which seemed so much more interesting. Then the big person saw her and got up, coming toward her. She seemed to want to catch her. The little one ducked under a pile of leaves, but she was hindered by her broken leg, and the big person kicked the pile of leaves, leaving her lying there, exposed and vulnerable. She had nowhere to run, especially with her injured leg.

She was scared at first; all she saw and heard were strange noises and strange shadows from something that loomed over her like a giant. The big person made noises in a language she didn't understand. The little one tried to run, to get away from the terrible giant, but a foot which seemed at the moment to be larger than her own entire world was thrown out in front of her, and the giant scooped her up into a blanket and carried her away from her familiar forest. She took her to her home and threw her, still wrapped in her blanket, in the corner of a screened-in porch. She went inside the house and left her there in the dark.

Since that day, the little one had lived in that dark corner of the big person's screened-in porch, sleeping under the white wicker chaise lounge and waiting for food. There was no source of food or water on the porch, so she became completely dependent on the big person for her survival. Without the big person, she surely would have died.

When the big person came out on the porch each evening, she usually brought food and threw it into the corner. That is, on a good day this happened. Days frequently passed, however, when the big person failed to bring her any food at all, and she just sat under the chaise lounge and waited—maybe tomorrow. On some days, she never even came out on the porch at all.

The little one was completely unable to leave and completely at the mercy of the big person. With her bad leg and the screened-in porch, she had no escape route even if she had some place to go or the nerve to try.

On this particular evening, she waited patiently. What else could she do? Even though the big person had saved her life, the little one was still a prisoner. Tonight, she could see that there was a light on in the house. Usually, the light meant there would be something—some morsel at least, to hold her over for a day or so. She watched from the safety of the wicker lounger. She was about to give up, when at last, the door opened and the big person came stomping out onto the porch.

The little one peeked out from under the wicker chaise, still afraid to venture out onto the open floor of the porch. Her time in the forest had taught her that you could never be sure there wasn't a predator lurking in the shadows.

The big person came directly over to the chaise and threw some small morsels of food under the chair. The first two went careening off into the corner of the room, but the third caught firmly in the little one's web, and she jumped forward and began spinning the fly with her two front legs, holding it in place with the second pair.

At first, the fly flapped its wings and legs furiously, trying to escape the sticky fibers of the almost invisible web. But as it spun, the web ropes became tighter and tighter until any movement became futile. When the brilliant little yellow and black garden spider had completely immobilized the fly, she stopped and bit deeply into its thorax, injecting venom which would not kill it but would render it completely paralyzed, unable to move or even to attempt to escape. She could then eat it at her leisure, sucking the fly's body fluids while it was alive and fresh.

The big lady squatted down and watched this circle of life for a few minutes. The fly gradually died, its life fluids blending with those of the spider. One life given up for another, not with any gesture of goodness or kindness and neither in a gesture of evil or bad but simply cogs in the wheels of nature. I must live so you must die. If you don't die, I can't live. Then the big person got up and walked back into the house where she would await her own predator and the next phase of her own fate.

CHAPTER 1

THE OVEN BUZZER WENT OFF

T'he oven buzzer went off for the third time at 12:15 a.m. Felicia Jernigan washed her hands before she handled any of the food she was preparing. She just couldn't stand the idea of touching a live fly, but when she made a pet of the small injured garden spider, she was able to get past her revulsion like a young mother does after her first few diaper changes. *A girl's gotta do what a girl's gotta do*, she thought, using one of her mother's favorite sayings. And if you take on a pet spider, you have to get past getting sick at your stomach at feeding time. But you still wash your hands, and occasionally you have to cover your mouth while your stomach complains and tries to empty itself.

She had learned to stun a fly by popping it with the tail of her dishcloth. That way, she could feed her pet spider live food. At first the only way she could feed it was with dead flies, squished by the fly swatter. Then, with a little practice she could knock a moth or fly out of the air with the tail of the cloth. Finally, she was able to get a live fly about one out of every three tries.

Now, though, she had to change her role from that of feeding a live fly to her pet garden spider to preparing food for her husband. She smiled to herself as she thought of the eerie similarity between feeding flies to the spider on her porch to preparing food for the insect she had married.

She took her third pan of homemade rolls out of the oven and put them in her bread warmer, covering them with a barely damp towel. Preserved this way, they would stay fresh for a while. The first two pans had dried out over the span of the evening, and she had tossed them in the trash. Craig was frequently late, and he always insisted on oven-fresh, warm homemade bread, no matter what time he got home. After a couple of hours in a warmer, the bread lost its freshness, and she knew he wouldn't like it. She had learned that it was better to throw out the two-hour-old bread and bake another pan than to take a chance on serving Craig stale bread.

He had ordered lasagna for that evening. It was lucky for her since this could be kept fresh easily, and Craig got home late so often that she never knew when to expect him. She checked the lasagna, in the microwave on the lowest intermittent keep-warm setting. The towel covering it was still a little damp, and it was still okay.

She had long ago given up on trying to serve steak even though it was the favorite of both herself and Craig. It was impossible to keep it edible, much less tasty, for very long after it is grilled. The excellent filet mignon, which he had ordered online, carefully seasoned, marinated, and grilled to perfection with singed edges and pink center, morphs into a less than mediocre tough roast after only a couple of rewarmings in the microwave. Felicia knew that from experience; she knew better than to try to serve Craig a tough steak.

The salad in the refrigerator was still crisp but wouldn't be for much longer. She had even remembered not to put the ice in the glasses yet. She was a fast learner. It only took once, serving Craig drinks that were watered down by stale ice, to know never to do that again. She would fill the glasses with ice when she heard him come in the front door and not a second before. The table was set, and the candles were ready to be lighted. She listened to the soft mood music while she waited. So far, so good.

Felicia wanted this to be a perfect meal; in fact, it had to be perfect. She didn't think she could stand another episode like the last one, when the rolls had been rewarmed and chewy. It had taken her two hours to clean up the mess in the kitchen, and the bruises had kept her inside for a week.

Today, she had taken extra time to be sure everything was perfect. She had carefully applied her makeup and had gone to the bathroom mirror to check it several times. She had bathed early in the afternoon and put on the grey miniskirt with the red flower pattern, which Craig seemed to like so much. She had done her hair in his favorite French roll and wore his favorite perfume. Now she went back to the bathroom one more time, to make sure her makeup hadn't smudged while she cooked and rewarmed dinner. It hadn't. Everything was still perfect. If only Craig would get home, she would show him she could fix a perfect meal.

Felicia had always been proud of her looks. Five feet four inches tall and 118 pounds, she had worked to keep her figure after college. And she had succeeded. Her long dark hair topped off her beauty, and she still had the picture-perfect looks of the college cheerleader that she once was.

She was realistic about her looks though; she realized they had been a major asset, even in childhood. They had helped her to be successful in dance classes and later to be chosen for student council and yearbook staff. More importantly, they had helped her to land Craig. She was intelligent, and well above average in looks, but she had never had enough self-confidence. She had special skills in music, playing both the violin and the piano, and was in the high school concert orchestra. But she berated herself, needing constant reassurance that she was not only adequate but exceptional.

She took as much pride in her home as she did in her own looks. Their single-story home in Lewisville was always spotless. She had decorated it herself. She had chosen the furniture herself and had even made wall decorations from her favorite craft store. She shopped at antique stores, flea markets, and even garage sales and had a knack for finding inexpensive small pieces that seemed to highlight her own furniture perfectly. She had always had a knack for home decoration anyway, *so why spend Craig's hard-earned money for professional advice that she might not even like anyway*, she thought. Even in college, her girl friends were envious of her ability to make her dorm room attractive on her limited budget.

Sometimes she would spend an entire day shopping, often without even a purse or a checkbook, aimlessly wandering, not thinking, not even feeling. In the back of her mind was always the realization, though, that she must get back well before Craig, early enough to get everything ready for him.

Craig rarely complimented his wife on her housekeeping or cooking, but at work he bragged about her. He had trained her well; he knew that he could bring a business guest home for dinner even at the last minute and frequently did. He knew she would never embarrass him with a messy or unclean house. He knew she had certainly better not, at least.

The couple had met at the University of Texas. She was a sophomore music major, and he was a junior in business and journalism. Both were hard workers. She played keyboard and sang with the Outfit, a small country and western band, at a night spot called the Corral. She also taught private piano lessons in children's homes when her schedule allowed.

Craig was two years older but only one year ahead in school. He was trying to get a business and journalism degree but had difficulty with several classes his first and second year, so would graduate at least one or two years late. Both not only worked hard but partied hard, frequently staying out until well after midnight. Felicia was still able to keep her grades up in spite of an active evening life, but Craig frequently missed classes after a long night out and never made higher than a C+.

They met at Craig's fraternity, at an end-of-year toga party. They were immediately attracted to each other and, after an evening of beer and partying, spent the night together in his room at the frat house. Their relationship never seemed to falter. They moved into a duplex together two weeks later and were married after only a year, the summer after her junior year.

All their friends agreed that Craig and Felicia were perfect for each other. They seemed to thrive on each other's company and gradually limited their social contacts. Eventually, they only kept company with each other, to the exclusion of all their prior friends. They no longer seemed to need the parties or the alcohol. With the change in her social life, Felicia became more serious about school, and her grades went from her usual B's to a mix of A's and B's. Even Craig's grades picked up considerably. Never a good student, he at least began to attend all his classes and never received less than a C on another final grade. They would graduate together, it seemed.

Midway during their senior year, a brawl broke out at the Corral while Felicia's band was playing, and Craig insisted that she quit her job with the group. It just wasn't safe there anymore, he decided. She had been teaching piano in children's homes anyway, to supplement her support from her mother and was making enough money with that to get along.

Later, Craig convinced her that it would be safer to get a piano at home and let the children come to her instead. That way, he said, children who didn't have a piano at home could take lessons. It seemed to make sense. Their duplex neighbors both worked evenings, so the noise wouldn't be a problem. So Felicia shopped the *Green Sheet*, a weekly free personal for-sale paper, until she found exactly what she wanted and bought a ten-year-old used spinet piano for less than half what she would have paid for it in any store.

Craig took a job at Chaparral Cafe, a steak house on Sixteenth Avenue, with its reputation for having some of the best steaks in town. He only made minimum wage, but he could triple that with tips and avoid the taxes as well. He had a ten-year-old Chevy Malibu that he had received as a high school graduation gift. It was anything but cool, but it was dependable. Now, with Felicia working at home, they only needed one car. Craig suggested they sell his Malibu and keep Felicia's newer Mustang. They had both been gifts, so they were both paid off and her newer Mustang was still in warranty. The Chevy brought enough to pay for the piano and furniture for the duplex.

Craig used the Mustang after that to commute to school and to the restaurant every evening. With the sale of his older car, Felicia no longer had her own transportation and gradually came to stay at home, eventually depending on Craig even for most of her errands and shopping. Since they lived near campus, she walked to her classes or rode a bicycle. Except for classes three days a week, then, she was then essentially homebound.

On the surface, their relationship seemed to be everything you would want. But gradually, Craig seemed to become more tense, to open up less in talking with Felicia, and to spend a lot of time staring at the television like he was in a daze. He also began calling at various times of the day, for no reason. Felicia sensed that something was amiss, but tried not to let it get to her.

During the summer after his junior year, Craig worked as a cub reporter for the local Guardian Press, a weekly sheet specializing in local social news and paying for itself through small business advertisements and want ads. Mostly, he covered fishing contests, county fairs, and parades. It wasn't much, but it was experience in the business and a way to get a journalism credit on his curriculum vitae. And he did enjoy the work more than he had the drudgery of the steak house.

After graduation, with his new degree in journalism and a little field experience, Craig started the task of finding a full-time job where he could use the training. After six months of sporadic interviews and keeping the wolf off the door with the Guardian Press job, he was able to land a position as police reporter with the *Lewisville Journal*, about forty miles north of Dallas and about ten miles from his mother-in-law. It would require a move but not too far, and it looked like a good place to start a family.

The *Journal* was a real newspaper, not just a private, struggling neighborhood sheet like the Guardian Press. He felt like he was making progress.

With their limited finances, they were able to buy a small home in nearby La Vista, where a real estate dollar carried more weight. Craig had a knack for reporting and rapidly developed a reputation among the *Journal* reporters. Even the police liked him; frequently he could get information when others had failed. Life looked good.

Now, Craig was about eighteen months into his new position as police reporter for the *Journal*. His long-range goal, of course, was a job with a major metropolitan newspaper. He had written a couple of fairly good articles that had been picked up by the UPI. He was trying hard to get his reputation developed.

Just six months earlier, he and a college buddy, now a narcotics squad detective with Dallas Police Dept., had written an article on drug trafficking in the Dallas and surrounding metropolitan area. The report had resulted in arrests and imprisonment of several local small-time dealers who were active in Lewisville, and had helped to establish him as a serious, if inexperienced, investigative reporter.

But as all reporters learn, he felt he had to watch his backside. Certainly there was no love lost between him and the rough elements of the drug trade. But although the offers from major papers had failed to materialize so far, he didn't mind too badly. He felt that he was paying his dues, and he would get his big chance eventually.

It was after-midnight now, and Felicia began to worry. Craig should have been home by at least seven. Although he sometimes had to work late because of an unexpected crisis, he rarely worked past 6:00 p.m. She tried to have dinner ready by six-fifteen every day, so if he came in a little early, it would be ready. But now it was after midnight, and he still wasn't home. It was common for him to be late, but this was much later than he had ever been before.

She was beginning to worry. Had something happened to him?

Or was he just testing her again?

CHAPTER 2

ELLIE CONLIN HAD ALWAYS BEEN . . .

Ellie Conlin had always been a serious student, making excellent grades until spring break her senior year in high school when she got pregnant on a skiing trip to Snow Mass. She was almost three months pregnant when she graduated, hiding her small baby bump under her loose dress and graduation gown. Only her closest friends knew about the pregnancy. She had even been able to hide it from her mother until a few weeks after graduation. Thank goodness for loose sweaters.

Her boy friend was a leather-jacketed motorcycle mechanic who had dropped out of high school two years ago, six months before his graduation. When he learned of his impending fatherhood, he panicked. At first he just stayed quiet and didn't come around as much, but after about three months he left town. He decided he wasn't into Ellie as much as he thought, and certainly wasn't into marriage and teen parenthood. He had found a construction job in Louisiana, and simply rode off in the night on his bike. Ellie never heard from him again. Felicia Conlin was born Christmas morning, 1965.

After graduation, Ellie worked at various waitress and secretarial jobs to support self and baby but was determined to go to college. Then two years after high school graduation—with a combination of loans, grants, and part-time work—she was able to start at Central Community College, just a few miles from home. After three years getting two years of credit at CCC, she transferred to North Texas State University in Denton in September 1968,

7

majoring in premed and English. Four years later, she graduated with honors. Little Lisha-Lou, as she fondly called her daughter, was then eight years old.

Ellie worked for a year after graduation from North Texas, substitute teaching in third grade in McKinney, Texas. She started to medical school at the University of Texas Medical Branch in Galveston, September 1975. She made excellent grades, especially in pathology, and even worked in the Galveston County Medical Examiner's office between semesters.

After her graduation in May 1980, she stayed at UTMB for a rotating internship and a family practice residency. She was able to moonlight a few extra hours in the ME's office during the residency to supplement the small salary the Galveston house staff received. She never partied or dated. Her life consisted of her residency, her part-time job, and her daughter.

During Mom's medical school and residency, Felicia attended public schools in Galveston. She was never very interested in her mom's medical studies, at least certainly not for herself. Instead, she loved music and liked to perform for groups. By the time she was a junior at Ball High, she was singing and playing keyboard for an amateur high school band. Although they were young, The Islanders sometimes got paid for playing at school parties and a few private functions. Felicia finished Ball High in 1984, the same spring that Ellie completed her residency. Mother and daughter graduated less than two weeks apart. Not only were they mother and daughter, but the closest of friends.

The two took a month off after their graduations for a much-needed and even more-deserved vacation in Florida. Neither had ever been to Disney World, and it was the icing on the cake of their graduations.

Ellie opened a private practice in Richardson, a man-made bedroom community about thirty miles north of Dallas, on I-45. Felicia stayed in Galveston for the summer after high school graduation to play with her group, and left for Austin in August to start college at the University of Texas. Ellie was happy with that choice: a good school, close enough but not too close. Of course, Ellie helped her move into the dorm. Tears, but good tears, the kind a woman doesn't feel bad about shedding.

Ellie had never married, at least not to a man. She was not gay but simply had no use for men. She had been burned once, badly, so instead of marrying, she wedded herself to her medical career. She had always been mother, friend, and confidant to her daughter, at least until the last six months. Even before, over the past year, she had noticed a change in her daughter. She had become somewhat withdrawn and rarely visited or called anymore.

Felicia had lost a few pounds, and Ellie wondered if she was depressed. She had never used drugs, but it was no secret that there was a period in college when she had really liked alcohol, and her mother wondered if she was having that kind of a problem. She had only skirted the issue a couple of times on the phone though, asking the generic, "how's the marriage going?"

Felicia hadn't seemed to want to talk about it, so her mother hadn't pushed the issue. Her daughter would talk to her about it when she was ready if there was even a problem in the first place. She was probably imagining it anyway, she thought: a typical yuppie Mom, trying to make sure her kid has a perfect life (protect her from the stresses of life that made a woman out of you).

More recently, no matter how she tried to communicate, she couldn't seem to make a connection with her daughter. Her once outgoing, happy daughter seemed to have lost interest in anything related to her mother and even in things in general. So they gradually drifted apart and had barely spoken for several months.

CHAPTER 3

FELICIA'S PROBLEMS WITH CRAIG . . .

Felicia's problems with Craig had begun gradually, almost imperceptibly. Craig did most of their shopping, and she was usually able to get to her classes at the University on the bike Ellie had given her for her fifteenth birthday. After Craig sold his car and Felicia quit working for the Outfit, there seemed to be little other reason for her to leave the duplex.

Over the months, Craig had begun to develop a jealousy of any telephone calls Felicia received, of any visits by repairmen, and even of the rare errands which might force her to leave the duplex. At first she was completely honest with him, telling him of any visits by repairman or delivery boy as he asked. But as his jealousy increased and his criticisms became more severe, she began to feel that she needed to protect herself from his verbal assaults. She was confused; she had never given him any reason to question her love or loyalty for him.

Craig had become more and more jealous over the months after graduation, and the once sweet love he had for Felicia was spoiled by his accusations and bitterness. It seemed to get worse as he tried unsuccessfully to get a full-time reporting job. He began to imagine any telephone call to be from an unknown paramour. If she received this many calls while he was home, how many more must she be getting while he is at work?

The frequent dinnertime sales pitches from telemarketers fed the fires of his fury, especially after he had a couple of drinks. He refused to answer the telephone himself; that was the wife's job. But when a call came in, he sulked and accused her of infidelity. As the jealousy and accusations increased, Felicia began to hide things from him. When the telephone rang, it was automatically from her mother. The white lies seemed her only protection from his accusations.

Finally, he had landed the *Journal* job. Felicia hoped that the new job and the move to a new location would help their relationship. And in fact, it did . . . for a while anyway.

Even though he liked his new job, and things were looking up, they still didn't have much money, so they made the move from the Austin duplex to the single story house in La Vista in a rental truck with a couple of dollies. It was about eleven miles from his work, but for a once-a-day trip that didn't seem too bad. It seemed a perfect place, and Felicia looked forward to adding her own touches to the décor.

Even though she worried about Craig's tension and slowly developing jealousy, she never worried about him ever becoming physically violent. It just didn't seem in his nature. She had never seen him strike out physically; even in their bar-hopping days when fights were common, he was always able to keep his cool. Once, when an actual fight broke out, he grabbed her hand and led her outside to the car. He seemed to want to avoid any physical conflict and even more wanted to protect his wife.

One evening, just a month after their fourth anniversary, the daily barrage from telemarketers was unusually bothersome. Already upset from a bad day at work, Craig became even angrier when the first call interrupted their dinner. He had stopped for drinks after work and had already downed two more beers before sitting down to dinner.

"Your boy friend calling again?" he asked through a mouthful of meat loaf and mashed potatoes. "Can't he get my schedule down straight? I'm always home this time of the day."

"You know better than that. I can't keep these people from calling. That was from some long distance company, wanting us to change services."

"Yeah, I'll bet!" He went back to eating but was sulking.

After only a few minutes, the phone rang again. "Hello, Jernigan residence," Felicia answered.

The person on the phone was doing a marketing survey, she said. "This is not a good time to call," responded Felicia. "We're eating dinner." Immediately she realized that in front of Craig that was the wrong answer.

"Hang up the damn phone!" Craig ordered. "He can call you tomorrow when I'm at work! You need to tell him my hours so he won't call when I'm here!"

Felicia replaced the receiver. "You know I don't have any boyfriend. You know I haven't seen anybody but you since the very first day we met. Where do you get such an idea?" The inside corners of her eyes were beginning to be filled with the tears which would begin to spill over her cheeks shortly.

"Sure you haven't! I believe that like I believe I'm gonna get the Pulitzer fuckin' prize next year! You can't fool me! You're too much of a hot pants to just sit at home on your pretty little ass all day twiddling your thumbs while your husband is out busting his butt trying to support you in style! You don't fool me a minute!"

As luck would have it, the third telemarketing call interrupted their argument. When he heard the phone ring, Craig jumped from his chair. "Keep your seat! It's my turn! I'll tell that son of a bitch where to get off . . . Hello!"

"Hello! This is . . ."

When a man's voice answered, Craig went ballistic. "I know who you are, you bastard! Don't you ever call here again!"

His face had reddened and the vein on his forehead stood out like it wanted to burst. He seemed possessed. His muscles bulged under his tee shirt. A bead of perspiration began to glisten on the thinning area above his brow. He jerked the phone receiver hard, and the wall unit came loose and fell loudly to the tile floor. He rushed toward Felicia, pushing her out of her chair onto the floor. She fell hard, striking her elbow first on the edge of the table and then on the hard floor. She grabbed at the table, trying to catch her balance, but only caught the edge of the red plaid place mat. It came with her, pulling her dinner, silverware, and glass of wine on top of her. The glass broke when it hit the right side of her head, cutting deeply just above her ear. Craig stood over her with clenched fists. "I told you I'd find out! He can't call here every night and get away with it!" But as he started to strike her with the back of his hand, he saw the bright red blood, flowing freely onto her shoulder and blouse. He was shocked by the amount of blood from the cut over her ear and was stopped in his tracks.

"Oh my god! I'm sorry! Oh my god! You're bleeding! Oh my god! Oh Lisha! What have I done? I didn't mean it! Oh my god!"

He rushed to find something to put over her ear to stop the bleeding. The first thing he found was paper towels. He wadded up a handful and pressed it over her ear. It seemed to slow down the flow of blood but didn't stop it completely.

"We've got to get you to the emergency room! You're gonna need stitches. My god, I'm sorry! I don't know what came over me. I'm so sorry! Oh, god, I'm sorry!" The shock of the fresh blood seemed to have the same sobering effect on him that four cups of coffee might have had. The previous slur in his voice seemed to disappear immediately.

Felicia accepted his apology, trying to accept for the moment that it indeed was an unintended accident. In his contrition, he helped her into her car, all the time expressing his ever-lasting love. He replaced the paper towels that had become bloodstained with a clean white terry cloth towel, taking care not to get any blood on the soft tan leather upholstery.

The trip to the nearest Medical Center doc-in-a-box was only a seven-minute ride, and for once Craig stayed within the speed limit. He knew police had been patrolling I-45 and didn't want to be delayed by a speeding ticket. Especially considering his DUI three months ago, which he had carefully kept secret from Felicia. If he was stopped again, he would have to explain the DUI to her, and he might even be arrested. That would be just what he needed! *If it's not one thing, it's three others,"* he thought.

"It just occurred to me, what are we gonna tell them at the emergency room? I sure don't want some nosy nurse to know we were arguing. It'd be hot gossip. What are we gonna tell them?" Craig asked, meaning, of course, what are *you* gonna tell them.

"Don't worry. I'll just tell them I knocked a glass out of the cabinet cleaning. I won't spoil your nice, clean reputation," she said with a cynical smirk. But Craig was still worried. He knew how ER gossip spread. He should know; it was his business to help spread it.

They pulled into the doc-in-a-box minor emergency pavilion of La Vista Medical, Craig frantically honking the horn for help. The bleeding had stopped, though, and the triage nurse seemed perturbed that he was so anxious about what seemed to be a minor injury. Felicia was wheel-chaired into a minor surgery room while Craig was told to go to the patient registration office to fill out forms.

"Can't I stay with her?" he asked.

"You can come on back as soon as you sign the papers. We'll take real good care of her while you're gone!" The triage nurse was a very large and very black woman, about fifty years old, with a threatening demeanor if you're on her wrong side but the very picture of protection and kindness to the unfortunate victims she cared for. She wore a dark blue scrub shirt and pants over white sneakers.

The black leather fanny pack hanging loosely over her right hip served as a holster for her protruding bandage scissors, just like Roy Rogers's leather holster had served for his six-guns for so many years. Her burgundy stethoscope hung from around her neck, labeled "McCarty" in the small white letter cubes strung on a baby anklet that the newborn nursery used to identify its wards and that the nurses used to make their own personal ID tags. It projected a stark contrast against her dark wrist. Her image to Craig told him that he would be wise not to press the issue with her too strongly.

She turned then to Felicia, who had stopped bleeding but was still very bloody. She had seen countless abused women in the emergency room and was immediately suspicious. Her persona, threatening to Craig, became kind, soft and protective to Felicia. "Now, young lady, tell me what happened to that pretty face of yours?" she asked.

Craig fidgeted apprehensively while Felicia recited her carefully prepared story. He nervously walked the two steps to her side, expecting McCarty at any moment to throw him out the front door or to pound him into the floor. He cautiously put an arm around his wife's shoulder as she answered the nurse's questions.

"Oh, stupid me!" Felicia seemed almost cheerful, but falsely so, in her attempt to cover what had really happened. "I forgot I had just mopped the kitchen floor and was trying to get a glass off the top shelf of the cabinet. I guess I just slipped on a wet spot on the floor. Anyway, the next thing I knew I was on the floor. I must have pulled a glass out of the cabinet. It hit me and broke on my head. It bled like crazy, but we got it stopped with a bunch of paper towels. How does it look?"

"It's pretty clean. It isn't bleeding anymore."

"Will I need stitches?" Felicia asked.

Craig was relieved to hear her story, and knowing he would be able to duplicate it when he was asked the same questions, he reluctantly left the emergency room, insurance card in hand. He seemed to want to loiter outside the door but was ill at ease, so he slowly walked on down the hall toward registration.

After Craig was well out of hearing range, McCarty pulled the door closed and sat on the rolling stool by the examination table, close to Felicia, almost whispering. "Okay, honey, you can be honest with me. How'd you really get hurt? This 'pulled the glass out of the cabinet' story sounds like a load of bull to me."

Felicia became indignant. "What do you mean? I'm telling the truth! What makes you think I'm lying? You have no right!" Tears began to pool again in the corners of her eyes. They weren't spilling yet but looked like they would any minute.

"Now, don't get your dander up! If I'm wrong, I'm sorry. But Old Nurse McCarty has been around for several dozen trips around the sun, and she has seen lots of girls get hurt real bad before they wise up and tell somebody about their problems. I've been around enough to get a sense about these things, and the look in your eyes tells me you're having some trouble that you're not quite ready to talk about yet."

Felicia began to cry softly while she still resisted McCarty's suspicions. "You let me alone and just do your job! There's nothing going on! I'm telling the truth. Just get the doctor in here to stitch me up and leave me alone!"

"Listen, hon, don't get upset. But you should see the terrible things we see here every day. Some scared li'l thing just like you comes in, busted up, won't tell us what's happening, and we can't do a thing for her till she comes clean. Then when she comes back in here later, she's really hurt. Broken bones, busted face, you name it. Once in a while, even DOA. I just don't want to see something like that."

"Nothing's going on! I told you what happened. Just leave me alone! Either get the doctor in here and leave me alone or I'm walking out of here!"

"Okay, you win. But just remember, in this business, sometimes, if you're lyin', you're dyin'!" But McCarty suspected that Felicia's almost hysterical reaction indicated a deeper fear that Craig would find out and she would be in even worse trouble than she was now.

"*Soundeth to me like she doth protesteth too mucheth,*" McCarty mused to herself, smiling subconsciously at the mental game she frequently used to take her own pressure off. Otherwise, sending women back out to get hurt and maybe killed would be more than she could stand.

Felicia realized at the same time that her reaction was too extreme. If she wanted them to think she wasn't lying, maybe she needed to back off. "Really, I understand you're just trying to help. God knows what kind of stuff you nurses must see here in the emergency room. But really, I'm telling the truth. It was just a silly accident. Nothing's going on between my husband and me. We love each other very much. But I really do appreciate your concern. It's good to know there are people like you that want to help women in trouble. But I'm not one of those women, you can believe me."

McCarty studied Felicia's expressions, especially her eyes. *Now me thinketh she goeth the other wayeth too mucheth*, she thought. *I'd better keepeth my eyes open for her. She'll be back. But there's not a damn thing I can doeth about it in the meantime.* She opened her fanny pack and handed Felicia a card for the Women's Shelter, with a twenty-four-hour hotline number for women in trouble.

"Here, hon. If you don't need this, maybe you know somebody who does. But keep it handy, would you, just in case. And you remember, if and when you're ready to get some help, you come call me."

On his way back from patient registration, Craig stopped at a pay phone in the hallway between ER and radiology and ordered a dozen yellow roses, Felicia's favorite, to be delivered the next morning. When he returned to the ER, Dr. Ron Price had arrived and was putting drapes over her scalp. He had already shaved and prepped the small area just over her ear.

The surgical light caused a bright golden glow on the betadine-painted area. The odor of alcohol and betadine scrub permeated the room, and Craig felt nauseated, almost like he might faint. Hospitals, clinics, emergency rooms always reminded him of standing in line as a first grader, waiting for the mean old nurse to stick his arm for some dumb immunization shot and always made him think he was about to pass out. Thank goodness he hadn't. At least not yet.

The doctor looked up at him questioningly as he entered the door. The bleeding had stopped. "I'm Dr. Price. You Mr. Jernigan?" He looked suspiciously at Craig but didn't make any comment about his suspicions. McCarty had already briefed him while Craig was in admissions filling out papers.

"Yeah. Glad to know you," Craig answered as he took Felicia's right hand in his own and sat on the rolling stool the nurse provided for him. He appeared for all purposes to be the loving husband, just wanting to be there for his wife. Price, though, suspected otherwise. But he felt unable to say anything, knowing that McCarty had already been through it with Felicia.

Price began to inject the lidocaine to anesthetize the area for suturing. "Sorry for the giant bee sting. You'll just feel this for a second and then it'll be all numb," he said to Felicia. He injected in several places, proud of his technique of moving the injections sites carefully so that each time the needle pierced the skin, it was in a spot already numbed by the previous injection.

"My patients only feel the first needle stick," he explained to Felicia and Craig.

Great, Craig thought; *it's behind the hairline and won't show. We're gonna get out of this okay yet.*

After the doctor had put the seven stitches into her scalp and covered it with a sterile bandage, he told Felicia to wait a few minutes before she left, to be sure she would be able to walk without getting dizzy. During that time, she and Craig were left alone.

"I love you, Lisha, and I'm so sorry! I don't know what got into me. It'll never happen again."

"I know. It's okay," she said, actually beginning to believe him. "I know you've been under a lot of stress at work. I'm sure that's what happened. Maybe we need to take a long weekend in Galveston. You need the rest. We could get a cheap motel room and watch the surf for a couple of days." She remembered her life in Galveston during her mother's medical school. But quietly she wondered if that carefree peace she had enjoyed as a child would really ever be hers again.

It was after eight am when they arrived. As they pulled into the driveway at home, the delivery van also pulled in, to deliver the roses. Felicia tried to believe that maybe this incident would be a turning point, that Craig would realize he was wrong and would be the same old guy that she had fallen so deeply in love with in college.

Indeed, over the next few days, she could not have asked for a more attentive, loving husband. The evening after the accident, he put her to bed and made sure she was comfortable. Craig loved to cook, and he had a special risotto and pork loin dish that he was especially proud of. Tonight he took extra care to prepare it perfectly. He served it to her in bed with steamed vegetables and a glass of chardonnay wine.

"This is perfect!" Felicia said. Her heart wanted to believe all was perfect, but her mind urged her to use caution. After dinner was completed and the dishes put away, Craig joined her in bed and they made love as he continued to apologize for his tirade and to promise that it would never happen again.

It was almost six months before Craig lost his temper with her again. During that time he often seemed agitated and grumbled to himself but always caught his temper just short of ignition. He let the telemarketers call, with no more than a grumble under his breath when Felicia answered their unwanted calls. But he had become progressively pickier about his clothes, frequently throwing a freshly starched and ironed shirt onto the floor if he found a wrinkle or a stain.

The first she would know of his displeasure was when she found the freshly laundered clothing crumpled up on the closet floor. At first, he would simply toss the shirt on the floor and reach for another, not saying more than a soft grumble to himself, leaving the shirt for Felicia to find later. But lately he had been more vocal with his criticisms.

He got up later than usual one Friday morning, and the first two shirts failed to meet his inspection. As he wadded them up and threw them across the room, he cursed loudly. Felicia came through the door into the bedroom just at the moment that he realized that those were the only two clean dress shirts in the closet. The rest were in the wash.

His face again was reddened, and the vein on his forehead seemed ready to pop. As she walked into the room, he whirled and slapped her with the back of his hand hard, knocking her off her feet.

"Goddamn it! Can't I even have a clean shirt to wear! You're so goddamn stupid! You sit here on your goddamn lazy ass all day with nothing to do but my clothes, and you can't even do that right! Do I have to teach you how to wash clothes?" With that, he grabbed the shirts up in one hand and her left arm with the other and began to drag her through the house. Luckily, the laundry room was just off the hallway to the bedroom, so he didn't have to drag her far.

Felicia was frightened; he was so out of control, just like the other time on the telephone. She was unable to get her balance as he dragged her through the hallway. Her flailing right arm hit the large sixteen-by-twenty-inch wedding picture that her mother had framed for them while they honeymooned in Jamaica. The picture came crashing from its position on the foyer wall to the floor, shattering the matte glass and bending the ornate frame at an angle that made the picture bulge out like a ridiculous 3-D cartoon. When they entered the laundry room, Craig shoved her down to the floor hard.

"You just sit down there and watch! Obviously, I've got to show you how to do this!" He threw the shirts into the four-year-old Kenmore and set the dial on small load, hot/warm. He added two full cups of powdered Tide on top of the shirts and a full cup of liquid bleach to the dispenser in the corner of the washer. In his anger, he spilled a few droplets of bleach directly on the shirts.

When he realized this, he became even more outraged and threw the bottle of bleach across the small room. It hit the wall over Felicia's head, and spattered droplets of its caustic liquid over her head and back. The bottle then bounced off the wall and fell directly on her head, the bleach pouring over the back of her neck and cascading down onto her clothes.

She cried out, in fear more than pain, and tried to get up to get the bleach off her skin and clothes. But Craig had not finished.

"Now look what you've done! You've messed up the whole room. If I have to do your work for you, can't you even stay out of the way?" With this, he again backhanded her, knocking her face first into the dryer. Her right brow struck the corner of the dryer, causing a short but deep cut. Blood spurted out, spilling onto her white blouse and the floor.

When Craig saw the blood, he suddenly again became repentant and began to apologize as profusely as the blood that was pouring out.

"Oh my god! Oh my god! I'm sorry. Are you okay?"

There was a clean towel on the dryer. He quickly grabbed it and pressed it on Felicia's brow to stop the flow. The cut, though deep, was short, and as soon as the blood had time to coagulate, the flow stopped.

Felicia's tears mixed with the blood, and her face was covered with a streaked, watery blood. She sobbed uncontrollably for a full ten minutes as Craig continued to apologize and promise that it would never happen again.

"I don't know what got into me. It's all the pressure at work. It's all I can think about. Please forgive me! It'll never happen again!"

The cut was short enough that this time it didn't require stitches, so they were able to avoid the ER trip and the embarrassing questions. She was able to get the edges together adequately with butterfly-shaped Steri-Strips that Craig picked up at the Walgreen Pharmacy a couple of miles from their house. He continued to apologize and beg her forgiveness, and again they made up by making love, Felicia cautiously hoping, for the second time, that he had learned his lesson and that all would be like it was before.

Again, Craig continued his penitence for several days following the laundry incident, and again he continued to promise that he would never let it happen again. But by next morning, a dark black circle had developed around Felicia's right eye, a reminder of what had happened. This time, there were four more round bruises on the inner side of her left upper arm, the typical bruises of an abusive husband, whose strong fingertips dig into the soft flesh of a woman's upper arm when in uncontrolled anger he grabs her forcibly. When Craig saw her black eye, he made her promise that she would not leave the house until the eye looked normal again.

"I'd just die if anybody saw you like this," he said. "It was just an accident, but the neighborhood bitch-meister team wouldn't understand. Tell me you won't go anywhere till this goes away!"

"Okay! I know you didn't mean it. I promise I'll stay home the next couple of days. I only have one more class this week, and I haven't missed any, so I'll skip till Thursday. Nobody will see me."

She stood there, contemplating for a moment, before she continued, "But Craig!" she said. "This just can't ever happen again! You've got to get control of yourself!"

"Oh! I guarantee it. Just give me a chance. I'll show you. It'll never happen again! I promise."

After Craig left for work, Felicia went back to the laundry room to survey the damage and clean up the mess she had been too upset the evening before to clean up. As she expected, the shirts were ruined by the direct spill of bleach on them. Of course, her blouse and jeans were ruined as well. She placed them all in a tie-top garbage bag and dropped them into the large barrel outside the back door. Luckily, the bleach spill didn't reach the carpet in the hallway, so she was able to mop it up from the laundry room floor.

Luckily also, the wedding picture itself was not ruined, except for one corner. A shard of broken glass had made a scratch on the picture directly over Felicia's left hand. The scratch on the picture was so positioned that it almost obliterated the ring on the left fourth finger, which had only been there for a few minutes when the picture was made. She laughed to herself cynically as she looked at the small cut on the otherwise perfect picture. *Is somebody trying to tell me something*, she thought to herself as she carefully picked up the broken pieces of glass, trying to avoid seeing her own blood for the second time that day. *Well*, she thought, *I can take it to a good framing shop and get it fixed later.*

She was able to repair all the laundry room damage without getting out of the house. Craig had plenty of other shirts; several were actually hanging on the rack he had installed in a corner of the laundry room at the time of his explosion, ready to be worn. Luckily, they had escaped being stained with either the bleach or Felicia's blood. She carefully inspected them and hung them in the large walk-in closet which they shared. She could replace the damaged shirts after her eye cleared up, she thought. Her own blouse and jeans were not critical; she had plenty of clothes.

The picture was okay, except for the where the new wedding ring had been scraped off her finger. Her mom had gotten it framed for her secretly, but later when a friend complimented her on the beauty of the framing, she had told Felicia where she had it done. When she called Ronnie at the Frame Gallery, she told him she had knocked the picture off the wall while vacuuming the hallway. Luckily, he still had the records from the original job, so he could redo it exactly the same and nobody would notice the difference. She put it under her bed for storage for a week until her black eye faded enough for her to cover it with makeup and be seen in public.

When she brought it to Ronnie, she was wearing makeup and sunglasses and a long sleeved shirt as well. The bruises on the inside of her upper arm were still a yellow-green color and could easily be seen with short sleeves. She had been careful to keep the bruises on her arm covered by a long-sleeved shirt. Even though the black eye had faded almost completely, she was afraid Ronnie would notice.

She repeated the story about the vacuuming accident, taking care to tell it in the same way she had earlier. Ronnie didn't ask any questions although he sensed the tension in Felicia's voice. Two weeks later she picked up the picture, framed exactly the same as the original. Ronnie had even repaired the small scratch over her wedding ring so that it could only be seen by very close inspection. She took it home and hung it back in the foyer. Craig never mentioned the picture.

Indeed, he seemed the perfect husband for nearly six months after the shirt incident. But then he began to get home from work later and later. He told Felicia his job with the *Journal* was more demanding every day, and complained about his lousy lot in life.

Actually, most days he was stopping at a bar for a drink on the way home. When he came in the door, he usually threw his jacket on the couch and then collapsed onto "old blue," the overstuffed leather lounger he had bought at a furniture warehouse, from a salesman determined not to let him leave without buying something. But though he had not planned to make a purchase that day and really couldn't afford it, the salesman was right, and the recliner had become his favorite piece of furniture. A floor lamp stood to its left, throwing light at just the right angle for reading and making notes but still not causing a glare on the TV.

Felicia brought his before-dinner drink, either a bottle of beer or his really favorite glass of peach flavored iced tea as soon as he sat down each evening and then brought his dinner on a tray. Thus, he was able to spend his entire evening in the recliner, getting up only to go to the bathroom and to bed. On many nights he skipped bed and slept in his clothes in the lounger.

He seemed to look so forward to his evening in the recliner that the particulars of his drink and dinner gradually took on an escalating importance, any gaffe causing him to grumble for the rest of the evening. If dinner wasn't ready when he arrived, he griped. If the bread was not freshly baked and warm, and the main dish steaming from being brought directly from the stove, he griped. If the ice was not fresh and crisp, he griped. Partially melted ice is a turnoff, he told her, and spoils the atmosphere.

In 1995, Craig was promoted to senior police reporter at the *Journal*. With the new promotion and better salary, they were able to move from their small house in La Vista to a larger and newer home in a nice neighborhood in Lewisville, just five minutes from work. Felicia hoped the move and more money would ease his stresses and help to smooth out the wrinkles in their lives. The home, a ten-year-old single story, was larger and brighter and had an extra study that would make a perfect nursery when they were ready for a baby. But unfortunately, the promotion seemed to bring even more stresses, and things at home didn't get any better.

Felicia complied with Craig's new dinnertime pickiness as well as she could, feeling that anything she could do to make the household run more smoothly would help. It was her job to make his evenings relaxing, she felt. He worked so hard and asked so little (as he frequently told her). But it gradually became more and more difficult, even impossible, to time the dinner so that it was complete but still fresh when he arrived. After all, he rarely got home the same time twice in one week, so it was impossible to predict when the dinner needed to be ready. Often the main dish had cooled off too much or was dried out from being re-heated several times. The bread was the hardest to have ready at an instant's notice. She threw out more bread than she served.

At first, if dinner didn't suit him, Craig just snarled and left the table, usually with a comment under his breath, comparing Felicia's cooking to his mother's, and his wife's inability to cook, clean, etc., as well as his mother could. But Felicia had visited his mother's house several times and knew that his mother was a terrible housekeeper. Maybe she did better in her younger years before alcohol and depression made their irreversible mark on her daily life. But now, you could barely walk through the house for the clutter, and it looked like the carpets hadn't been vacuumed for six months. But Craig only remembered the earlier years, when his mother had apparently kept a neat, clean house.

Even though Felicia had really liked his mother at first, she developed such a resentment that she could hardly stand to visit her. She herself began to believe that she could never come up to the standards that Craig remembered from his childhood and his mother's better years. By the time they had been married only a year, she had gotten used to his pickiness and griping.

"I work all day at the *Journal* while you just sit here on your ass! You have nothing else to do. You ought to at least be able to fix dinner right. I've told you how I want it fixed, just like I'm used to at home!" It didn't help Felicia to remind him that this was his home now, not Carol's mobile home in Ferris, about seventy miles south of Dallas. And the clean, bright home he remembered from his childhood was not the home his mother had now.

Gradually, Craig's pickiness became more violent and sometimes seemed to have an element of planned cruelty. At first, dishes of food were thrown into the sink but later onto the floor if it didn't come up to his expectations. Eventually, if he was particularly upset, he threw the plates of food into Felicia's lap and even into her hair.

One night after a movie, they realized that Craig had accidentally locked Silly Cat, Felicia's ten-year-old Siamese, in the closet, and she had soiled the carpet. Craig became enraged and kicked her across the room. Then the next morning, against Felicia's wishes, he took her to the veterinary hospital that they used and had her put down, making up a story about her escapades that seemed to make the euthanasia sound more reasonable to the vet.

The dinnertime ritual and rules developed gradually. At first, he came home just a few minutes late, maybe an hour at the most. But this Wednesday, six months after the move to Lewisville, his desk was slow, and he got home about 5:15 p.m. This was almost a full hour earlier than usual, and she had not yet put the bread into the oven. She was preparing pan-baked chicken. She had seasoned the two skinless breasts with paprika and pepper and had browned them to a perfect golden glow in her cast iron skillet. She was now ready to add the vegetables and oregano, but the mixture needed about a half hour to bake when Craig arrived.

Craig had stopped for a couple of drinks at the Old Man on the Square Bar & Grill. He came in and sat down in Old Blue and asked for his glass of peach tea. She brought it, and he asked what was for dinner.

"We're having pan-baked chicken. You know, we had it a few months ago and you liked it. But you got home so early, it isn't quite ready yet. It'll be about thirty minutes."

With this, Craig became livid. "Goddamn! Why can't you have dinner ready for me when I get home? I'm hungry now, not in thirty minutes!" He got up, threw his glass of tea across the room, and stormed out the front door. As he did, he shoved her backward; she toppled hard over the back of the couch. She cried out in pain and surprise as her neck and head hit the coffee table in front of the couch.

He stood over her, glaring, his fists clenched, his forehead again red, the bulging vein again signaling his anger. "If you are so goddamn lazy and stupid that you can't have my dinner ready when I get home, I'll go somewhere else to eat." He angrily pulled out of the driveway, throwing gravel as he gunned his two-year-old white Avalanche that he had traded her Mustang for just the year before. He didn't come home until almost midnight. Felicia was already in bed but could smell the liquor on his breath as he entered the bedroom.

He stormed in, too loud for Felicia to play possum and make him think she was still asleep, and roughly threw back the covers. He grabbed the front of her pajamas and jerked her to a sitting position in the bed.

"What are you doing in bed, you lazy bitch? You don't go to bed till I'm ready to go do bed, you understand . . . *Do . . . you . . . understand . . . me?*" he snarled, pausing between each word for emphasis and intimidation. Pulling her out of the bed, again by the left arm, and dragging her to the dining room, he forced her to sit in a chair and listen.

"We're gonna have an understanding, you and me! You don't have anything to do but sit here all day on your lazy fat ass! All I ask is that you get my dinner, and I want it when I get home, not whenever you fuckin' get around to it! Understand?"

Felicia was frightened and didn't answer, except to sob quietly.

"Do you understand me?" Craig slapped her hard on the face. "Answer me! Do you understand me?"

"I understand," she sobbed, frightened. "I understand." She had never seen him quite like this before.

"Now, let's lay some ground rules." Craig's lowered his voice and spoke in such a slow menacing tone that he frightened Felicia even more. This was a new voice, one she had never heard before.

"Let's get our roles straight here. My job, you see, is to go to work every day and pay for all this shit that you seem to need, to buy you this goddamn fancy house you had to have, to make your miserable little life happy. I deserve a little peace and quiet when I get home. And I'm going to have it. Now, we get to your job. All you have to do is to make sure I get that little peace and quiet when I get home from work. That's all you have to do. That's your only purpose in life, to give me just a little peace and quiet so I can relax and get my job done, so I can pay for all this goddamn shit! Is that too much to ask?"

Felicia still sobbed quietly; she was too stunned to answer.

"Goddamn you! You answer me when I ask a question! Is that too much to ask?" He stood up and slapped her again with the back of his left hand, this time his class ring cutting into her lip. She thought the ring might have chipped her tooth and wondered for a moment if the blow had also chipped the red stone in his class ring. She started to fall, but Craig grabbed her by the front of his burgundy plaid pajama top, which she had worn to bed. He caught her before she fell out of the chair and onto the floor.

"I said! . . . Is . . . that . . . too . . . much . . . to . . . ask?" Now he was standing over her, fists clenched, yelling at the top of his voice. "I want an answer!"

"No, no, no! It's not too much to ask. Please . . ." She was almost unable to speak but finally was able to answer his demand between snubbings.

"All right . . . that's better . . . ," he hissed as he slowly relaxed his grip on the pajama top and lowered himself back into the ladder-back captain chair. "Now, let's talk about this a little bit." He slipped back into the new voice she had just heard for the first time, low, slow and menacing. His face was still red, and a drop of spittle glowed at the right corner of his mouth. Perspiration made his face shiny, and his five-o'clock shadow became even more menacing. He leaned closer, his face within inches of hers, and his foul liquor breath made her try to turn away.

The odor of his alcohol breath mixed with the odor of her blood made her gag. She tried to turn her head away, but when she did, he caught her hair, one hand gripping each ear and jerked her head back to face him directly.

"You look at me when I'm talking to you!" the strange, unfamiliar voice ordered. She thought he looked like he was crazy or possessed by the devil. Her nausea from the odor of blood and alcohol was almost overwhelming.

"You can consider this your very first real lesson from ole Craig. This is where we start some of ole Craig's good ole-fashioned home schoolin'. Now you just listen to me. Craig is the *teacher*, the law, the rule maker, the judge; and little miss Felicia is just the student, the kiddygarter ya might say, and from now on, *teacher*'s word is gonna be law around here. You see?"

"I see," she murmured. She wasn't even paying attention to what he said but would agree to anything, just to stop the barrage of anger.

But a murmured answer wasn't enough. Craig immediately slapped her hard, and not expecting it, she screamed loudly.

"Do you see?"

He bent over her, and their faces almost touched despite her cowering, almost fetal position. "You make me do that! You don't ever pay attention to anything I say. That's what I have to do, just to get your attention. Just like a damn mule, ya get their attention with a two-by-four across the bean. Now! Do . . . you . . . see!"

"I see," she said, much more clearly this time.

She couldn't believe this was happening; the man she loved and married had become someone she didn't know at all, and she was terribly frightened. She didn't know what was going to happen but wanted it all to be over and would agree to anything he said. *Just let him stop and leave me alone*, she thought.

"Teacher has to have an understanding, you see? Obviously, you're so goddamn stupid teacher has to set some ground rules. Here they are. Number one, teacher wants dinner when he walks in the front door . . . not an hour later, not a week later, not a year later but when he walks in the front fuckin' door!" As he spoke, he grabbed her by the hair on each side of her head, her ears caught tightly in his grip.

"Teacher don't want to sit here and starve to death while you sit on your lazy ass and file your fucking fingernails. And he wants his dinner fresh and hot. He wants bread right out of the oven. He don't want any of your goddamn tricks. He don't want some stale shit that's cooked yesterday or last month. He wants it fresh, like right out of the oven. He don't want some of that rubbery shit that's been redone a dozen times in the goddamn microwave! *Understand?*"

Frightened, she meekly whispered, "I understand."

"I can't hear you! Do . . . You . . . Understand?"

Louder, she said, "I understand! Please, Craig! My ears!"

"That's better," he said and finally began to ease his hold on her ears. "Second, students don't get to go to bed until teacher gets to go to bed. If teacher has to stay up till midnight trying to earn enough money to support you in the goddamn luxury lifestyle you have to have, you have to stay up too. Since that's all you have to do anyway. You understand?"

"Okay, I understand," she said clearly, afraid that he would again tighten his grip on her hair and ears.

"Third, teacher wants his laundry done right for a change. He don't want wrinkled shirts, and he don't want any goddamn stains on them. Is that perfectly clear?" Still the unfamiliar, threatening voice.

"Yes, yes . . ." By this time, Felicia wasn't even able to listen to what he was saying but knew she had to agree to anything he said. "I understand."

"Now, fourth thing, or fifth thing, or whatever the fuck number the next thing is, I didn't marry some goddamn slut who sits around all day eating chocolates and watching soap operas in a goddamn tee shirt and blue jeans. I don't give a hot fuck what you do when I'm not here, but when I get home, I want to see something a little better than blue jeans and a goddamn tee shirt. I work hard to pay for all those goddamn expensive dresses you have in your closet, and I want to see them. You can get dressed for me once in a while, I guess. I think I deserve at least that much out of you, if you can't do anything else right. If that's all the good you are anyway, you can at least look decent. Okay?"

"Okay," she sobbed. "I didn't know. I didn't know."

"Well, now you do! See what I mean? You're so goddamn stupid! I have to spell out everything; you don't even know how to dress right."

Felicia continued to sob quietly. She couldn't believe this was happening. Her lip and mouth hurt, and the lip was still bleeding a little. But the blood didn't seem to stop him the way it had the other times. And her ears still hurt where he held them; he had pulled on them so hard that she was afraid he would rip them off.

"Okay, those are Craig's ground rules, for now. That's just the first set of ground rules, for the professor's ole fashioned home schooling." He laughed, thinking somehow that he was being amusing. "Now, let's talk about what's gonna happen if you don't get your lazy ass in gear and keep up your end of this goddamn marriage." He gripped her head tightly again with both hands, his fingers still in her hair, pulling her ears so that their faces were only two inches apart. The ears still hurt from before, and now he was viciously pulling on them again.

"Are you listening to me? Are you hearing what I'm saying?" He shook her head sharply when she hesitated; she felt like her ears were being torn off her scalp. "Are you listening?"

"Yes, I hear you," Felicia sobbed uncontrollably now, afraid not to answer, remembering how badly it had hurt when he had slapped her and the heavy class ring had bitten into her face. Her lip was still bleeding, and by now she was sure that the ring had chipped a front tooth. Her tongue not only tasted the blood from her busted lip and gum but told her that the tooth didn't feel right, like a child who has lost a baby tooth, and the tongue hasn't gotten used to the new architecture yet.

"All right, then. Here we go. First off, this little lesson tonight is nothing. Just let me see another one of your typical lazy ass jobs on my shirts. That'll be a lesson you can write home about. But even that will be nothing compared to what'll happen if I come in and have to sit around this goddamn shit hole house starving to death because you're too goddamn lazy to get my dinner on time. Is that too much to ask?" Again, he pulled her ears hard, jerking them back and forth until she answered. "Is it?"

She screamed again at the sudden excruciating pain in her ears as he seemed to try to tear them from her head. "Yes . . . I mean No . . . I understand. I understand. It won't happen again, I promise. Just please let go of my ears. You're hurting me. Please let me go! Please . . ."

"Don't you tell me what to do, you ungrateful bitch! I'll show you what hurt is! I'll do whatever I want to do. This is my goddamn house, and I'll run it any way I want, understand? I pay the goddamn bills here, and I'm the teacher here. If you think your measly little piano money helps, I've got news for you. It ain't helping one little bit! I'm teacher here, not you, not your shitass mother, not nobody. I'm the *only* teacher here. Do you understand me?" He again shook her head back and forth, this time slamming her face onto the dining room table.

"*Do . . . you . . . understand . . . me?*"

Felicia thought her nose was broken. The pain shot through her face as the blood began to flow from her left nostril, like the pain she remembered as a child, when she swallowed too big a bite of ice cream. The kind of pain that made her want to scream but hurt too bad to scream. She felt paralyzed for a matter of seconds. Unable to answer him at first, she finally did cry out in pain, but this only enraged him more.

He jumped up from his chair, knocking it backward until it fell to the floor with a loud crash. Still holding both ears, his hands tangled in her dark and now bloody hair. He jerked her up savagely, lifting her feet several inches off the floor. He whirled around, slamming her head and shoulders against the wall, her feet still six inches off the floor. Her 118 pounds seemed nothing to him. She gasped for air, unable to breathe, much less answer his demanding question. He coarsely threw her over a chair and onto the floor, the chair tumbling over on top of her. He began to take off his heavy leather belt.

"Goddamn you! I'll teach you to answer me when I ask you a question!" He began to whip her with the belt, first over the neck and face, and then when she rolled up in a ball, he attacked her back and legs.

"*Do . . . you . . . understand . . . me? Do you understand me?*" he repeated over and over as her belted her. She was unable to get free of the belt and cowered in the corner of the room, screaming each time the heavy belt struck her thinly covered back and her bare legs until he finally tired. He threw the belt at her and kicked at her in the final gesture of his drunken rage. The toe of his shoe glanced off her shoulder and caught her squarely over her right eye. The old scar on her right brow was reopened but more deeply and a full inch longer, and again the fresh river of blood flowed onto her pajama top and onto the floor. The pain in her shoulder from the glancing kick was so severe that she thought it must be broken.

Before Craig saw the blood, he stormed out of the house for the second time that evening. Again he spun the pickup's wheels, and again she heard the now familiar sound of gravel pelting the window panes. This time, the gravel broke through one pane, and several small stones fell to the floor of the foyer. But Felicia was oblivious to these new sounds; she was still reeling from the pain of Craig's whipping and the final kick. He didn't return that night.

She was stunned and had been knocked almost unconscious. She didn't know what to do. She knew that any call to police or a women's shelter would only make her situation worse; it might even endanger her life. But she had to have help from someone. She could no more stop the flow of blood from the cut on her eyebrow than she could the flow of her tears. She caught up a corner of the pajamas and pressed it against the cut with the heel of her right hand, trying to slow down the bleeding.

She hobbled to the bathroom to survey the damage. She saw in the mirror that it was worse than she thought. The cut extended up past her eyebrow, a full inch on to her forehead. It was deep too; she would surely need stitches again. She put a towel over it and pressed hard for fifteen minutes. But when she took the pressure off, the blood was still flowing freely.

Finally, she gave up. She had to have help. Since the move to Lewisville, she had barely left the house. She still was without a car of her own and had not started giving piano lessons again yet.

"Anyway," Craig had told her, "you don't need to do that anymore; I'm making enough money for both of us. What you make teaching piano isn't a drop in the bucket."

Since he did the majority of the grocery shopping, there was rarely a reason for her to leave her house. The only neighbor she had met was Tom Palmer, two doors down. He was manager of an office supply store in Plano, and she had only spoken to him twice since the move. She didn't know him well enough to call him in such a situation, and she thought he was on vacation anyway. She was terrified to call 911. She knew a police report would embarrass Craig, and he'd really be pissed then. No telling what would happen when he found out. So she finally gave in. There was only one person she could call.

CHAPTER 4

IT WAS 2:30 AM

It was 2:30 a.m. when Dr. Conlin was awakened by the persistent ring of her cordless bedside telephone. She tried to ignore it, but it kept ringing. She enjoyed being a family physician but had to admit that the middle-of-the-night calls made her wish sometimes that she had stayed with pathology. There, you rarely had your sleep interrupted.

She had heard the story too many times to count that a pathologist's patients rarely called after midnight. But the advantages of family practice, working with couples as well as children and being able to see just about everything that medicine has to offer, usually tipped the scales away from the somewhat more impersonal specialty of pathology.

But it still wasn't easy and was getting less easy every year to be roused out of a deep sleep from a warm bed to answer a nurse's questions or to go to the hospital for an emergency. She finally picked up the receiver, and sleepily whispered, "This better be important."

"Momma . . . I can't make it stop bleeding!" the distraught feminine voice mumbled between sobs. Felicia had not reverted to her childhood name for her mother since the spring of her twelfth year, when she was delirious from the high fever. Now she sounded delirious again, this time not from fever but from being in terrible trouble, her back against a rock, with nobody to turn to except her mother.

"Lisha, what's wrong, honey?" Ellie recognized the weeping voice of her daughter, and the rush of adrenalin brought her immediately to full alert status. "What is it?"

Felicia could hardly speak. She sobbed with her entire being, like a child who has mashed her finger in a door and the pain has begun to ease up, but her shattered emotions are still out of control. "Momma . . . Oh, Momma! I . . ." But she was still unable to control herself enough to make any sense.

"Lisha, it's okay. It'll be okay. Just tell me what's wrong. What happened?" It was getting difficult for Conlin not to become just as hysterical as her daughter. "Is Craig there? Has something happened to him?"

"I can't make it stop bleeding. I don't know what to do," Felicia wailed. Her face was reddened, and she perspired profusely. Her hair was matted now, the red-brown stain streaking the dark brown hair like flames invading kindling. The mixture of blood, tears, saliva, and her running nose had stained her chest. The top two buttons of the pajamas had been missing for nearly a year.

Craig liked the extra bit of spice the missing buttons added to her already gorgeous bedtime appearance, and he had asked her not to replace them. Now, instead of revealing a glimpse of the tops of her full breasts, the unbuttoned shirt exposed the red-brown dried streaky stain of blood, sweat, and tears. Her sobbing had caused the cut on her brow to reopen, and fresh blood now mixed with the darker partially dried stains on her pajama top and chest.

"Felicia, try to tell me what happened. Are you pregnant?"

"No, Mom, not that kind of bleeding," she was able to say between sobs. "It's my head." She again was wracked with uncontrolled weeping and could not speak for a full minute.

"It's okay, Hon," Conlin tried to get her into control. She knew she should call 911. "I'm coming, Lisha. It'll just take me a few minutes to get there. Let me call 911 first, and then I'll call you again from the car." She had the cordless house phone in one hand, connected to Felicia, and her cell phone in the other. She had 911 on the screen and was ready to push the send button.

"No! No! Don't call them! You can't call anybody! You've got to help me!" Her frightened voice made Ellie join her in the flood of tears that followed.

"Okay!" Conlin conceded, but Felicia's warning caused her stomach to tighten into a cramp as she listened between the lines and was suddenly struck with the full realization of what she desperately wanted to deny. She knew now why her daughter had seemed so withdrawn recently. "I'm leaving as soon as I can get dressed. Has Craig hurt you?"

"Oh, Mom! I'm so scared!" Felicia sobbed. She didn't have to respond; Ellie knew the answer.

"Where is he now?"

"I don't know. He was drinking, and he ran out and left. I don't know where he is."

"Okay, I'm leaving right now." Conlin had already grabbed the pair of dirty sweats and socks from the floor where she had dropped them after her evening jog and put them on with Reebok's and a white UTMB sweatshirt while she talked to Felicia on the cordless phone. Then she got into the car, still holding the phone to her ear.

When she started the motor, she hung up the cordless phone and redialed Felicia's Lewisville number from the Bluetooth connection she had programmed for her cell phone in her midnight blue BMW SUV. Afraid Craig might come back, she stayed on the line with her daughter for the entire fifteen-minute drive to her house.

Traffic was sparse at 3:00 a.m., so she made good time. She burned her flashers as she drove through the three red lights on the freeway. She knew that licensed physicians could legally speed when responding to an emergency in Texas, but she still hoped she didn't get stopped. She didn't have time or inclination to explain her situation to the cops, so she kept the speedometer below 80.

She arrived at 3:15 a.m., her best time ever. All the outside lights were on, and she could see a broken window pane in the panel next to the front door where the rock from Craig's spinning tires had hit it. She honked the horn at the same time rushing out of the car and up the steps. Felicia had given her a key, but her shaking fingers were barely able to get it into the locked door. She turned the key, opened the door, stepped inside, and turned the deadbolt. Then she realized that was foolish; Craig had his own key. The usually reassuring deadbolt was useless to keep him out.

There was still blood on the floor, and the brightly colored flowers on the dining room wallpaper seemed to have added a burgundy pattern which Ellie hadn't remembered from the last time she was there almost six months ago. She felt like she was going to have a heart attack when she realized it was her daughter's blood, still a dark red on the wall, with droplets partially dried but still seeming to search for a pathway downward to the floor.

"Lisha-Lou, honey, where are you?" she called out, using her childhood nickname for the first time in many years. When she didn't see her, she stepped through the doorway carefully to avoid tracking the blood onto the carpet. She was anxious to see but at the same time dreaded what she might find—there was so much blood. What had happened to her only child?

"I'm in here, Mom, in the bedroom," Felicia answered weakly.

Felicia's mother found her curled up on her side on the bed, a white towel pressed against her forehead, the pajama top covered in blood. Blood also stained her bare legs. She had not taken time to cover them. The bedspread had been turned down, but she was lying across it and uncovered. She had been almost successful in stopping the flow of blood, but still a large stain showed through the towel.

"Oh, Mom! What am I going to do?"

Her mother was unable to speak, suddenly overwhelmed by the realization of what her only daughter had been going through. She grabbed her in her arms. "It's gonna be okay, honey, it'll be okay," she tried to reassure her, not really knowing if it would or not.

Ellie was able only to sit on the edge of the bed and hold her and rock her back and forth as she had so many times as a baby and small child. They both cried on each other's shoulder: Ellie quietly, with the tears of a mother grieved by her baby's pain, and Felicia loudly, with the heartbreak of a child who has been in terrible trouble, who has finally broken down and told her parent about that terrible trouble.

Finally, after nearly a quarter hour, they both were able to control their tears. By then Ellie's sweatshirt was stained not only with both women's tears but with her daughter's fresh blood and running nose as well.

But when she pushed her to arm's length to survey the damage, she saw for the first time the entire picture of the cut over her eye and the welts from the belt on both legs. "Oh my god! What has he done to you?" A torrent of tears came again, from both women this time. They held each other tightly for a full three minutes before Felicia finally snubbed herself into control.

"We've got to get you out of here, Felicia. You can tell me about it later. I don't want you to be here when Craig gets home. I'm taking you to the emergency room to get that cut fixed. That cut's gonna need stitches."

By then, the cut over Felicia's brow had again stopped bleeding, so its repair was not so emergent as it had been. Ellie grabbed a blanket and covered Felicia. Toiletries and undies could wait, or she could run to a store later for replacements. Safety was her only concern at this point. She would feel much better after they were on the road and a couple of miles away. Even if Craig headed back now, their paths probably wouldn't cross, with their head start.

As she expected, Felicia was at first adamant in her refusal to go to the emergency room. She was not ready to make her tribulations a public spectacle . . . not yet, anyway. But her mother was determined to get her to a safer place for the time being. She had a close friend, Dr. Ken Perdue, working in ER that night, and she knew she could trust him to keep his mouth shut about it. Finally, she was able to convince Felicia that she had to go to the emergency room.

"Baby, you have to come spend a few days with me. I have the guest room all fixed up for you. You have to get away from here till you figure out what you're going to do. I understand you don't want to call the police yet, but it isn't safe for you here. What if he comes back?"

"I don't think he'll hurt me again, Mom. It's just the stress at the paper, and he got mad and went out drinking tonight. I'm pretty sure he won't hurt me again."

"You don't know that. Please come with me. We can leave him a note. I'm afraid something terrible will happen to you. I'd die if something happened to you."

Felicia finally relented. "I guess you're right. I guess I'll come with you at least till my head feels better."

While Felicia ran to gather what she would need for a few days at her mother's house, Ellie tried to wipe the stains off the hardwood floors and tried to clean the blood off the wallpaper before it dried. But she immediately realized that the harder she tried, the more damage she did to the paper. The wallpaper would have to be replaced. The blood could not be removed without leaving a large stain or a hole rubbed in the paper. So she abandoned her efforts and helped Felicia gather underwear and clothing for a few days away. She helped her change into a pair of long pajamas, both tops and bottoms and a dark blue thin cotton robe which would cover most of her welts. Even though it was December, in north Texas the night was barely chilly. All she needed was something to protect her from the little breeze that had been blowing after midnight. Then they left through the front door and got into Ellie's car, locking the door behind themselves and looking around the area carefully to make sure they didn't see Craig's car.

During the twenty-minute trip back to the Richardson, both women were completely silent. Ellie loved her BMW, and this was a time that she really appreciated its quiet, smooth ride. The salesman had told her she only had to aim it down the road, it would do the rest. This time, Ellie kept the cruise control set at the speed limit. There wasn't any need to rush anymore. Felicia didn't want to talk; she laid her head back on the headrest and pretended to sleep. The smooth trip in the comfortable car, once they hit I-45, was almost hypnotic. She actually did doze off in her exhaustion, for a few minutes of fitful sleep, rousing only slightly at red light stops.

Ellie was quiet too, afraid that if she started talking she wouldn't be able to stop. She didn't want to risk alienating her daughter, so she painfully held her tongue. She had little personal or even professional experience with abused wives, but she knew that the violence tended to escalate, and she was afraid for Felicia's life.

She knew that the bruises and lacerations could be inflicted in a sudden fit of uncontrolled anger. But the welts bothered her even more. She felt that the welts were a sign of a deeper, more sinister, more evil mind. She felt that if Craig could whip her daughter with a belt, there was no telling the potential extent of his violence.

Her only real exposure to abused wives had been the young woman she had counseled the year before. Her husband had said many times during their turbulent relationship, "If I can't have you, you can be goddamn sure nobody else will." The day after their divorce became final and he was finally forced to accept the fact that he would no longer have her, he had made sure nobody else would; he had pulled his car beside hers in her apartment parking lot at two-thirty in the morning, as she got home from work, rolled his window down, and shot her in the temple.

Ellie had testified in the man's murder trial and had done her part to help put him in prison for many years to come. The experience of losing her patient in such a violent way had affected her, and she hadn't yet quit thinking about it. She wondered, wasn't there something she could have or should have done to prevent it.

And now, her daughter might be in a similar fix. *My god*, she thought, *how could I be so blind, not to notice the signs in Felicia! Well, I know now, and that'll be the end of that!*

As they neared Memorial Hospital, Ellie gently nudged Felicia's shoulder. "We're almost there, hon." The car's CD player spun James Taylor's song of loneliness and friendship.

When you're down and troubled . . . and you need a helping hand . . .

Ellie knew she could depend on Perdue to fix Felicia's laceration, but she would have to work on him to make sure he kept his mouth shut about it. Being in practice locally herself, she was fully aware of the gossip and consultations that went on in the doctors' dining room. Even though physicians are sworn to confidentiality and usually adhere to it religiously, for some reason, they don't consider talking to other doctors as a breach of confidentiality. She would have to make sure he agreed not to tell even his colleagues.

and nothing, no nothing is going right . . .

How blind I have been, she thought. *Sitting here in my nice packaged suburban practice, thinking everything was rosy while all the time my only daughter has been living in hell. God, how stupid can a mother be?*

Close your eyes and think of me . . .
and soon I will be there . . .

I'll make it up to her. She has to know that I'm here for her, and I always will be. Why didn't she call me sooner? Didn't she trust me?

Felicia, dozing off and on, subconsciously heard Taylor's music as well. Though relaxed and dozing, she could only get fitful rest, realizing that her charade was over. Somebody else besides herself knew about her troubles.

To brighten up . . . even your darkest hour . . .

Darkest hour! she thought. He really knew what he was talking about. She didn't think she could ever remember a worse time in her life. She never knew her father, so never missed him. She had only had a couple of boyfriends before Craig and wasn't serious about either of them, so she wasn't accustomed to dealing with lost loves. This problem with Craig had been her only really serious trouble.

You just call . . . out my name . . .
and you know . . . wherever I am . . .

Conlin knew her daughter pretty well, she thought. *If Felicia is ever forced to choose between mother and husband, even such an abusive husband, I might just come out wearing a second place ribbon. I'll have to use all the diplomacy I can muster to keep Felicia from ever feeling like she has to make that choice.* As she turned into the Memorial emergency entrance, she determined in her mind not to let that happen. *I'll help, but I have to let Felicia make her own decisions, regardless. I'm not going to be that kind of a mother!*

She gently nudged Felicia's shoulder. "We're almost there, hon."

Luckily, at four o'clock in the morning, the emergency room was empty. And Conlin had remembered correctly; Dr. Ken Perdue was on call in the ER. She quickly registered Felicia and insisted that she be brought back to a minor surgery room immediately. Being on staff at the hospital helped her avoid any major wait in the waiting room. Dr. Perdue came in after just a few minutes to assess the damage.

"Hi, Ellie! What's happened to your kid?" he asked cheerfully even though he too had just been roused after being asleep for less than a half hour.

"Hi, Ken! Felicia bumped her head and looks like she's gonna have to get a couple of stitches."

Being an emergency physician, Perdue was much more experienced in dealing with abused women than Conlin. He immediately recognized the welts and insisted that he examine Felicia without the protection of her long garments. He left while she changed into the short-sleeved open-back hospital gown. When he returned with a nurse, he examined the tender areas of Felicia's upper arms and saw the four telltale round bruises, all lined up in a straight row where Craig's stronger fingertips had gripped her. He looked over her back and upper legs where the belt had left welts, now reddened and swollen. He noted her sore shoulder where the glancing kick had left her a tender dark memento. He thought it would be okay but would get x-rays to be sure.

He ran his hands over her entire scalp, looking for lacerations or bumps that Felicia might not have even noticed in her terror. He was startled when she pulled back and winced as he touched her ears. They were still very tender after their rough treatment, and when he pulled the hair back to look, he saw that both ears were bruised and reddened.

He looked at the laceration over her eyebrow and saw the now-darkening circle under her eye. "What did he hit you with?" he asked.

"How did you know?" Felicia asked, not only stunned that he could tell by so casual an examination but frightened that somehow Craig might find out that she had spilled their secret even to a physician.

"Sweetie, you aren't the first banged-up housewife I've ever seen," Perdue softly told her. "I have two jobs here. First, I have to fix your eye and make sure there aren't any other injuries that need care. Then we have to make sure this doesn't ever happen again."

By then, Felicia had regained enough composure to slide back into her cover-up. "Oh, I'm going to be okay. Just fix me up. I'm sure this won't happen again. It's just that there's been a lot of pressure at work lately. We just need some time off. We'll be okay!"

While Dr. Perdue washed off the cut and injected Xylocaine into it, to numb it so that he could start the stitching, Stacy, the ER charge nurse, called the Women's Outreach Shelter, and a volunteer abuse counselor was soon on her way to the hospital. Stacey knew that the Shelter was one group of volunteers who actually get out of bed and come out to help a victim, day or night. As he finished the last stitch and placed the bandage over Felicia's eyebrow, Myra Carpenter arrived in the ER.

Stacy came in and held Felicia's hand, "Hon, we have somebody here who's been through the same thing you're going through. She came out here to talk to you and help you decide what to do. We don't want this to happen to you again. Is it okay if Myra comes in to talk to you a few minutes?"

"What do you mean? I didn't want anybody to be called! Mom, you promised!" Felicia seemed to border on hysteria. "I can't tell anybody. It'll mess up everything! I don't want to talk to anybody!"

Despite their gentle pleas, she was adamant; she would not speak to Myra. Stacy went out and told her, "I'm really sorry we got you up. I thought she would want to talk with you."

"Don't worry about it. When I was in the same boat, it took me four trips to the ER and finally a broken wrist to make me give up and get some help," Myra answered. "Just give her the Shelter business card. Tell her we stay open all night. Any time she needs help or any time she wants to talk to somebody, we'll be there for her." Sounded a little like what the singer had told her over the radio speakers just an hour before.

Felicia was still both frightened and angry. She felt she had been betrayed and needed her mother's reassurance that she had nothing to do with the call to the Shelter. Even with that reassurance, she still didn't fully believe her.

Perdue tried to help; he assured Felicia that his team always called the Shelter whenever an abused wife came to the emergency room with injuries, but nobody would force her to talk with them until she was ready.

"But remember what I tell you," he said. "This will not get better until either your husband gets some help or until you get away from him."

He came closer to her and placed his hand over hers, speaking in a soft, understanding voice. "We see this all the time, kiddo. You aren't the first person we've seen with this kind of problem. Believe it or not, you're not even the first one we've seen today. There's help available for you. If you aren't ready today, call when you are. Call me, call the Shelter, call your mom, call anybody. But don't let this go on!"

Felicia didn't answer but began crying again, placing her head on Perdue's shoulder. He was an old friend; he had been in Ellie's class in med school and had watched Felicia grow up. She didn't have any uncles, since Ellie was an only child. And she never met her father. So except for Perdue, she was fresh out of favorite uncle / father figures.

Perdue's frustration was in realizing that abused women are like alcoholics; you can't help them until they are ready for help. He was helpless. He had someone very important to him, trapped in a web of abuse, and he could do nothing to protect her from the spider that he knew was lurking in the corner, just waiting for next time. He could repair the damage but was powerless to prevent it from happening again and even worse the next time. Mom was powerless, the Shelter was powerless, even the police were powerless.

CHAPTER 5

THE TRIP HOME

The trip home from Memorial Hospital down I-45 to Richardson Parkway, and east a couple of miles to Ellie's neighborhood usually only took about ten minutes. Neither woman spoke during the trip. Conlin wondered what her daughter was thinking. So far as she knew, nobody had confronted Felicia in such a direct manner about her home situation before tonight. Ellie was glad that Perdue was on call in the ER. He had always been such a good friend. She knew that he had held a secret crush on her, but she had refused to get caught in another romantic trap after the fiasco of her teenage pregnancy and her betrayal by Felicia's immature father.

After graduation, while Ellie stayed in Galveston for her residency, Ken had gone to John Peter Smith in Fort Worth for internship and emergency medicine residency. Not knowing where he wanted to settle, he had worked for Coastal for five years, doing locum tenens emergency room and family practice work until he finally moved to the Richardson and a full-time ER job at Memorial. He hadn't even known that his old friend was in Richardson until a month after he started there, and she came in to see a patient late at night.

Ellie couldn't believe that she had been so completely oblivious to her daughter's problems. She felt so stupid. How could she have missed the signs, she wondered. There must have been things she could have recognized, if only she had been looking. She would make it up to her, if she would only let her.

Felicia was too numb to think and laid her head on the gray leather headrest of the car. James Taylor had held his thoughts for their return, and when the motor hummed to a quiet start, the CD automatically resumed spinning. He picked up exactly where he had left them when they arrived at the emergency room, and the ignition key stopped his music. He continued to pledge his support.

I'll come running . . . yes, I will . . . to see you again . . .

She listened without speaking, quietly being lulled by the faraway promises of the singer. In her dreamlike state, she almost believed that she really could call on him if things ever really got bad enough. *But god,* she thought, *could they ever get any worse?*

Winter, spring, summer, or fall . . .
all you got to do is call . . .

Felicia had gone through a lot without calling anybody and finally had called the only person she knew she could always depend on, she thought. She finally felt so safe in Mom's car. The heater was beginning to warm her up. She had gotten chilled with just pajamas and robe and the cool December north Texas breeze. It really felt good. It seemed almost like all her worries were gone.

And I'll be there . . . yeah . . . yeah . . . yeah . . .

Oh, god, she thought, suddenly flashing back to the present, *can I get any farther down? How did I ever let myself get into such a mess? It all seemed so right, and now it all seems so wrong.*

Oh, ain't it good to know, you've got a friend . . .

She readjusted her position on the gray leather. The cut over her eyebrow was beginning to throb, and she was finding other sore spots she didn't realize she had. The bright welts from the belt were separated from the leather of the car's luxury seats by only the thin cloth of her robe and pajamas.

People can be so cold . . .
  They'll hurt you . . . and desert you . . .

The music made her cry. Everybody said they would help, that she could call them anytime, but could she really? This was her problem, and she had to handle it herself.

They'll take your soul if you let them . . .
  Oh yeah, but don't you . . .
    Let them . . .

Ellie passed the statue in the middle of the esplanade on Richardson Parkway, of the father and son fishing, and approached the Enchanted Woods turnoff. She had always liked the figure. It portrayed a small child fishing with his father, both having the times of their lives. The expression on the father's face made you think probably the fish weren't biting, but who cares anyway? Ellie thought it reminded her of how her life should be, relaxed, carefree, just out fishing, relaxing, who cares if the fish bite. Until now, she thought she had found that life in Richardson.

Ellie looked over at her daughter and remembered driving her back and forth to preschool, then elementary school. How on the way home she talked awhile then lay down for a few-minute nap. How she hated to interrupt the blissful sleep of her tired child. How she frequently passed her neighborhood and drove around a while, just to prolong the ecstasy of little Lisha-Lou's sleep. Now again she drove right past the Enchanted Woods turn, instead driving to the end of Richardson Parkway, left on Grand Park Avenue, back around sweeping Palmer Road, and back west to I-45 and north again to Richardson Parkway. The circular trip allowed an extra forty-five minutes for Felicia to nap but also allowed Ellie that time to plan her strategy. She had to handle this carefully. She wanted Felicia to see that she must get out of her abusive relationship, but she knew if she pushed the issue, she risked losing her daughter altogether. She had to let her know she was her friend as well as her mother.

Ain't it good to know . . .
  Ain't it good to know . . .
    you've got a friend . . .

45

This time, after she passed the man and son fishing on the esplanade on Richardson Parkway for the second time, she turned left onto Enchanted Woods Circle. When she turned into her driveway on Rio Frio, she decided to garage the car to keep it out of sight from the street. The garage was detached but had a six-foot privacy fence between the corner of the garage and the house, and she could get Felicia in without having to expose her to the street. She didn't know if Craig might be waiting for her and didn't want to take any chances.

She helped Felicia into the house through the back door and led her to the upstairs guest room. The house was not extravagant but tastefully decorated. A visitor could easily tell how Felicia came to have her good styling sense. It was open and airy; one could see into the backyard as soon as he entered the front door. The large panes of glass that made up the bottom half of the living room wall made it seem that the entire house was open to the recently manicured backyard. The rose bushes at the edge of the garage and the lake on the other side of the wrought iron fence made a visitor feel immediately welcome.

"Where are we, Mom?"

"We're home, baby. We've just been driving around awhile to let you sleep. How do you feel now?"

"I'm sore, and I'm really tired," Felicia answered, and the realization of her situation again caused her to cry, this time quietly.

Dr. Conlin led her daughter into the brightly lit master bathroom in the back of the first floor. The mirrors covered the entire wall above the dual sinks and were surrounded by theatrical type lights. There was a large Jacuzzi platform tub, and she knew a hot bath would feel good. She drew the bath water, got clean towels out, and began to leave the room. Ever since Felicia had begun to develop, she had always been very modest, and Ellie thought tonight would not be different, especially with her soft body covered with bruises and welts.

"Here, Hon, get a nice hot bath and call me if you need anything. I'll be right outside."

"Thanks, Mom . . . and thanks a lot, for being there for me. I don't know what I would have done without you. I was so scared." The reminder caused Felicia to begin to cry again, this time softly, as a child who has almost quit hurting but is still heartbroken. For the second time tonight, she relaxed and let her head rest on her mother's shoulder and wearily accepted the mommy's hug that she so badly needed.

"Stay with me, Mom. I know I'm a big girl now, but I really need you to stay with me right now."

"Sure, hon, I'm here. I've always been here. I always will be here."

Felicia got into the tub and covered her chest and belly with a hand towel while she lay back and let her mother gently massage the shampoo into her bloodied hair. Ellie took care not to let the shampoo and bathwater ruin the bandage over the new sutures. The bathwater turned a muddy reddish brown as the remaining clotted blood gradually dissolved. Ellie noticed two bumps she hadn't seen before. Felicia hadn't even realized they were there. There was also a small laceration at the crown of her head, but it was shallow, and Ellie decided it would heal without stitches.

The second floor guest room overlooked a balcony but didn't connect directly with it. Ellie thought it was the safest room in the house and led Felicia to it. It seemed nearly impossible for Craig to bother her there; the window was well away from anything he could climb up and was too high to reach without a long ladder. She doubted that he would try to come in through the window anyway but felt she had to be careful. She didn't know what mood he would be in, and if he could deliver such a beating, she didn't know what else he might do.

The queen-sized bed was covered with a patchwork quilt and had a white lace dust ruffle. The quilt was an heirloom from Felicia's great-grandmother, all hand sewn from her children's clothes during the depression. The filmy curtains contrasted with the quilt but matched the dust ruffle. The bed had large posters at all four corners and a cedar chest at the foot. Felicia knew that the chest held many mementos of her own childhood and infancy. She loved that chest above almost all of her mother's possessions. She had spent many happy hours just going through the treasures in the old chest, remembering her happy childhood at Mom's house. It occurred to her now what memories would she store there from today.

Ellie turned down the bed, and Felicia wearily crawled in. There would be time tomorrow for more talk and decisions. But for now, she needed rest. Ellie sat on the edge of the bed and stroked her neck, being careful not to touch the painful places where she was bandaged or where the bumps lay. Her only child was sleeping soundly within less than five minutes.

The next morning, Dr. Conlin called her office and told Darla, her receptionist, that she would be out for at least a couple of days for a family emergency. She asked her to find coverage for her practice. There were several family physicians that she traded call with, and Darla could call around and get one to cover her hospital rounds. The office patients could be rescheduled, and any emergencies could be sent either to another friendly physician's office or to the emergency room. She was careful not to say anything which would lead anyone in the office to suspect the nature of her emergency.

When Felicia woke at 8:30 a.m., Ellie brought her downstairs to a breakfast of scrambled eggs and salsa with homemade biscuits and orange juice. She ate with relish and seemed to want to talk. "Mom, I can't believe I've got into this mess," she started. "I thought Craig was perfect until this kind of stuff started happening."

"Oh, baby, you mean this isn't the first time?" Ellie knew that wife beating was something that gradually escalated, starting off mild and finally rushing to a crescendo of unspeakable violence. But she tried to think that this night was an isolated incident in Felicia's life. She was visibly disturbed to realize that her daughter had put up with abuse and had not told her. "I feel so ignorant. How did it happen right under my nose, and I didn't even know it? Why didn't you tell me?" she asked even though deep inside she really knew the answer.

But when she asked her, Felicia clammed up and refused to talk about the previous problems any further.

"What can I do to help?" Ellie asked her daughter. She knew she couldn't suggest any solution such as separation or the Collin County Women's Shelter; that kind of suggestion coming from her mother would automatically be wrong. Felicia had to decide for herself. But somewhere during the next twenty-four hours, Ellie hoped to convince her daughter to get out of the situation permanently.

Felicia was determined that she could work it out herself, however. She was adamant in her refusal to call the Shelter, much less the County Sheriff's Department. Craig was in the news business, and she had heard the reporters gossip about what happens when abused wives try to get help.

Just like most sheriffs' offices in North Texas, there were unconfirmed tales of officers siding with the abusive men. Many times, the abused wife had been arrested and the abuser left alone to sleep it off, especially if the investigating office found that both had been drinking. In fact, Craig was good buddies with several of the deputy sheriffs. They would never believe that he could be mean to his wife like this. And if they believed it, they would think she must have done something to deserve it anyway.

There were even stories around town that a couple of the deputies' wives themselves had occasionally visited the local emergency rooms with strange bruises and lacerations. Some people even believed that a former sheriff himself had a wife with a tendency to fall down and get black eyes a lot. She wasn't ready to face that, no way, Jose. Conlin had no reassuring answer for her concerns either. As a physician in practice locally, she too had heard the stories in the physicians' dining rooms at both local hospitals. And as a physician, she was in a position to know that the gossip was more than rumor; she had heard Ken Perdue talk more than once about local dignitaries whose wives got knocked around occasionally. He should know; he had patched the wives up himself several times.

Ellie finally gave up; she could not talk Felicia into making a report, and she realized that if she persisted, she risked alienating her even further. Felicia even refused to consider family counseling; she could never get Craig to go in for counseling. And she was afraid of making him mad by suggesting it. So Ellie decided she had to accept the things she couldn't change and work with what she had left. All she could do was try to make sure Felicia was physically safe and let her know that she could always come home if there was trouble.

Craig called Felicia at her mother's house late that afternoon. She had left him a note saying that she was okay but needed to get away for a couple of days; she hadn't said where she was going. But he figured she must be at her mother's house. She didn't have any other friends or family she could call in a crisis like this. He had made sure of that! He had discouraged any other friendships since the move to Richardson and figured there was nowhere else she could go. He was right, of course; she didn't have anywhere else. Felicia had talked with her mother about what they should tell him when he did call, and they had decided not to try to hide her, so when he asked to speak with his wife, Ellie didn't interfere.

"How you feeling, honey!" he started.

"I'm better, no thanks to you!" Felicia answered sarcastically. She was able to be bolder, now that she was fifteen miles away, in the safety of her mother's home. "What do you want?"

"I just wanted to make sure you were okay. When are you coming home?" he asked. He no longer used the new voice she had heard the night before, the low, slow, menacing one. But now he used still another voice she didn't remember ever hearing before; this one was sugar sweet, like some parents use when they don't really know how to talk to their small child.

"Is your head okay? I didn't know you had hurt yourself till I came back home after work today and saw the blood on the wall. Are you okay?" She half-expected to hear him say, *"Daddy missums little Lisha-Lou."*

She noticed his subtle hint that her injuries were her own fault, that she had "hurt herself." But she knew that wasn't true. She hadn't hurt herself. Craig had hurt her. But it wasn't worth getting into, not right now at least.

"I'm okay, I guess. I had to get my head sewn up again."

Oh god, Craig thought, *she has already been to the hospital, and there's no telling what she told the nurses there. It's time for damage control.*

"Oh, Babe! I'm so sorry. I'll make it up to you, I promise. Did you tell them I did something to you?"

"They're not stupid! I didn't have to tell them. They figured it out themselves. But don't worry, I made them promise not to report it. Old Dr. Ken was there. He's Mom's old med school buddy. He knows how to keep quiet. You don't have to worry your poor little innocent head about it. I didn't make any trouble for you."

"Oh god! Thanks! I'll make it up to you. Really! You'll see, it'll be different this time. We just need to get away for a while, maybe take a trip or something. It'll all be okay if I can get some of this stress off. You'll see. I promise, I'll make it up to you. When are you coming home?"

"I'm not sure what I'm going to do yet. I just know I can't take much more of this. This shit has got to stop." She had never used such language with Craig before, but it felt good.

With her suggestion that she might not be coming back, his voice took on another tone yet, one filled with apprehension and concern.

"Please come back, Babe! You know I can't live without you. I'm sorry. It's just the pressure. I love you so much. I'll make it up to you, you'll see. It'll never happen again. Just come on back! I'll kill myself if you ever leave me . . . I can't live without you!"

He had made this suicide threat before every time that he had to apologize and talk her into staying with him. And like most abusive husbands, he had cried, and begged her to forgive him, and use round-about ill-logic, like how can I prove I'll be good if you won't let me come back home? The obstacle to this reasoning, of course, is twofold. First, the abuser has usually already had dozens of "second chances." And then, if she lets him come back it could be the end for her.

And like most abused wives, it usually worked. She was just a little afraid that he would carry out his threat. But as in many similar abusive relationships, she had nothing to worry about. It isn't the abuser who might not survive the relationship, it is the abused spouse.

She heard his voice break up slightly, like he was trying not to cry. How he was able to scare up a few crocodile tears, she had no idea.

"How do I know it'll be different this time?" she asked. "You say that every time. How do I know this time will be any different from before?"

"I'll show you. Come on back. I'll show you. How can I prove it to you if you don't come back? I love you so much! Come back, just give me a chance to show you. If it isn't okay, then you can leave, but at least give me a chance to prove it to you!"

With this, he had begun to break her resolve. In her distraught mind, he was at least making a little sense. Maybe she was being unfair. Maybe he deserved just one more chance. Not that she hadn't already given him many "just give me a chance to show you" chances. If she stayed away forever, she would never know. Maybe just one more chance. Maybe . . . But as Nurse McCarty had said, if she didn't get away from him, maybe she would be dyin'.

They finally hung up the phones with no decision made. But Craig had succeeded in making her doubt her decision to leave him. She was at least considering going back with him, giving him one last, ultimate, final, absolutely last chance. When Ellie realized this, she became frightened for Felicia's safety and discarded all her earlier plans for subtlety and psychology. She realized she was losing the battle and had to take a chance; she had to try once more to talk some sense into Felicia. If she never spoke to her again, there was nothing she could do about it, but she couldn't let her make this crazy decision and go back to him without one last try to get her back on the road to sanity and safety.

While she hoped that Craig was telling the truth and everything would be peachy, her rational mind also kept reminding her that there was a good chance he wouldn't change. That if she was wrong, she was taking a chance of getting hurt really bad.

"Felicia, you just can't go back yet. You're gonna get hurt really bad next time. Stay here awhile at least. Talk to somebody about it. Give yourself a little time to think about it. Give him a little more time to sober up some more and cool off. I'm so afraid for you!"

"He's not drinking now. He never drinks at work, and he's been at work all day. I don't think anything's going to happen. I can handle it." Ellie had lost. Felicia was going back, and there was nothing she could do about it.

"Oh my god, Felicia! Please at least wait a few days! A few days won't hurt anything. Give yourself some time. If you don't believe me, talk to somebody else. Call the Women's Outreach. They have counselors there." She felt desperate; she knew she was losing the argument and may be losing her daughter as well. She felt she had lost all control, not only of her daughter's safety but of herself as well. Deep in her subconscious, she kept thinking of Janet and the early a.m. phone call.

"I told him he could pick me up tomorrow morning. That'll give us both another night to think about it. Mom, I really think this time has taught him a lesson. He really sounded like he was sorry. I'm sure we'll be okay," she lied.

Ellie couldn't speak. She knew the decision had been made and that she could do nothing to change it. But worse than that, she knew that it wouldn't really be okay. She knew it would never really be okay again.

Not tonight, not tomorrow, not ever!

CHAPTER 6

THIS PARTICULAR TUESDAY

This particular Tuesday afternoon, Craig Jernigan especially wanted to get home on time. The Mavericks were playing Chicago at home at eight pm. The game had sold out early, so it would be broadcast locally. It would be the first time the Mavs' three all-stars would be together to face Jordan, Pippin, and their entourage since last season. Even though he lived in the Dallas area, Craig had been a Michael Jordan fan for years and hoped that the Bulls would walk all over his home team.

With his new job at the Lewisville Journal, he could afford some of the luxuries he had wanted all his life. And one of those luxuries was a partial season seat at the Mavericks' stadium. He didn't want to miss tipoff for this game especially.

But nothing had gone right today. He had been working on an enterprise article comparing the ambulance services in various medium-sized suburban counties in north Texas and was almost a week behind schedule. He had spent half the afternoon in his weekly conference with the city editor, getting a chewing-out for being behind schedule. Now it was four-thirty, and he was still waiting for a return call from Joey Wilson, the Denton County fire marshal for a follow-up on a recent restaurant fire investigation. It looked like he might still be at the office at the eight o'clock tipoff time, he thought.

It was four-thirty when his phone finally rang. Craig took the necessary information from Wilson, got the words transformed from audible to visible, with the help of his word processor, turned off his lights, and headed for the exit. He was the last person out, and at four forty-five, the building's main lights were already off. The on-at-dusk light sensor for the employee parking lot had not clicked on yet, and the overcast sky left the area in that in-between dimness, too light for headlights but too dark to read. And way too dark to be safe.

He would barely have time to run home, shower and dinner, and fly down Central Expressway, to get to Reunion Arena in time for tipoff. And that's only if the traffic cooperated. Good thing this wasn't Friday; might take two hours to get there if he had to fight Friday afternoon traffic.

As he exited the building through the rear door, he made sure to key-lock the door behind him. The *Journal* was in a section of Lewisville which invited break-ins. The employee lot was at the side of the building, about fifty yards away from the back door. It was deserted except for his white two-year-old Chevy Avalanche and a rusted-out mid-sixties Volkswagen minibus in the opposite corner of the lot.

Craig had traded Felicia's Mustang in just three months ago and had almost broken even on the newer car's payments, considering the absence of repair bills on the older Ford.

He loved the Avalanche, with its big V-8 motor and rear-wheel drive power. He had always liked pickups. With their heavy motors in the front, the back was relatively light, and you could spin the wheels without even trying, especially in gravel. He realized he just hadn't gotten all of his high school teenage macho bravado out of his system, but he didn't care. This was still his favorite car of all times.

The VW minibus, with a banged-up rear end and the rear door held closed with bailing wire and gray duct tape (duck tape in his old neighborhood), parked fifteen yards away, with a short hedge partially obscuring it from Craig's view. It had been driven through mud and was so dirty that the license plate was obscured.

It was a faded-out pale blue, originally called baby blue, and had the remains of large homemade flowers painted on the sides, somewhat blurred by the longstanding dirt. It looked like it hadn't been washed in years. A peace symbol on the rear door, originally hand painted in black, was so faded it was hardly visible. The arms of the symbol had faded so that it looked more like a drooping Mercedes three-point star than the symbol used for nuclear disarmament, peace, and nonviolence.

Craig guessed one of the *Journal*'s employees must have run out of gas or couldn't start the miserable thing and had just abandoned it. *God*, he thought, *what a wreck! A real white-trash express! I hope they don't leave it there for long. Property values in this neighborhood just dropped by 20 percent*, he thought and chuckled to himself at his silent joke.

He pushed Unlock on his remote entry clicker, opened the driver's side door, and reached in to put his burgundy leather briefcase in the backseat. It was a promotion present from his supervisor when he had made senior police reporter. He heard a footstep crunch the loose gravel but did not turn fast enough to see the darkly clad figure come from the direction of the hedge and the old VW.

He never saw the stun baton in its upward arc toward his head and barely felt it as it hit the back of his right shoulder. What he did feel was a sudden excruciatingly painful electric shock that started at his neck and shoulder and then pulsed through his entire body and all four extremities. He completely lost control of himself and fell to the ground, paralyzed and dazed, wetting his pants as he fell. In the brief millisecond before he lost consciousness, his mind flashed to the thought of a stroke. Then everything went black.

After a few minutes, as the effects of the 150,000 volt stun baton began to weaken and Craig began to rouse a little at a time, he could feel his legs being tied together but was unable to see. His mind was unclear, and he was unsure at first of where he was.

He was confused and bewildered, and the thought that he might have had a stroke, and would be blind and paralyzed produced a terror in his mind worse than any he had ever felt before. But his confusion and fear took a new dimension as he felt ropes tugging on his ankles and then dragging him along the ground. He felt the ropes cutting into his ankles as he was dragged by the feet, first across the gravel of the rough parking lot and then over a small patch of dirt. The tail of his shirt had come out, and gravel was accumulating under his shirt and cutting into his skin. He tried to reach down to his ankles but realized that his hands were tied behind his back. He tried to wrench them free, but the cable tie handcuffs cut into his wrists. The ties were so tight that he had no chance of freeing them.

The ropes pulled him up, upside down, his head banging on gravel and asphalt until his shoulders hit the sharp edge of something hard and cold, and his head completely cleared the ground. He heard the whine of an electric motor as he was pulled even farther up until his head cleared the sharp edge as well. Then he felt a shove and was dropped hard on his head onto a splintered wooden surface.

His legs and hips were still suspended in the air; his head and shoulders were all that rested on the floor. He was still confused but gradually realized that he was in a vehicle. He heard the rusty side door of the van squeak and then slammed shut. After a few seconds, he heard the driver's door open and then close as his abductor got into the vehicle.

Lying as he was, partially suspended, he could feel the bare wooden floor of the minibus against his face and arms. The floor was littered with trash; and there was a mixed odor of gasoline, cigarettes, and stale hamburger. Some type of tape had been put over his mouth.

As he regained his senses, he realized that he probably wasn't blind, but something had been put over his head, something cloth but so black and so thick that no light came through it. It was tied tightly under his chin, so he was unable to squirm out of it. Although the cloth allowed for air passage so that he could breathe adequately, he gasped for air and felt claustrophobia for the first time in his life. His terror escalated as he imagined that he was suffocating.

As he realized he was being abducted, his panic rose even higher. So far, his captors had not made a sound, except for the initial crunch of the footstep on gravel. He tried to yell, to ask what was happening and why but was unable to produce any more than a muffled, "Hmm . . ."

The tape almost prevented him from breathing as well as talking; it had been clumsily placed over not only his mouth but also part of his left nostril. He found himself still gasping for breath. He rubbed his hooded face on the floor, trying to rid himself of the tape. Unable to get it off, he finally was able to get it at least off his nostril and finally was able to breathe more normally.

His captors never spoke. He heard a motor start and realized he must be in a van or truck. He had a foggy memory of an old beat-up van, was it a Dodge or a Ford? His memory was much too blurred to be dependable. He assumed that he must be in the van. There was too much room in the floor for this to be just a car or even a car trunk.

The vehicle backed out and started forward. It coughed and sputtered a couple of times. It sounded like an old junker. Probably it was the same filthy old wreck he had seen for just a second before he felt the shock from the stun baton.

He could tell from the transmission sounds that the vehicle had a standard transmission and the motor whined when the gears were shifted.

The exhaust was loud; the muffler must have dropped off years before. The body rattled badly. He tried to remember if he had seen the van previously, but his memory was so clouded he had trouble even remembering the color. All he could visualize was it was old and dirty, and he thought there was a flower or something painted on its side, but it was partially camouflaged by years of unwashed dirt.

He kicked out, and his manacled feet hit the rear doors of what he assumed was the old van. The combined odor of stale hamburger, onions, gasoline, and cigarettes nauseated him. It was so strong that he felt that someone was blowing onion and cigarette breath directly into his face. His hooded head hurt badly, and his neck and shoulder throbbed both from the physical effects from the baton's vicious blow as well as from the high voltage it had sent through him.

Finally realizing he was unable to pull free from his restraints, he lay as still as he could for the rest of the ride. He only moved when the van went around a curve. Partially suspended in midair as he was, every sharp turn slung him from one wall to the other like a crane swinging a wrecking ball into a wall at the end of the crane's long chain. He crashed repeatedly into the unpadded walls of the vehicle.

He was chauffeured for what seemed like almost an hour although actually it was barely half that. During that time the effects of the stun baton's voltage wore off, and he was able to regain better control of his mind and body. His head still ached terribly; every heartbeat sent a throb that made him feel as if his skull would explode.

He again tried to pull his hands free, but it only made his wrists hurt more. He tried to bend his knees so he could reach up with his manacled hands and untie them but was unable to reach that far. He worked with the ties on his hands but soon realized it was futile. His captors had used plastic cable ties, and they could not be untied like simple ropes. His maneuvers only caused his back and wrists to hurt more. He thought his face was bleeding from hitting the edge of the van's floor but trussed and hooded as he was, he could only guess.

He tried to think of who might be kidnapping him and why. He was not rich himself, but he did have an uncle who had made several million dollars in an oil venture a few years ago. If they only knew. There was no love lost between him and his rich uncle. He probably wouldn't pay a dime to save his loss, so the ransom idea was probably not reasonable.

Had he pissed off someone so badly that they were kidnapping him for revenge? Was this a get-even from some of the drug dealers that his article had helped to put away? If so, he thought, he was in real trouble, and he was very likely being taken out to be killed.

But it was too soon for any of that bunch to be out on parole already, he thought. He guessed some of their friends might be trying to get revenge on him though. His thoughts were still not very clear, and he had trouble remembering.

Was somebody at work mad at him? The only person he could think of was Charlie Ross, a mid-thirties loser who had thrown one of the larger rural routes for about the past year. He had an old beat-up van too that he used for the route . . . *was it blue or white?* He couldn't remember, except that it had been wrecked and not repaired.

Craig had gotten him fired just yesterday morning after a confrontation in the parking lot. Ross had parked his dilapidated old van too close to Craig's still-shiny truck and had made a small ding in the passenger's side door when he carelessly threw open the van's driver's side door and got out. Unfortunately, Craig had still been in his car and had been infuriated.

"Damn it! You've put a dent in my damn car! If you can't be careful, why don't you park that ugly thing somewhere else?" he had shouted through the partially closed window of his car. Ross had been embarrassed but, in his typical surly manner, had merely waved Craig off and started to walk away.

In his anger, Craig had mistakenly thought that Ross had flipped him the bird. He had become enraged and had gotten out of his car and run toward him. "Don't just walk away from me!" He had grabbed Ross's leather jacket and pulled him back toward the cars. "I want to see how bad you've screwed up my paint job."

Although Ross was much larger than Craig, he had allowed himself to be pulled in between the cars. "Don't look like much to me," he had said. "Leggo my arm." He had shoved Craig away with ease and had again begun to walk away. But when Ross had shoved him, Craig had lost his balance and fallen over the back of the truck and onto the right rear corner of Ross's vehicle.

The van had been wrecked previously, and a torn edge of twisted metal protruded from the rear left fender. As he fell, Craig reached for something to hold, something to help him regain his balance. All his hand reached was the jagged metal of the torn fender. He fell to the ground as the rusted metal edge cut into the palm of his hand. It was a deep cut and bled heavily.

"Come back here, you chicken shit!" the irate Craig had insisted, but Ross had continued to walk away.

Tom Stockton had just assumed the evening security shift and came out the exit door to patrol the parking lot when the scuffle was almost over. All he saw was Ross shove Craig, and even that he only saw from a distance. When Craig saw Stockton, he ran up to him, holding his bleeding hand up to his chest, hysterically complaining about being attacked by Ross. The hand bled so ferociously that it was easy for the guard to believe Craig and to back up his story to the boss later that morning.

The incident was reported to the circulation manager, and resulted in Ross being fired the next morning. Although he expected to be pink-slipped, he came to work the next day to collect his papers for his route as usual. But when he arrived, the route had already been reassigned, and he was told to report to the circulation manager's office.

There he was informed that he was fired, effective immediately, no grace period, no second chance, no gold watch, no going-away party. Just a check with his back earnings. And to add salt to the wound, a reminder that he was being fired for cause and would not be able to collect unemployment on his work at the paper.

As Ross left the building, he had passed Craig in the hallway and had turned to him and whispered between clenched teeth, "You're gonna be sorry you ever tangled with Charlie Ross, you son of a bitch!"

Craig had never liked Charlie anyway and made no bones about it. The guy was only borderline competent, but he had never done anything bad enough before to justify getting him fired. He was an obnoxious smart ass and always looked sweaty. He rarely combed his long greasy hair and only shaved once or twice a week.

In good weather, he wore tank tops, exposing a demon tattoo on his right shoulder and a chain design around his left upper arm. In cold weather he wore denims, black boots, and a black leather jacket with a Harley Davidson emblem on the back with the word Bandidos just above the waist. To top it off, he was six foot two and at least sixty pounds heavier than Craig. And very little of it fat. Whether by design or not, he presented an image that Craig detested, and that scared him just a bit.

Fortunately for Charlie, his customers had always seemed to like him. Even though he was frequently late to pick up his papers, he had fewer complaints on his route than anybody else did. In fact, in spite of starting out late, he could usually get the papers delivered and be back at the shop as soon as the others who started on time. Craig couldn't understand why his customers didn't complain though. He guessed he must be banging a few of the housewives along the route.

Anyway, for whatever reason or for no reason at all, Craig couldn't stand Charlie Ross. He suspected he was an ex-con although he had no real proof. With his muscles and tattoos, he fit Craig's image of a con. He also suspected Charlie was what he called a mental defective or maybe a drug addict. He had long wondered if Charlie might be a criminal on the run. Now, he imagined Charlie to be a serial murderer, just waiting, planning for Craig to be his next victim.

After the incident in the parking lot, Craig always referred to Ross as Chicken-shit Charlie, both to his coworkers and to Felicia. Only his embellishment of the story bore little similarity to the actual events of the day. It was lucky they had gotten rid of Ross when they did; he was probably a serial killer just waiting to pick out his next victim. And of course, it was damn lucky for Ross that Stockton had stopped it when he did. Craig was just getting ready to spread his ugly ass all over the parking lot.

Regardless of who his captor was, though, Craig now realized he had to think clearly if he ever hoped to get out of this alive. He had kept rubbing his face, through the hood, against the filthy wood of the vehicle's floor, enough so that the duct tape was finally off the corner of his mouth. He finally could make some semi-intelligible sounds and at least could breathe better. His head rested against something soft, and with his next breath, he realized it was a pile of dirty sweats. He pulled back, trying to get away from the foul odor, but it didn't help. The floor had rusted out and been replaced with a poor grade of plywood and now was littered with trash.

The cable ties had cut sharply into his wrists, and they were hurting. His pulling on them had only made them cut in more tightly. He had no idea where he was being driven; the black hood over his head had completely ruined his sense of direction. He only knew that the van had turned both left and right several times and that he had ridden over several miles of smooth concrete and then even more on a rough unpaved gravel road. Being confused by whatever had stunned him at first, he had no good idea how long the ride had taken. He tried to remember Charlie's address from his employment records, but couldn't.

"Where are you taking me?" Craig screamed when he finally got the tape far enough off his mouth to be able to talk. No answer.

"Why are you doing this?" Still no answer.

"Who are you?" No answer.

"Ross, you chicken shit son of a bitch, you'll never get away with this!"

At that comment, his captors answered by turning the van sharply to the left, without braking, onto another unpaved road. Craig was thrown across the floor and slammed hard into the wall of the van. There were no seats in the van, so his sudden roll was unchecked. The sides were unfinished, and the sharp steel edge of the frame cut into his shoulder. He thought his shoulder might be bleeding but was unsure. Finally, the van came to a stop, and he was able to sit up for a moment.

He heard the van's front door open and then close, and then he heard the side door squeak open. The ropes on his ankles were jerked roughly, and he heard his captor walk away. After a couple of minutes, he again heard crunching of gravel under foot and felt tension on the ropes on his ankles. Suddenly he heard the whine of another more distant electric motor, and the ropes on his ankles again jerked him around and then slowly pulled him out of the van. His head hit the ground hard as he was pulled out of the minibus. Again, the ropes cut painfully into his ankles as he was dragged across the ground, he didn't know how far. He felt gravel cutting into his back, and then the gravel was gone and he felt grass and dirt being ground into the fresh scratches and cuts the gravel had left.

Finally, he was pulled over a few feet of smooth concrete and up several steps, onto a wooden surface. As he unwillingly ascended the steps feet first, his hips, and then his elbows, and finally his head bumped in succession over each of the six risers on the steps to the porch. His head bumped hard on the stairs several times, and he felt blood coming from his nose. His elbow scraped hard against the door threshold and the pain shot through his body. He thought the elbow might be broken.

"Why are you doing this?"

"What do you want with me?" But still no answer.

"Who are you?" he now screamed.

After Craig was completely inside the building, he was pulled up by the ankles, into a partially hanging position, upside down, with only his head and shoulders resting on the floor. He was left that way for a few minutes, and could hear his captors walking around in the room. He felt and heard the legs of his pants being cut and then torn away, and he could tell that at least one of his captors was wearing gloves. He really couldn't tell if there were several captors or only one. He felt his shirt being cut and ripped off, and his shoes and socks were removed.

After another few minutes wait, he was suddenly snapped to a horrified electrical wakefulness when a whip struck across his chest. It cut deeply into his skin, and he screamed in pain. More blows came in rapid succession over his now bare legs and arms. Again he screamed, both in pain and in questions to his tormentors. Again, no answers came; he only heard a heavy "hmmfff," as the person behind the whip put his entire strength into his work, grunting with each morbid effort.

The whipping only lasted a few minutes. The beating had not neglected any part of his body; the only areas receiving any protection at all were his hooded face and the small portion of his trunk that his torn pants still covered. He was relieved but still frightened, still not knowing why he had been abducted or who was responsible. He felt the abject terror of the realization that he was completely at the mercy of a brutal assailant who could and would do whatever he wished with him.

After a few minutes, the ropes suspending him by the feet were relaxed, and he was allowed to lie on the floor. His gloved assailant then placed another rope around his chest under his arms and, with this, hoisted him up into a standing position. The ropes, but not the cable ties, were removed from his ankles. His captor then, standing behind him, pulled him backward into a wooden chair with sturdy arm rests. He struggled, trying to tip the chair over, but it would not budge. He realized that it must be nailed to the floor. He then felt his elbows being taped to the arm rests, he assumed, with some kind of duct tape. His knees were similarly taped to the legs of the chair, his ankles still tied together with the cable ties. He sat spraddle-legged, his knees taped apart on the edges of the chair, and his feet bound together.

He felt several loops of tape being placed tightly around his chest and shoulders, binding him so tightly that he could not turn in his chair, much less hope to rise out of it. When his elbows and chest were securely taped and he was unable to move to defend himself, he felt the plastic cable ties being cut from his hands. Both hands were then taped, open, palm down, over the ends of the arm rests, like he was gripping the wood. Then the ties on his ankles were similarly cut, and his ankles taped to the legs of the wooden chair. He was then left there, fixed, for several quiet horrifying minutes.

He listened intently but could hear no footsteps, no rustling of the wind, nothing. In the stark stillness and quiet, his terror escalated to a level of panic he had never before felt. He continued to struggle intermittently with his bonds, but he succeeded only in making his wrists hurt, the tape cutting into the skin of his wrists and elbows. He cried out several times during this otherwise quiet period, now begging for mercy. But still, no answers came.

He did not expect the blow when it finally and suddenly came. It was without warning, enough time having passed since he was tied in the chair that he had let his guard down. His hooded head drooped on his chest, wet and shining from the perspiration of pain and terror, but cool from the exposure of his damp sweaty skin to the night air. There was no heat in the building. His frightened pause was suddenly interrupted when a seventeen-ounce wooden T-ball bat struck him flatly across his face, breaking his nose. He screamed in pain and in terror. More blows fell every few minutes, striking not only his face and ears but also his shins and forearms, at varied intervals. He never knew when to expect the next blows, so was unable to steel himself for them. Finally, the blows with the small bat stopped. Nothing happened for a while; he couldn't tell how long.

When he felt the next blow with the whip, he jerked so hard that he felt like he had broken his neck. The blows rained down hard and rapidly for a full ten minutes, over his face, shoulders, arms, legs, every part of his body. Each blow brought a scream of terror and pain from the victim.

Then the blows stopped for a while, all the while Craig both waiting for and dreading whatever would come next as he alternated moaning in pain with begging for mercy. He believed now that he was going to die and, at this point, only wished that his death could come quickly so that his torment could end. He had stopped asking who and why but only begged for the blows to stop. He quietly prayed, for the first time in many years. It had been so long since he had prayed; he wasn't really sure how to do that anymore.

His clumsy attempt at silent prayer was suddenly interrupted when the next unexpected blow with the small bat came across the left side of his face, this time breaking his lower jaw and loosening several molars. More blows to the face came, and he spat out two front teeth, almost choking on the foamy blood.

The small bat was perfect for inflicting nonfatal injuries, cutting deeply into his scalp without knocking him unconscious. The hood was little protection for the clubbing from the small but hard bat. He felt blood running down his face, onto his shoulders and chest. His screams went unanswered.

He was allowed another period of rest before the final attack, but he was unable to relax, tensed the entire time in anticipation of the next blow. He tried to beg his captors to stop, identify themselves, tell him why this was happening. Anything. But his fractured jawbone and the injuries to his teeth made his pleas all but unintelligible. Still he never heard a word from any of his captors.

During his times of partial consciousness, Craig still worried that he was being beaten to death. His confused mind wandered from one possible assailant to another. Why wouldn't Ross answer him, *the bastard!* Nothing he had done to the jerk was enough to warrant anything like this. The article he had written about him wasn't that bad. But how did he get out of prison so fast? Or was that somebody else?

In his confusion, Charlie Ross blended with the drug dealers he had exposed. Try as he might, he couldn't get them straight. *Who was that article about anyway,* he thought. Maybe that's what this is all about. Those sons of bitches have already gotten out of prison, and they've come to even up the score. *Fuck the parole system in this damn state,* he thought, again chuckling at his private, feeble attempt at wit.

I sure sized up Chicken-shit Charlie right the first time though, he thought. *What a fucking psycho! I wondered how many other people the son of a bitch has murdered,* he wondered. *I bet there are bodies buried all over this goddamn house—maybe in the walls or basement? I bet that's what he has planned for me! How long will it take them to find me, out in this god-forsaken shithole of a house!*

The bat had made a small half-inch tear in the front of his black hood, just to the edge of his right eye, and if he turned his head just right, he found that he could see to the right through the small peephole. He could tell the room was dimly lit and could see a window with a dark curtain. He assumed it was still dark outside, but couldn't tell for sure.

He heard the ticking of a clock and was able to see the edge of a fireplace and mantle where it sat. At the edge of the fireplace he saw an outdated flowered wallpaper, faded and pale from age. A large corner of the paper next to the mantle was torn loose and curled over. The hardwood floor was littered with trash, like somebody had moved away and forgotten to clean the place up. He could see no doors or furniture from his miniature peephole. Trussed and hooded as he was, he could only see the narrowest sliver of the room. He could only see what was directly in his line of sight like he was looking through a telescope on a fixed pole that would neither rotate nor tip up or down.

When finally his head began to droop from exhaustion and he began fitfully to doze off, the final barrage started. He was suddenly brought back to reality when the next blow came; it was with a much larger bat or board or something, or maybe the bad guys were just hitting him harder with it. Anyway, whatever it was, it came across his lower chest and produced such an intense deep pain that he knew his ribs must be broken. He coughed and screamed with pain, but still the blows continued and still his captors said nothing. When he coughed, there was blood, and he could hardly catch his breath. As he gasped for breath, he choked on the blood and thought that it was surely almost over; now he would surely die.

As he tried to get his breath, his captor switched their attack; the next series of blows from the small bat came to the backs of his hands. As hard as he tried, he was unable to wrench them free from the tape and move them out of the way of the blows. After several hard blows to both hands and elbows, he was unable to move his fingers. He knew his hands must be broken. The tormentors then moved to his bare feet, taped to the legs of the unmoving chair, with a series of excruciating blows to the insteps, toes, and ankles. Despite his screams, the blows continued until Craig knew his ankles and feet had to be broken as well.

Another short period of fitful rest followed, probably only a few minutes. Then the blows to his shins that followed made Craig realize that the first were only practice shots. These were so strong they had to be with a baseball bat. The pain was unbearable. Mercifully, he finally passed out with the blow that broke his right tibia.

CHAPTER 7

EARLY IN THEIR MARRIAGE

Early in their marriage, sex had been very fulfilling to both Craig and Felicia. But for Felicia it had gradually became a drudgery. How can a woman feel sexually attracted to someone who treats her so badly, someone who so obviously has no respect for her? But she had learned to go along with his demands. She had learned not to resist. She knew there was no point in refusing to have sex. The few times she had refused him, Craig had slapped her, hard, and then forced her to have sex anyway. There was no point in refusing.

Frequently, after an episode of "home schooling," Craig apologized and turned his brutality into a make-up and make out session. Felicia meekly conceded with confusion. Deep in her heart, she silently hoped that each apology and subsequent lovemaking session would signal an end to the abuse. But in her mind, she realized that refusing Craig brought its own retribution. It was better to allow the sex and be able to roll over and go to sleep than to refuse it and face another episode of "instruction."

Now it was 2:00 a.m., and still she hadn't heard from Craig. Maybe he had worked late and then gone directly to the game. But he should still be home by now, even if . . .

Only once before had he gotten home as late as midnight but never this late. That had been the time he "tested" her by staying out until midnight and found her already in bed. He had given her the "don't go to bed before teacher goes to bed" lesson that time. She was sleepy now but not sleepy enough to chance another lesson from teacher.

She still remembered vividly. "Well, you get a big fat fucking F for your test," he had said, his face over hers, and his breath smelling of alcohol and old food in unbrushed teeth. "I guess you must need a little more of my home schooling! Get your lazy ass out of bed!" This was the worst beating she had received up to that time.

Felicia had learned her lesson well. She knew not to go to bed even if Craig stayed out all night. As a teenager in junior high, she had learned a trick to keep from going to sleep in study hall. She practiced her gymnastic routines in her mind, by visualizing them. Now, she had again learned to use that technique of mental gymnastics to stay awake waiting for Craig, this time visualizing a cheer she had learned at a summer cheerleading camp.

Left side cheer stance . . . "Ready . . ."
Side Lunge . . . Right L . . . "Get on . . ."

She switched the CD player off and tuned in a local C&W station. She carried the remote control for the unit in her pocket so she could instantly switch back to Mozart if she heard Craig's car on the gravel driveway.

Squat . . . "Up . . ." High V "Are you ready . . ."

She wondered if this is the kind of thing that prisoners in solitary confinement did, to pass the time, to prevent going crazy. But then, she thought, this is a kind of solitary confinement after all. She felt she had to stay fresh and clean for Craig so she couldn't really go through the full motions and jumps of the cheers. But she couldn't help letting her fingers do the walking, mimicking in miniature the positions her arms and legs wanted to take. She walked around the kitchen, whispering the chants and thinking of older, freer times.

Cheer stance . . . Clap . . . High V . . . "Are you ready . . ."
Front lunge . . . Toe touch . . . "To . . ."
Front Lunge . . . "Fight . . ."

She had enjoyed her college cheerleading. It was the only outside activity that she had insisted on keeping after she met Craig. Her girl friends were very important to her, but since graduation, she had failed to keep in touch even with Angie, her best friend for several years previously. She was too embarrassed to call her. And Craig would have a fit if she started spending time on the phone with the girls. What did she need with old girl friends anyway when she had him?

Front cheer stance . . . T . . . "Let's hear it . . ."
Rt side cheer stance . . . "For the . . ."
Rt punch . . . "Longhorns . . ."

She checked the lasagna again; it wouldn't last much longer, even with the microwave on the lowest keep-warm setting. Soon the dinner would be ruined, and she would be in trouble. *Why doesn't he come home*, she thought. She even considered leaving. There seemed to be no way she could avoid another installment of Craig's home schooling. A tear came to her eyes, as she continued to work the cheer in her mind.

Clap . . . Front lunge . . . Clap . . . "Tonight!"
Side hurdler . . . Herkie . . . Side hurdler . . .

And over and over again, she visualized every cheer she could think of, from both college and high school, and even went over some of her grade school gymnastics routines. Thus she managed to stay awake for the next several hours and was still sitting in the dining room at 5:30 a.m., still fully dressed, with makeup straight, fighting to stay awake, when she heard a car's wheels turn into the driveway, crunching on the loose gravel in front of the garage.

She looked and wondered why Craig had turned his headlights off. She heard the wheels slide over the gravel as the brakes locked and then heard a car door open and then slam twice, a few seconds apart. The car backed out, spinning its wheels, and she heard the gravel hitting her front door as it was thrown by the spinning tires. Then it was quiet again, except for the crescendo-decrescendo roar of the gear changes as the car sped away. Felicia ran out in the dark to see what was happening but could hardly see the blurred form of the speeding vehicle, barely illuminated by a distant streetlight. It was already a block away, and with no lights, it was not recognizable to her. She didn't think it was Craig's car though; it was too boxy.

Thinking it probably was a car full of teenagers on the prowl, she turned in the dark, to go back into the house, almost tripping over the crumpled and broken figure of her husband, lying in the grass. At first, she didn't recognize him, but when she realized who it was, she screamed.

Tom Palmer had come out to pick up his morning paper and heard Felicia's screams. He rushed over to help and then ran back into his house to call 911. Craig was unconscious, and Felicia at first thought he was dead until she heard his raspy attempts at breathing and saw the pink bloody froth from his mouth.

Palmer came back, bringing a blanket to keep Craig warm until the ambulance arrived. "What happened?" he asked. "Is this your husband?"

In her hysteria, Felicia couldn't answer him yet. Her mind was on the nearly lifeless form of her husband. She thought that Craig must be dead or if not he soon would be. There was so much blood. She sat on the grass, clean dress and all, and cradled Craig's bloody head in her lap. The pretty gray miniskirt was now covered with blood; it was pooling in her lap under his head and spilling onto her stocking-covered legs.

"Oh, Craig! Oh, Craig! Who did this to you?"

Craig was unconscious and couldn't answer. His right leg was folded in a bizarre angle below the knee, obviously broken. His hands had been tied behind his back again with the cable ties, and his ankles were tied together, but the hood had caught on the branch of a shrub at the edge of the driveway. It still hung morbidly from the branch late into the day, a grim reminder of his capture and torture.

The 911 report was relayed to all officers in the area, and two uniforms, Hauser and Bayden, came to investigate. They happened to be cruising a few blocks away when Craig was dropped off and were on the scene less than two minutes after the emergency call came in.

"What happened here?" Hauser asked. "Is he alive?" He bent over to feel Craig's neck, to see if he still had a carotid pulse. Finding one, he radioed in for an ambulance and backup. He didn't know what he had; the bad guys may still be in the neighborhood. Again, "What's going on here?"

Felicia was unable to answer in her shock. Palmer tried to tell Hauser what he knew. "I was coming out to get my paper and heard this car burning rubber getting out of here. Then I saw Mrs. Jernigan come out. I saw the car, but it had its lights off, so I couldn't tell anything else about it. It might have been some kind of van or something, but I'm not sure. It was still dark, and no lights."

Hauser radioed again, this time to alert all cars to watch for a speeding vehicle with its lights off. With a little luck, they might just catch this guy before he can get far.

Hauser continued to ask questions while Bayden cut the nylon wrist cuffs off Craig's hands and ankles. Carefully, he tried to position him more comfortably, taking care not to do more damage to his broken legs and hands. "They'll need a backboard. No telling what's happened here," he said, concerned that if the victim had a neck or back injury, a move might paralyze him.

Hauser asked what else Palmer had seen.

"Well, I didn't see the man here—I guess it's Mr. Jernigan—at first. Mrs. Jernigan looked like she was trying to figure out what was happening and walked out to the end of the driveway looking at the car driving off. Then she went ballistic when she saw her husband lying there. We both thought he was dead. Lord, I've never seen so much blood before."

As he spoke, they heard the high-pitched whine of the Denton County ambulance, and its emergency lights met those of the patrol car. The ambulance stopped a block short of the scene, the EMT's calling ahead to make sure the area was secured, no weapons were seen, and they could safely evacuate the victim. Hauser was able to reassure them that the site was secure, and the red-and-white box wheeled in, lights flashing and siren squealing.

Senior paramedic Boyd Dickens and EMT paramedic Ed Webb jumped out of the ambulance and brought their equipment kit to Craig's side.

"Does anybody know what happened?" Dickens asked as he checked Craig's pupils and pulse. His pupils were constricted; dilated pupils would have told him that there was probably irreversible brain damage. His blood pressure was so low that he couldn't get a reading, and the pulse was rapid and thready.

"He was dumped out here in the yard from a vehicle," Hauser reported. "Looks like somebody really worked him over. We don't know anything else yet."

Dickens looked at Felicia. "You his wife?"

"Yes," she nodded, crying fitfully. "Is he going to be all right?"

Dickens ignored her questions, firing several back at her without looking up from Craig. "Any medical problems? Is he taking any medicines? Any allergies?"

Felicia was only able to shake her head. She seemed frozen, unable to speak.

"Looks like he's in shock," Dickens said to Webb.

"Yeah. I see a compound of the right tibia. Maybe a spleen too," Webb responded as he rapidly pushed two large bore needles into separate veins in Craig's left arm. "We'll need the MAS Trousers." He connected clear plastic bottles of saline to both IV needles, left the lines wide open, and hung both bottles high on a pole, letting the lifesaving liquid flow into Craig's failing circulation as rapidly as possible.

While Webb started the IV's, Dickens ran back to the truck and brought out the Military Anti-Shock Trousers, a transparent wraparound balloon apparatus which could be inflated and pressurized around the victim's legs and abdomen. They placed the MAS trousers on the back board and then carefully moved Craig on top of it. They then folded the trouser fronts over Craig's legs, closed the velcro straps, and inflated it.

The effect was predictable. The inflated trouser pushed blood out of his legs, back into his circulation, and combined with the rapid infusion of intravenous fluids, caused his blood pressure to rise to a low normal level. They also served to decrease the active bleeding, and to stabilize the broken lower legs so that they wouldn't be further damaged during transport.

Together, Dickens and Webb pulled Craig up on the backboard and moved him into the ambulance. Then Dickens placed a breathing tube into Craig's trachea, through his open mouth, and connected him to a positive pressure ventilation system. He listened to his chest to make sure the tube had been inserted into the correct location and that both lungs were being ventilated. He taped the tube down and signaled for Webb to move out, and they began the short trip to Lewisville Regional, sirens screaming and blue-and-white strobe lights flashing.

Felicia followed in the backseat of the patrol car, adding another set of lights and sirens to the not-yet-awake neighborhood.

Dickens looked at his watch. "Hmmnn . . . in and out in nine minutes. Not bad!" he said to Webb.

Only five miles away from Lewisville Regional, the ambulance arrived seven minutes later, sirens screaming all the way. Craig was taken to Trauma Room #1, and Felicia was instructed to wait outside. Although Craig had multiple fractures and was still unconscious, his worst problem was inside. In spite of the MAS trousers, he was rapidly going back into shock from internal hemorrhaging. Blood was crossmatched and a transfusion was rapidly begun. Dr. Michael West, a general surgeon, happened to be in the building when the call came from the EMT that there was a severe multiple injury case coming in, in shock, and he met them in the ER. He did a quick evaluation and determined that he was bleeding internally, probably from a ruptured spleen and ordered him prepared for surgery.

Felicia went to the waiting room as the nurses rapidly wheeled Craig to the elevators and to OR #5. She stopped in a quiet corner and pulled her mother's cell phone number from the speed dial on her cell phone. It was now 6:45 a.m.; Ellie should be awake, getting ready to start her morning rounds before her 9:00 a.m. office schedule. She may already be on her way to work. The phone was answered on the first ring.

"Hello! This is Dr. Conlin."

"Mom, I'm at the ER. Craig has been hurt. He got beat up real bad. I don't know if he's gonna make it or not. He's in surgery. I think he's in a coma!"

"My god!" Ellie gasped. "How? ... Who? ... Listen, I'll be right there. Are you in Lewisville?"

"Yes, at Lewisville Regional. The ambulance just now brought him here. Oh, Mom! It's terrible. He looks real bad!"

"I'll be there in twenty minutes," Ellie reassured her. "I have to get dressed."

As she hung up, Felicia saw a uniformed policeman and a middle-aged man in denims approach.

"Mrs. Felicia Jernigan?" the officer asked.

"Yes, I'm Felicia Jernigan," she answered.

"I'm Detective Jack Simonton," the man in denims said, showing her his badge. "You can call me Smitty. This is Detective Steve Franks. Do you feel like talking to us while you wait for your husband to get out of surgery?"

"Sure, I guess so. My mother's on her way." Felicia seemed bewildered and frightened in her bloodstained dress.

"Is your mother Dr. Ellie Conlin?" Simonton asked. "She's a friend of mine." Actually, he had only met her twice, but his comment seemed to put Felicia at ease. He was dressed casually, with jeans, a denim jacket, open neck white shirt, and full quill ostrich skin boots. He was a large man, at least six feet four inches, and obviously kept himself in good condition. His full face beard had a scattering of gray, giving a salt-and-pepper texture. His hair was dark brown but had escaped most of the graying that had aged his beard. They went to a consultation room adjoining the OR waiting room for privacy.

"Have a seat," Simonton offered. "Want some coffee or a donut or anything?"

73

Felicia suddenly remembered she still hadn't eaten dinner from the evening before and realized she was starved. "Okay," she responded.

"Let's go down to the cafeteria. They serve the best artificial eggs here that you'll find anywhere. Some of the bacon tastes so good, you'd almost think it was real." Felicia smiled back as Simonton tried a dumb joke. "There, that's better. They can page us overhead if they need us."

They took the elevator down the single flight to the cafeteria. They found it almost empty, so there was no waiting. Smitty and Franks took scrambled eggs, toast, and bacon while Felicia took a dish of cottage cheese and covered it with freshly thawed strawberries. They asked for a private area and were directed to Classroom A, just behind the cash register.

They ate silently for a couple of minutes until Simonton broke the ice. "How long have you and Mr. Jernigan lived in Lewisville?"

"Just about six months." It took her a moment to get her mind on the questions that Detective Simonton was asking. "Craig works for the Lewisville Journal. He just recently got a promotion to senior police reporter, so we moved from La Vista to Lewisville."

"Yeah, I remember him. He's called me a couple of times about cases I'm working. When did you see him last?"

"Yesterday morning, when he left for work."

"Don't be offended, but except for all the blood, you sure look better than most people do at this time of the morning. Are you going to work?"

"Oh, I don't work. I guess it does look silly, but I haven't been to bed yet. I was worried when Craig didn't come home, so I've just stayed up waiting for him."

"All night?" Franks spoke for only the second time, glancing momentarily toward Simonton with a knowing/questioning look.

"Yes," she answered, turning her head toward Franks.

"Did you call anybody, ask if anybody had seen him?" Simonton asked questions while Franks continued taking notes.

"No, except I called my mom after I got here."

At that moment, Dr. Ellie Conlin entered the hospital through the special doctors-only ID badge-controlled back entrance, straight from the physicians' covered parking lot, and saw her daughter as she hurried past the cafeteria en route to the emergency room. She rushed over and hugged her tightly, and both women cried. The officers waited patiently for the women to regain their composure.

"Oh, Lisha, Baby! Do they know anything yet? Is he going to be ok?" she asked.

"They think he may have a ruptured spleen. He's bleeding internally! Do you think he'll make it?"

"Let me go check on him." One advantage of being on staff at the hospital was that she could go to surgery and talk with his surgeon. "I'll let you know, soon as I can find out anything." She left, took the stairs to the second floor operating suite, and changed into surgical scrubs. She looked at the surgical scheduling board and saw, "Jernigan—West—Room 5." She put on a surgical mask, cap, and shoe covers and entered OR #5.

"Hi, Mike! How bad is it?"

"Hi, Ellie! Sorry about this. He's stable at this end. We've already got the spleen out, and we're working on a little tear on the medial edge of the liver. Lost a lot of blood but looks like we've got it under control now."

"Thank God!" Conlin whispered and said, "Thanks for your help!" out loud to West.

"He's got a tibial compound fracture and a lot of smaller fractures that we're gonna wait till he's stable to fix. Arnie Tabor's gonna splint the legs as soon as I get through so he can have room to work. We've got him on a shitload of antibiotics. That's all he needs, an infected compound fracture." Other less serious injuries, including multiple other fractures and lacerations, were not life-threatening and would have to wait until after surgery. They would all be cleaned and bandaged and repaired later, probably in ICU.

"What's his neuro status?" Conlin asked, looking toward Raymond Barnes, the anesthesiologist.

"Well, it's hard to say. His pupils are okay, and everything seems to be working. But we'll have to see what his MRI shows and how he does after surgery. We've got him on steroids already to keep his brain from swelling. So far so good though, Ellie," he answered.

She left the OR, not wanting to put any pressure on the physicians taking care of him. "Sure appreciate your help. It's lucky you were both so close by."

"No extra charge!" West quipped, not turning his eyes away from the task at hand.

"Take it easy, Ellie!" said Barnes.

"You need anything, you got my number," said West.

Conlin stripped off her cap, mask, and shoe covers and went back to the waiting room where Felicia and the officers waited. "He's stable for now.

They've taken out his spleen, and they're sewing up a little tear in his liver. He should be okay." Her eyes failed to maintain contact with Felicia, showing her concern that she might be overstating Craig's prognosis.

"Are you sure?" Felicia needed more reassurance.

"Well, we'll have to wait to see how fast he wakes up. They can't tell much about his neuro status till they do a CAT scan or maybe an MRI later. So far, so good though. I'm sure he should be okay. We just have to wait." She sat next to her daughter to await further reports and to wait for the surgeon. Simonton and Franks left, promising to check back later in the day.

Craig's lacerations eventually required a total of almost two hundred stitches, and he received eleven pints of blood. In addition to the compound fracture of his tibia, there were fractures of several bones in his hands, ankles, ribs, and face. His nose was broken, and his right ear was almost completely gone, hanging by a half-inch span of skin. He had lost most of his front teeth and had a broken jawbone and multiple other facial fractures.

He spent a week in the surgical ICU, not waking up for the first forty-eight hours. Simonton had questioned Felicia, trying to determine if Craig had any enemies that might want to hurt him. She had no helpful ideas. So far as she knew, except for a few pissed-off paperboys, Craig didn't have any real enemies.

He had told her about the conflict with Charlie Ross, and she related that to the detective. None of his coworkers at the *Journal* could add any better suggestions either. He had written his drug-trafficking expose just six months earlier; maybe this was a get-even message from some of their friends. There had never been a ransom demand, so that probably wasn't the reason. The van's tires were too slick to leave any kind of a track they could use for identification, and it had left so fast that none of the witnesses saw it well enough for a description. They would all just have to wait for Craig to wake up.

Felicia was finally able to visit and see Craig in SICU about 3:00 p.m. He looked so helpless and so sick. His face was bandaged, but what she could see was almost completely black-and-blue. One leg was in a long cast and suspended from an orthopedic frame. The other leg had a short cast, covering his foot and reaching up to mid-calf. Both hands were also in casts. He had a large bandage on his stomach and another wrapping completely around his chest. He had drainage tubes in his chest and stomach and other tubes in what seemed to be every conceivable bodily orifice. He was connected to a maze of monitors and was breathing only with the assistance of a respirator. He seemed for all practical purposes to be dead.

She had not been able to stop crying since she found him in the yard. She was alone with Craig when, just after 4:00 p.m., Simonton returned. Conlin had gone to work, planning to return later in the afternoon.

Simonton came into the SICU, put his arm on Felicia's shoulder, and gently pulled her out into the hall. It was apparent from his demeanor that he kept a high opinion of himself. But it wasn't a cocky ego, more of a confident, fatherly kind of strong self-assurance. He had long ago been divorced by a wife who couldn't tolerate the stress or schedule of a detective's life and lived alone. His two daughters were also at the University of Texas, and his only regular communication with them was through his checks for their tuition and dormitory.

"Hi, Mrs. Jernigan," he said, showing Felicia his badge. "Are you feeling strong enough for a few more questions? I know this is hard for you, but if we're gonna catch the scum who did this, I've got to have some information. Can you help me a little? I don't know when we'll get to talk with your husband."

"I don't know . . . I feel like I'm going to vomit."

Simonton led her to a chair in the waiting room and asked a nurse for a cold washcloth and a glass of water.

"Any better?"

"I'm getting a little better . . . Why did this happen? Who would do such a thing?"

"We don't know yet. Do you know if anybody was mad at your husband? Did he have any enemies?"

"Not any major ones that I know of. Sure, everybody has people they don't get along with. But this . . . I can't imagine anybody mad enough or crazy enough to do this."

"Have you had any threatening phone calls? Any calls that didn't make sense? Anybody calling and hanging up after you pick up the phone?"

"No, not that I can remember. Craig might have had some calls like that, but he didn't mention it to me."

"Has your husband ever had any problems with drugs or alcohol?"

"No . . . Oh, he drinks some, but don't all men? He doesn't stay drunk all the time. Mostly weekends. And he's never done drugs. You'd think I'd know, wouldn't you?"

"Wives don't always know. But I'm not saying he did. I'm just asking some routine questions for the record. You know . . ."

"I'm sorry! I'm just so upset. Nothing like this has ever happened before. And they're still out there. How can I go home?"

"We'll watch your home tonight. You might feel better if you went and stayed with your mother a few days."

"I have to be here when he wakes up! I can't leave."

"I understand. Do whatever you need. Just a few more questions. Who keeps the checkbook? Has he made any unusual deposits or withdrawals lately?"

"No. But I might not know. He keeps the checkbook, and I usually don't see it. What are you getting at?"

"Just routine questions, like we have to ask everybody, ma'am. I'm not accusing anybody of anything. Has he talked about any problems at work?"

"No, I don't think so. Except that guy he got fired the other day. I forget his name. Sounded like a real smart-ass, according to my husband. Always late for work, sloppy clothes, didn't bathe very often. Craig finally got tired of it and fired him. He talked like it really pissed the guy off. Said if looks could kill, you know."

"Did he make any threats?"

"Well, he did say something like "You'll be sorry," or something like that? I think Craig was a little scared of him. Talked like he was Hulk Hogan or something."

"Do you know where he lives? Have you ever talked to him?"

"I don't know. I guess the paper has his address, the employee files, I guess, but I don't know where they are. I never saw the guy. Do you think he did this to get even?"

"I don't know, ma'am. He's as good a lead as we have so far . . . the only lead, in fact."

"I want you to find whoever did this!"

"We'll find him, you can bet on that. And in the meantime, get some rest. If you insist on sitting out here at the hospital, at least let them get you a blanket and pillow. And call me if you think of anything else."

"Okay. And thanks. I didn't mean to be snotty with you."

"Goodnight, ma'am."

"Oh yeah! I just remembered. The guy he got fired . . . You know, the smart-ass. His name was Charlie. I don't know his last name. But I remember Craig calling him Chicken-Shit Charlie."

Conlin returned about 5:00 p.m. She had canceled several non-urgent appointments and arranged for another colleague to cover her practice for a couple of days until they knew how Craig was going to do. Felicia was still in the SICU waiting room. When she saw her mother, she breathed a sigh of relief and welcomed the hug that Ellie gave her.

"Mom, they just about killed him! He's still in a coma. He hasn't even moved a finger or opened his eyes yet! They still can't tell if he'll be okay or not! They can't even tell me for sure if he'll live or not! I'm so scared!"

Ellie put her arms around her daughter again, and together they sank into one of the large, soft couches in the waiting room. Felicia wailed loudly while Ellie sobbed quietly, each woman's pent-up emotion seeming to boil over on the other's shoulders. After what seemed an eternity, they both began to feel better, and the crying gradually subsided.

Conlin had already stopped at radiology on the way to SICU. She had reviewed Craig's MRI with Dr. Don Miller, the radiologist who read the films. Other than a couple of questionable small blurs, there was no sign of any major bleeding inside his head. *Thank God for small miracles*, she thought.

She stopped also at the ER to visit Perdue. He was doing one of his occasional shifts at Lewisville Regional but had not been on call when Craig was brought in. He only knew about him through the physicians' lunchroom grapevine.

"Hi, Ellie!" he said, giving her a friendly hug. "How's everybody holding out?"

"Hi, Ken," she responded and returned his hug. She had long ago realized, living alone as she did, that sometimes the very best thing a friend can do is to simply put his arms around you and hug you tightly. If a picture is worth a thousand words, a hug is worth a million. The arms around you seem to form a shield, impenetrable by even the worst of the world's wicked woes, at least for the few moments that the hug lasts. She wanted this hug to last forever.

"I'm doing fine, I guess. Don says they didn't find any major intracranial bleeding, so hopefully he'll come out of it. It's Felicia that I'm worried about now. I want her to come home with me for a while, but so far she refuses. You know the kind of stress she's been under. Ken, she has barely spoken to me since I brought her in here six months ago. I have no idea what's been going on in her house or in her head either for that matter."

"Did she ever let you report it to the police?" he asked.

"No! That's what I mean. She hasn't reported it, they won't get counseling. She won't even discuss it with me. I tell you, I can't talk with her about it!"

"Well, I guess that's on the back burner for now. He sure isn't going to hurt her for a while now, at least. Maybe somehow you can talk some sense into her while he's in the hospital."

"No, I'm afraid to even mention it to her. I'm afraid if I push it, I'll lose her. I wouldn't be talking with her now if this hadn't happened."

"I'm sure you realize, we see this kind of stuff all the time here in the ER. You'd be amazed at the women we see here, beat up, making up stories about some outlandish accident. Low class, upper class, middle class, no class, it doesn't matter. I've seen them all. I can tell it every time. The husband comes in with her, acting like he's the most devoted man you ever saw, always with that shit-eating sugar sweet smile, patting her on the back, rubbing her neck, talking sweet talk. Refuses to leave her side. Acts like he cares too much, can't even go to registration. Truth is, he's afraid if he leaves her side for a minute, she'll tell the truth for once, and he'll be in deep shit. Sometimes I'd like to get a couple of guys together and take the bastards out behind a barn. I'd give them a dose of their own medicine."

"Be careful what you say," Conlin smiled. "Smitty will have you in for questioning!"

"Well, you know me. All talk, no action. I'd be the one to get caught. I'm too chicken to make a good crook."

"I've already checked on his MRI," Ellie told her daughter as she arrived in Craig's room in SICU. "It's okay, no major bleeding. We're just going to have to give him time to wake up. I'm sure he'll be all right."

"I hope so. I just wish he'd hurry up," Felicia said.

Ellie begged Felicia to go home with her, to stay with her a few days, at least until Craig got out of the hospital where she would be safe. Nobody knew if it was some kind of a kook who would be back or not. She reminded her of Craig's part in the report that put the drug dealers away and was afraid the attack might be in retaliation. If so, she warned, they might return and Felicia might not be safe. But instead, Felicia insisted on staying at the hospital until Craig woke up. So the two women stayed in the SICU waiting room all night, dozing a few minutes at a time and waking with a start every time the automatic doors to SICU opened.

The next morning, Thursday, Dr. West came to talk with Felicia and Ellie. "I'm afraid Craig may be bleeding internally, and we're going to have to operate again. We are optimistic, but obviously this is a very serious situation. We'll be back to talk with you as soon as we know anything else."

"Can we see him first?" Felicia asked.

By this time, Craig's mother, Carol Andrews, had arrived. Her live-in boyfriend, Jeremy Spears, had driven her the hundred and twenty five miles from Ferris, just south of Dallas, after Simonton had called. When she heard the news about Craig's abduction and beating, she had been in a state of hysteria and was inconsolable for several hours. But with the help of an extra Xanax, two beers, and several cigarettes, she was finally calm enough to get into Jeremy's car and begin the trip up I-45 to Lewisville.

The three women, Carol, Ellie, and Felicia went into SICU together. Craig was still motionless on the respirator with his chest bandages bloodied and the suction receptacle more than half full of bloody fluid. He seemed so weak and vulnerable. Felicia went over to him and kissed him on the forehead. "I love you, Craig. You can't die on me!"

Carol burst uncontrollably into tears when she saw her son and had to sit down when she first saw him in this condition.

Ellie put her hand on Craig's shoulder but seemed afraid to do more. Once Carol gained her self-control, she just watched from the corner of the room, crying softly to herself. They stayed the five minutes until Craig was wheeled back to the OR for the second time in twenty-four hours.

Simonton showed up just after Craig was taken to surgery for the second time. He was unaware of the complications.

"Hi, Doc! Hi, Mrs. J! How's he doing this morning? Is he awake yet?"

"He's back in surgery. He's bleeding internally again . . . ," Felicia answered.

"Sure sorry to hear that. Hope he does ok this time. I guess that mean I'll have to wait for him to get better. We don't have that much to go on so far."

"Do you think Charlie Ross had something to do with this?"

"We don't know. But we're gonna talk to him as soon as we leave here! We're also trying to run a check on those thugs he wrote the drug article about last year. But it's too early to tell anything. We're working on it! I can assure you, we'll catch whoever did this. I just hope we can talk to Craig pretty soon. He should be able to tell us a lot."

He looked at Dr. Conlin, who looked exhausted. She had raided the surgery dressing room, and both women had changed into scrubs for their overnight vigil and had neither time nor opportunity to clean up for the morning. "Could I get you ladies anything? Something to eat or anything?"

"Well, we are really wiped out, and it looks like Craig will be in surgery for another couple of hours," Ellie said. "Maybe some breakfast wouldn't hurt . . .

some coffee and a donut at least. Maybe we could go to the cafeteria for a few minutes. We sure don't want to leave the hospital until he's out of surgery and we know he's all right."

"Sure! Come on, my treat this time. They can page you when he comes out of surgery." Smitty led the women to the downstairs cafeteria, and they had a quick breakfast of bagels, OJ, and coffee before the message came over the pager system.

"Dr. Ellie Conlin, report to SICU . . . Dr. Ellie Conlin, report to SICU."

They rushed back to the elevators and down the long gray corridor to SICU. They knocked on the door and were greeted by Dr. West, this time a little more cheerfully than the last.

"I think he's going to be okay now. The bleeding wasn't near as bad as we were afraid it might be. It was just a small bleeder from the splenic bed, and we were able to get it easily. He got two more pints of blood. I don't think he'll have any more trouble. How are you all holding out?"

"Oh! Thank God!" both Felicia and Ellie said simultaneously.

"When can we see him?" Felicia asked.

"He's still unconscious, but you can go in now for a while. Try not to disturb him though. He's been through a lot. But you can talk to him. We never know just what unconscious patients can hear and understand. Tell him you love him and give him something to get well for," he knowingly looked toward Craig's wife.

Again, Felicia entered SICU. The smell of hospitals had always frightened her, and the smells here in SICU were especially strong, usually a combination of alcohol, disinfectants, medications, and sickness. Today a patient had just vomited, and that odor added to those already present. She fought back her own nausea as she went into Craig's private room. His nurse was draining his catheter bag.

Felicia noted that the urine looked bloody. Even though he was still trussed with all the same casts, tubes, and dressings, she thought his color was maybe just a little bit better. She imagined that he was ready to wake up and would soon be talking to her.

"Craig, if you can hear me, I love you!" she said as she stroked his right upper arm, one of the only parts of his body not covered by bandages, IV tubing, or monitor connections. She imagined she felt a slight movement in his arm but decided it was all in her imagination. She cried softly as she looked at his damaged face. She raised the sheet to see the rest of his body, at the same time keeping him adequately protected from the view of others in the room.

He had always been modest, and she knew especially that he would not want Ellie to have such a private viewing when he was unable to protest.

Felicia saw the pale brown rubber catheter as it exited the tip of his penis. It had been so strong and virile and now was just another almost inert orifice for the doctors to hook up to tubes for drainage and monitoring. She could hardly make the mental connection between this weak, soft, pitiful thing, and the rigid rod that had given her such pleasure in the early days of their courtship and marriage. After only ten minutes with him, she felt that if she didn't leave, she would explode. Watching, her mother realized the difficulty she was having and gently grasped her shoulders to guide her to the door.

"Come on out now. You gotta stay strong so you can help him when he wakes up. Let's go get some rest." This time, Ellie didn't try to touch Craig. Felicia reluctantly left with her mother. They made the fifteen-minute drive to Ellie's Richardson home, and both sank immediately into their beds without even changing clothes. Both were exhausted, having slept in the chairs the previous night.

Craig recovered from his second operation without complications, although due to the extent of his injuries, his recuperation was slow. He remained in SICU on a ventilator until Thursday afternoon when he was finally able to breathe on his own. He was given steroids to reduce brain swelling and antibiotics to prevent infection. A second MRI of his head still didn't show any major internal hemorrhages.

Felicia stayed with him almost constantly, going home only to bathe and change clothes. She was at his side when he woke up, three days after his abduction. He was frightened by the tube in his trachea until the doctors removed it. He wasn't sure where he was and he was confused. Felicia tried to explain things to him, and gradually he began to understand.

Ellie visited daily, more to support her daughter than to visit with Craig. She was still angry since she heard how he had been treating Felicia. She came in the evening, after work, and stayed until late each night. This was the first time she had been able to spend any real time with her daughter in a long time, and she was making the most of it.

She brought her a homemade brown-bag sandwich and a coke every evening and sat with her in the hospital coffee shop while she ate. Even though at this point she had little use for Craig, she did not criticize him to her daughter. She knew that while he was in his current damaged condition, Felicia would not accept any discussion of leaving him or getting him into counseling. So she seemed completely supportive, not only of Felicia but of Craig and their future relationship as well.

Carol took leave from her job until she knew her son was stable. She had worked for Dr. Susan Lieder, an ob/gyn in Ferris, for seventeen years, initially as receptionist and assistant and, for the past six years, as office manager. She stayed at a local Motel 6, despite offers from Ellie to let her stay with her in Richardson. Married and divorced twice, she had not had an easy life. Both of her husbands had been heavy drinkers and had been rough on her. Craig had been witness to their abusive ways throughout his childhood.

Carol had finally broken free from her second husband eight years ago but still depended on alcohol way too much. She had only been able to stop drinking three years ago when she met Jeremy. He had been the best thing that ever happened to her. He was a real man, she thought, one who managed his life and love through kindness and his own personal strength, not through force. He had encouraged her in her abstinence and had frequently gone to AA meetings with her even though he never drank alcohol himself. But Jeremy had gone back to Ferris to work after a couple of days, and she couldn't rely on his constant encouragement.

The two beers Carol had when she heard of her son's critical condition were her first in six months. Knowing her only son was critically injured was just too much, especially now with Jeremy gone. Even if Craig survived, he would forever suffer the pain of his injuries. She couldn't stand to see him like this, with machines and tubes running everywhere.

Without Jeremy's strong shoulder, she had stopped at the Green House Bar & Grill near the motel and now spent most of her days there. She still came to visit Craig at least once a day, but Felicia suspected she had broken her abstinence. She had known her too long to be fooled. Even though she was never drunk when she came to Craig's SICU bed, she had the same blank expression on her face that Felicia had learned to dread during her heavy drinking years. And she thought she got a whiff of alcohol once when Carol leaned over her to kiss Craig.

Six days after his abduction, Craig's vital signs were more stable than they had been any time before, and he seemed to be making daily improvements. He no longer had the chest or abdominal drain tubes and was breathing almost normally. The dressings were dry now, and he had avoided the infections that his doctors worried about. His black-and-blue bruises were beginning to yellow. The doctors had taken out almost all of his stitches. The damaged ear had been repaired by a plastic surgeon and was beginning to look almost normal again. His face and scalp still were covered by scars and always would be. The swelling around his nose was going down, and Felicia could see that he would have the look of an old boxer, with the bridge gone and the tip turned up. But now that he was awake and getting stronger every day, all those things seemed like small potatoes. He would survive, and nothing else really mattered.

After six days in the intensive care unit, Craig was downgraded to a regular private room for the next four weeks. At that point, because of the extent of his injuries, the doctors planned to transfer him to a rehab facility when he had recovered adequately before he could even consider going home.

A week after his kidnapping and injuries, Craig went to surgery for the third time, this time to repair the worst of his bony injuries. Plates and screws were used to repair his tibia, and a plastic surgeon teamed with a facio-maxillary surgeon to put his facial tissues and bones back together as well as possible. New casts were placed on his legs and arms.

Finally, the last tube was removed, the intravenous line that was feeding antibiotics into Craig's veins to prevent infection. He was cooperating well with his physical therapists and, by this time, was able to assist in moving himself from bed to wheelchair, although with difficulty. The nausea and vomiting had subsided when the antibiotics were discontinued, and finally he was able to take in normal solid food. It was hard to estimate his weight, with all his casts and tubes, but he looked like he had lost about fifteen or twenty pounds during the month of hospitalization. He was thinking more clearly but only wanted to get back home to his own bed. But he wasn't ready for that yet. He had rehab to go first.

Felicia gathered all the cards and letters he had received and moved them to a cart the rehab center volunteers had arranged. Most of the flowers had wilted but had not been thrown out yet. They drooped so badly that Felicia had no qualms about tossing them. But there were still a few arrangements that he had received later, that still had a few days of life left in them, so she moved those to the car. Of course, she kept all the cards that came with them so Craig could remember who sent what when he felt better. There were four ivy planters, but two of them had died, so only two had to be brought home.

There was also one teddy bear that Jeremy Spears had sent. He had undergone surgery himself a few years earlier and had received a cuddly bear from his daughter from a previous marriage. It was dark brown with a big red bow tie and held a banner that said, "Get well!" It had actually made him feel better, he thought, and he had kept it ever since.

When Craig began to wake up from his coma, Jeremy had gotten his old bear out of storage and brought it to the hospital. It was a little ragged from age with one glued-on button eye hanging loose, but the fake fur was still soft and the plastic he had wrapped it in had protected it from mice. One drop of super glue fixed the eye, and it was like new again. Like Jeremy, Craig also enjoyed the soft old thing. So Felicia packed it with all the cards to take home while Craig was taken by ambulance to Memorial Rehab, the rehabilitation center in Dallas that had been recommended

He cooperated with his physical therapy team and was in rehab for three weeks. He had to relearn walking within the constraints of his multiple casts and received massage and passive range of motion exercises daily from the physical therapists. Finally his medical team declared him ready to leave Rehab. He was ready to go home.

Ellie had brought her car to the rehab center for the trip to Lewisville. Although she hadn't told Felicia of her plans, and certainly not Craig, she planned to leave the car with Felicia permanently. So long as she kept the title in her own name, Craig couldn't trade it or sell it, and at least Felicia would have transportation when she needed it. Now that she and her daughter were on speaking terms again, she wanted to make sure that she had her own vehicle so she could leave in a hurry if things ever got bad again. But she would work on that later. For now, she was the perfect mother-in-law, giving help without advice. She had even been getting along with Craig ever since he woke up.

Felicia piled Craig's flowers, cards, and teddy bear on the top shelf of the cart, and his suitcase and clothes on the bottom. When the cart was fully packed and ready, the nurse's aide helped Craig out of bed and into the wheelchair. It still hurt him to move, especially his slowly mending legs, but he gritted his teeth and moved.

It was raining, but the rehab center had a covered awning for patient loading and unloading, so they were protected from the direct effects of the deluge. Still, it was mid-February, and even in North Texas, the misty breeze was cold. It was hard to keep Craig covered; a gust of wind caught his blankets. When they flapped up, he felt the cold sting of the seemingly icy mist.

It took all the efforts of Felicia, the aide, and an orderly to get him lifted out of the wheelchair with casts on all four extremities, but with their joint effort they were able to get him into the backseat of the already-warmed car. Covered again with dry blankets, Craig finally felt warm again. The trip, though, had exhausted him. He had only done the exercises the physical therapists had taught him in the hospital and was unaccustomed to all the hustle and bustle. He broke out in a cold sweat as they lifted him into the car.

Felicia had converted her small sewing room into a spare bedroom for Craig's recuperation. She had rented an electric hospital bed with the same orthopedic trapeze that he had used in the hospital. With his hands and forearms still in casts and his legs in longer ones, he had to hook his arms over the bar in order to use it to lift himself. But it was better than nothing. And those casts would be off in a few weeks. Felicia had set up his laptop computer on a hospital style over-the-bed rolling table and had added a small TV/VCR/ stereo as well. Of course, it would be a while until he could use the computer. At least until he got the casts off his arms.

Craig asked for more pain medication and then slept soundly the rest of the day and night. The next morning, Felicia brought him breakfast in bed—scrambled eggs and toast with orange juice and hot coffee. He was hungry, but it was difficult to handle the fork with both his hands in casts. Felicia had fed him herself during his hospitalization and planned to do the same at home until his casts were off. But Craig was uncomfortable, and had trouble cooperating. He turned his head away just as she brought a forkful of scrambled eggs to his mouth. It hit the corner of his mouth and spilled the eggs onto his hospital gown. Felicia was startled, not knowing what reaction to expect. But Craig laughed, "Look at me—I'm a two-year-old again!"

Felicia cleaned up the mess and offered to change his gown, but he refused. It was almost time for his bed bath and linen changes anyway. "Let me drink my coffee first, then you can change the gown. During the few minutes that they had struggled to get the eggs and toast into him, the coffee had cooled off enough to drink. Felicia had added his favorite hazelnut flavoring. "Ah! Damn! You can't get coffee like this in the hospital. This is good shit!"

Felicia sighed peacefully. She hadn't heard Craig be this agreeable in at least two years. Maybe everything will work out, she hoped.

Finally, six weeks after the assault, the day came for Craig's casts to come off. This was his first day out of the house since he got out of rehab. But he felt excited like he was being released from prison, and it was a nice, warm, dry late February Dallas morning. Ellie brought the car to the driveway, and she and Felicia were able to get him from bed to wheelchair to car with relative ease. At the doctor's office, he had new x-rays, to make sure the fractures were healing adequately. He was so glad to get the casts off. His wrists had been driving him crazy with itching, and the best he could do was to have Felicia run a bent coat hanger inside the cast. It did relieve the itching somewhat, but there were still spots that she couldn't reach with the coat hanger.

His wrists and forearms were pale white, having suffered through their entrapment in the casts without benefit of air or sun. The odor was pungent; there had been no chance for washing off the perspiration over the past weeks. But that was no big deal; his arms were finally free. There was still some distortion over the backs of both hands where the bones had been crushed, but he was able to move all his fingers, and he thought all the feeling was normal. It felt good to be able to wiggle his fingers freely again. He picked up a pen and tried to write his name. It would take some time to get the strength back, but it would all be okay.

He had another set of x-rays on his legs as well. They were healing on schedule. His doctor removed the long leg casts and replaced them with posterior fiberglass splints and walker heels. He would still need the wheelchair though. His hands were not strong enough to use crutches yet. But he could move around at home so long as he had a helper and a wall to lean against.

The trip home was smooth in the BMW. Craig wanted to drive and was frustrated when he couldn't. His hands, which itched for scratching for several weeks, now itched for something to do. But his feet were still in posterior splints, and he had to accept that he couldn't handle the accelerator or brakes dependably and would be an unsafe driver. So Ellie continued to be his chauffeur a while longer.

Craig was tired after the seemingly long trip to the doctor's office for cast removal and slept for more than three hours after he was helped back into his hospital bed. When he woke up, Felicia brought him his dinner. He had wanted Chinese food, so she had ordered his favorite almond chicken from Original Hunan Restaurant and had already picked it up to go. Craig was finally able to get to the kitchen without a lot of pain, so he ate his dinner there with Felicia. He was so thrilled to be able to feed himself that the dinner went without incident and without complaint. He even talked with Felicia for a few minutes.

"Maybe things will get better, now that he's feeling better," she silently wished.

After dinner, Felicia helped Craig into the bathroom and then closed the door and left him alone. This was the first time he had shaved himself or even urinated by himself since his abduction. He was able to remove the splints and get into the bathtub to soak in the hot soapy water. Felicia brought two glasses of wine and then stayed and scrubbed his back. Soon she was scrubbing everything else. Bathing together had always turned them both on, at least in their early days.

Craig reached out to kiss her and touched her breast. The sweater was off in an instant, and the skirt and panties followed. His expression silently invited her into the bath with him, and she just as silently accepted. She hoped to keep him happy as long as possible, and their sex had never been the problem. She was eager to make love with him.

They had to be careful with his legs. The doctor had told him that he should put no stress on them without the splints for another couple of weeks for fear that they would break them before they were strong enough to handle the pressure. So there was no way they would be able to get him up, into splints, and into bed without breaking the magic of the moment.

But they were experienced in making love in the bathtub. Felicia straddled him, and at least for a few moments their bodies and souls became one as they had so many times in the early years of the marriage. The ecstasy of their union formed an invisible shield that the recent events could not penetrate. Again, Felicia dreamed that maybe everything could still be okay in the long run.

The next morning, headlines on the front page of the *Journal* read,

"Assistant District Attorney kidnapped and beaten by unknown assailant."

CHAPTER 8

SIMONTON RANG THE DOORBELL

Simonton rang the doorbell at the Jernigan home on Saturday morning after Craig was released from the rehab center. It was 7:30 a.m., but this was important. Craig was spending a lot of time sleeping, and Simonton had missed him twice already. Luckily, Craig was not only awake but seemed anxious to welcome the detective. His spirits were still doing cartwheels after the prior evening's lovemaking session. Felicia answered the door.

"Hi, Mrs. J. Can I ask your husband a few questions? I promise I won't stay long."

"He's awake—been awake a couple of hours already," Felicia responded. "Come on back. We've got his hospital bed and traction set up in my sewing room."

"Hey, Smitty! Come on in!" Craig called from the next room. "Sorry I can't come to greet you, but you know how it is." He seemed more jovial than he should considering his condition. Maybe it was the Prozac he had been prescribed to ward off depression during his recuperation. But probably not. It was probably the sex.

"Hey, Craig! Nice to see you feeling better. Mind if I ask a few questions? There has been another abduction."

"You mean somebody else was kidnapped and left for dead?"

"Do you know Farley Jacobs?" In the usual method of law enforcement interviews, Simonton ignored Craig's question, replacing it instead with one of his own.

"I've heard the name. Isn't he somebody in the DA's office up in Collin County, in McKinney? I don't know him personally. Why, is he the victim this time?"

"He was in McKinney at one time, but he's been in the Denton County office for the past six months, in Denton. Have you ever worked with him or written anything on a case he was involved in? What's the connection between a former Collin County prosecutor and a news guy in Lewisville?"

"Not that I know of. But who knows? I haven't really written that much yet, and I don't know if any of them had a Collin County connection. But you can look at my stuff yourself. I keep everything I've ever written in a file at home. You can ask my wife. She knows where it is."

Felicia entered the den then with her mother. "Hi, Mr. Simonton," she said.

"Hi, Smitty!" Conlin was obviously glad to see him.

"Hi to you both! I was just asking Craig about a former Collin County assistant DA that was kidnapped just like Craig and left for dead after a night of beatings. Just thirty miles away, same modus operandi, stun gun, hood, tied up the same way, same kind of injuries. I hear he was transferred to Parkland and is still in surgery. I haven't been able to talk with the investigators yet, but the prelim is that it fits the same pattern."

"Oh my god!" Felicia was shocked and had to sit down. "Why are they doing this? Does this mean it wasn't Charlie Ross?"

"We don't know. That's probably right though."

Conlin was quiet, except to put her arm around Felicia's shoulder, to try to console her. "They're doing everything they can, Lisha. They'll catch them. I just know they will."

Then, to Simonton, "Do you think she's safe at home? Should I keep her at my place, or do you think she can be safe here at her house?

Simonton answered, "We've been doing frequent drive-bys ever since it happened. We haven't seen anybody suspicious. I doubt they'll be back. My gut feeling is that there is somebody really mad at Craig, somebody that he may have helped to put away, and now they're out and trying to get even. I don't think they'll come after Mrs. J."

"Are you trying to track down people that have just been released?" Conlin asked. "You should be able to get that information from the computer, shouldn't you?"

"We've got people working on it right now. We're looking at everybody they have both been involved with even at different times. Maybe somebody your son-in-law wrote about last year but was put away by Jacobs in a different case years ago, and he's finally just decided not to take it lying down and wants to get even with everybody."

"We haven't figured out why he's keeping incognito though. Most of the time if you are getting even with somebody, you want them to know who you are, even brag about it. Let them know you're finally getting even with them. This one's different. But he'll eventually tell us who he is or leave a clue. Or he'll make a mistake. They always do. It'll take a lot of computer time and a lot of pounding the pavement, but we'll find him. You can bet your sweet bootie on that!"

Ellie tried to look relieved for Felicia's sake, but Simonton knew she wasn't. He knew also that it may be a long time before they would ever feel safe again. Until he was at least able to find a motive. They would not be able to trust anyone until he cracked this case.

Felicia gave Craig a gentle kiss and an even gentler hug. He was still sore and had tender spots and bandages everywhere she tried to touch. Conlin came over and gave him a brief hug too, and the two women walked out of the den to show Simonton to the door, each arm on the other's shoulder.

At least for the time being, Felicia agreed to let her mother stay with her at their home in Lewisville. She felt safer with her mother there, both from physical danger as well as the questioning she expected from the press. As soon as Simonton was gone, the deadbolts secured and the alarm system armed, they both went to bed and slept several hours. Felicia insisted that her mother sleep in the master bedroom; she wanted to sleep on the couch in the den so she could hear any problems with Craig.

Sleep had been hard to come by with Craig in the hospital and running back and forth all the time. Felicia had spent too many nights curled up in that convertible chair/bed in his hospital room. It made an uncomfortable chair and an even more uncomfortable bed. It was nice to have a hot bath and at least to crawl up on a comfortable overstuffed couch. She thought that here in her own home, she could almost forget about Craig's injuries, and for just a moment, she could almost forget about the problems in her marriage.

But she went to sleep so fast, she found she was too sleepy to think about forgetting. She dreamed of earlier times when everything seemed perfect. At home with Mom as a child and later at home with Craig as his lover and wife. For a while, everything seemed okay . . .

Nobody could get her here,

with the doors locked . . .

and the eider down comforter and soft pillows . . .

and lacy curtains . . .

CHAPTER 9

FBI AGENT TOM BORDEN

FBI agent Tom Borden considered the second kidnapping and beating to be an indication of a common thread. Assistant DA Jacobs was presently in no condition to be questioned, so after the initial investigation, the first thing he wanted to do was to interview the original victim, Craig Jernigan. He had already composed a computer-generated time line of the crime reporter for the past year, and the DA's caseload over the past several years and found several that they had both worked on at various times. In fact, there were indeed a couple of cases that involved suspects considered evil enough to try to get even with a couple of small town do-gooders.

He made an unannounced visit to the Jernigans with his partner, the week after Craig got out of rehab. He rang the doorbell of their two-bedroom single story home at the edge of town. It was early, and Felicia answered the door in her bathrobe. Still frightened by everything that had happened, she kept the door closed and answered through the video intercom she had installed after Craig's abduction.

"Hello, ma'am. I'm FBI Agent Tom Borden. This is my partner, Agent Gary Schulman, and we'd like very much to talk with you and your husband."

"Hold your badge up to the camera," she responded. She was taking no chances. Borden and Schulman did as they were requested. "Give me a minute," Felicia said and turned to ask Craig what to do.

He slowly walked from the bedroom to the front door. He was still on crutches. "Let me see your badges," he said. Again, Borden and Schulman held their badges up to the camera, which was connected to a hidden 8-gig 96-hour loop DVR recorder. Craig figured that four days was plenty of time to capture anything or anybody that might show up unexpectedly. He had called a friend in the security business and gotten it installed free. Just in case, though, he brought the Glock 19 that he had bought almost a year ago when there had been a rash of break-ins in the neighborhood. Now was the time that it might come in handy.

Satisfied that the visitors appeared legitimate, Craig let Felicia open the door while he stood behind it, Glock loaded and ready. "Stop, and let me see your badges," Craig ordered. Finally satisfied with the identification, he returned the badges and dropped the Glock into the pocket of his bathrobe. Just in case, though, he kept his hand in the pocket.

"I'm sure you know why we're here. We need to ask you some questions," said Borden. "Mind if I come inside?"

Borden had identified three cases over the past two years in which both Jernigan and Jacobs had major roles in either apprehending the criminal or writing the story about the arrest. First, the Taliaferro murder, in which Craig was a latecomer in the investigation and simply put the story together from notes originally made by his partner, who started vacation the day before the arrests were made. The arrest was in Denton County, but the murder had occurred in Collin County, so the trial was held in McKinney.

Then the Brandon case, the bank heist involving an inept robber who was caught before he even got to his getaway car. This happened after Jacobs moved to the Denton County DA's office. He had been the lead prosecutor in that trial. This was Brandon's third felony, so according to the law in Texas, he went away for life. Craig had followed his trial and reported on it daily in the Journal.

But finally, Barry Phillips, the younger brother of two men who had just recently been released from Huntsville after conviction on a number of liquor store robberies. Barry was the psycho responsible for at least two abductions, robberies, and rapes in the west Dallas area and was considered a person of interest in one other. Craig had picked up on reported similarities between those assaults and a single incident involving the aborted abduction of a young woman from an underground parking lot.

This time, Phillips had unfortunately chosen a strong young woman trained in the art of self-defense, and all he got for his efforts was a pepper spray in the face, a blast from the loudest horn he had ever heard, and a really hard kick in the groin. Deputy Ben Ferrell happened to be on duty in the same block and responded immediately to the 911 call. When he arrived, Phillips was being held down by a couple of burly passers-by who had heard the horn blast and rushed over to help the lady in distress. Phillips was arrested almost immediately.

Craig was assigned the story and, two days after the arrest, went to the jail to interview Phillips. He was met by an extremely angry mid-thirties thin white man with a scraggly reddish beard, tattoos everywhere, and the craziest look in his eyes that Craig had ever seen. "I'm Craig Jernigan. I work for the Lewisville Journal. I wonder if I could talk to you."

"What's in it for me, mutha fucka?" said Phillips. "You get me outa here?"

"I don't have that kinda power," said Jernigan. There was something about the guy that seemed either familiar or odd; Craig couldn't put his finger on it. He had lost two upper front teeth in a barroom brawl the year before, and was left with a toothless scowl, added to his already crazed appearance.

"Then you turn your prissy little ass around and get the hell out, or you'll find out you're jacking with the wrong feckin' guy!" That was it. A vague hint of an Irish accent. Craig had an uncle who used the same language. That must be it. Although he really would like to talk with him, Craig realized he was on a dead end and possibly dangerous road and left without the interview. He was disappointed. He could report without the interview, using other sources, but felt that it would be a feather in his cap to be able to talk with the perp himself.

So he called Deputy Ferrell, who was riding on the high of a good collar with a lot of publicity, and was in a cooperative mood. They met over lunch the next noon.

"Well, good job, and congratulations, Deputy!" Craig said. He had only met Ferrell once before, and the circumstances were less jovial then. "You've got one crazy, mean bastard in your jail there!"

"Don't I know it!" Ferrell responded, with a laugh. "I think when they handed out the brains and good manners, he was hiding behind the door!" The tired old joke always seemed to get a chuckle.

"They musta handed out teeth that same day," Craig responded. "What have we got so far? Anything you can give me?"

Ferrell had always felt a little guilty for their first encounter and wanted to make up for his bad mood that day. About three months ago, Craig had done his homework on a B&E case and tried to get information that would let him organize his report. But Ferrell had been tired and pissed off at his supervisor at the time, so he only snarled at Craig. "You'll know that when I decide to let everybody know it. Please get the hell out of my way! I actually have something important to do"

So he was in a mood to make up for it and showed a new cooperative face to Craig. He told him as much as he knew about the incident itself, the victim, the surroundings, the crime scene, and the psycho.

Craig had kept up with the serial abduction and rapes and remembered that one of the victims described her assailant as wearing a ski mask but thought she saw some reddish beard under the edge of it. Another remembered that although the assailant spoke very little, she remembered being called a "feckin' cunt" by the man.

Ferrell's good mood had been contagious, and Craig had told him of the similarities between the two cases. This led to further investigation and the proof, first through circumstantial evidence, and then the line up, and finally by DNA evidence, and Barry Phillips was sent away for a long time. Craig remembered Barry's crazy expression at the trial as the judge passed sentence. As he was led out in handcuffs and leg restraints, he mouthed the words in Craig's direction, "Don't you worry! We'll get you, you son of a bitch!" His final gesture was a simple nod to his two brothers, Gordy and Vernon, in the back of the courtroom and then toward Craig. The trial was three months ago. Assistant DA Jacobs had been the prosecutor.

Agent Borden agreed that the two remaining Phillips brothers were the most fertile fields for investigation. Although he applied himself to other possible leads as well, it became obvious that his primary focus was on the brothers.

CHAPTER 10

CRAIG HAD BEEN HOME

Craig had been home almost a full month since his discharge from rehab. He still had casts on both legs, and his right arm, the worst injured, was in a sling. His incisions had time to heal, and the pain was simply a soreness. He had managed to keep his narcotic usage down to a level that he was not addicted or even dependent on the Vicodin or dilaudid. He followed his doctor's orders and took Advil or Tylenol unless the pain was really bad. He was on the road to complete recovery.

Felicia felt that she was still in love with him as abused wives frequently do and was even more determined than ever to make it right with him. She took care of him during his recuperation like he was her baby. And it seemed like everything was the way it started out years ago, during the good years. She fed him his favorite foods, kept herself looking pretty for him, and kept the house in proper order. When he progressed to a point of being able once again to make love, she took the reins and became the assertive one, to minimize his effort.

Finally, two weeks after his casts were removed, Craig finally felt energetic enough to turn on his computer and try to re-establish a connection with the world. Immediately after the computer went through the Windows opening tones, AOL notified him through the soft, gentle voice that everybody knows, "Welcome! You've got mail!"

He clicked on new mail and found that he had more than five hundred new messages. He began to scroll down the list, deleting the spam and looking briefly at messages that looked important and then marked them "keep as new" so he could have access to them later. Many of his friends had sent "get-well-quick" notes, attached to comments about what they'd like to do to the bad guys when he or they were found.

Of course, there were the usual assortment of things that other people thought were funny, forwarded to him from the Internet. He deleted those as he always did, being afraid to open attachments for fear of viruses. He had experienced one virus that had contaminated the data on an entire bank of computers at work, simply because somebody opened an e-mail from a stranger.

Halfway down the third page he noticed a message that simply said, "Congratulations!" That piqued his interest. He didn't recognize the source address. What had he done lately that warranted congratulations? Probably a scam, he thought, as he double-clicked on the word. Although he never opened attachments from unknown sources, he felt that just opening the message itself was safe.

But this! He knew in an instant that this was not spam or scam but a message meant specifically for him and for him alone. The message said:

≈ *Congratulations!* ≈
You have just successfully completed
"Homeschooling 1.01, a Tutorial for the Instructor!"

Oh my god! he thought as the reasons for his abduction and beating crystallized in his mind. He had never in his wildest imagination connected his beating with his treatment of his wife. But he now immediately knew why he had been abducted and tortured, almost killed. Simonton might as well give up with his other leads. It had nothing to do with his newspaper work or with any mutual defendant that he and the assistant DA were involved with. No, some do-gooder was mad at him for "home schooling" his wife, probably with her knowledge and possibly at her request. "Son-of-a-bitch!" he said, loudly enough that Felicia came running in.

"Is anything wrong?" she asked.

"Nothing, nothing!" he responded. "I just turned my leg wrong. It still hurts like a son-of-a-bitch if I stretch it the wrong way. I'm okay. I don't need anything." Quietly, he thought to himself, *Get the hell out of here, bitch! You're probably at the root of all this anyway.*

After she left, he pushed the door closed and continued to scroll through the message privately.

This certifies that **Craig Jernigan** has just successfully completed:

Homeschooling 1:01,
A Tutorial for the Instructor

This is a tuition-free one-day course, offered only to the most qualified students. Mr. Jernigan, you were chosen because of your long history and experience in the field.

Home Schooling 2:01, a more advanced two-day course, will be offered to students who continue to demonstrate a need for instruction. The Home schooling Institute will monitor your progress, and if it becomes obvious that you need the additional class time, you will again be given free transportation to the Learning Center for this additional tuition-free course. Again, of course, no registration will be required. The first eight hours of HS 2:01 will consist of a review of HS 1:01 with even more extensive laboratory demonstrations. The remainder of the course will be tailored to the student's specific needs. No additional training past HS 2:01 is planned; we do not anticipate that any students will actually survive HS 2:01!

Please note that the Institute for Home Schooling will not divulge this information to any person or agency. It is for the student to use as he sees fit, for guidance in future relationship issues as they present themselves.

Again, congratulations on your success, from the
Institute for Homeschooling!

That was it. He had been beaten almost lifeless in retribution for correcting his wife. Not only that, but he knew that if he ever struck her again, he was likely to be killed for it. But who was behind it? And what could he do with the new realization? He had to give this some really serious thought.

He continued to scroll through his e-mails, mainly making sure there were no more messages from the "institute." There were none.

What could he do? He could think of three possible scenarios. First, the most logical thing to do would be to call Borden and let him call off the dogs. It had nothing to do with the criminals he had written about, it was because of his marriage and how he handled his wife.

He could see the headlines, "Wife beater abducted, beaten!" He couldn't stand the publicity, and it would destroy his career. Since he worked for the Lewisville paper, they would try to keep the damaging publicity down. But he couldn't rely on the major Dallas papers. They loved to get trash on smaller papers.

So that option was out! It wasn't his problem. Let Borden worry about chasing the other dead-end leads. If he somehow managed to connect his abduction to the Phillips brothers, well, they were no good anyway; they deserved anything they would get. Let Borden go ahead; he can go after the maniacs. They all belong back in prison anyway.

The only advantage of that scenario would be that Borden might be able to give him some protection in case his attackers came after him again. But he doubted that the FBI would be very enthusiastic about protecting someone they considered a wife beater!

Second, he could confront Felicia, but that would lead to more than words, and if he wasn't careful, he had no doubt that whoever it was that did it the first time would do it again, and he probably wouldn't be so lucky the next time. That option was out. Whether or not she had anything to do with it, he had to play dumb with her. He could do that, at least for a while.

Or third, he could just sit quiet, keep his mouth shut, take advantage of all the sex that was being thrown his way, and get the hell out as soon as he was able. Leave in the middle of the night, move to a faraway place, file for divorce after a year or so, and forget the bitch. His record would be clean, no felony assault, clean employment record, and an extra-puffed reference from his *Journal* people since they still felt sorry for him and thought he just got clobbered because of his job. He'd be a hero, and probably get a raise in pay with a job move after this little episode. Yep, just hang out, keep quiet, and get the hell out of Dodge.

One week after he opened his special "congratulations" e-mail, a Denton County Sheriff's Department deputy was abducted and beaten severely.

CHAPTER 11

JUST TWO WEEKS AFTER JACOBS

Just two weeks after Jacobs was abducted and beaten and a week after Craig received his special e-mail from the Home Schooling Institute, Ben Ferrell, the Denton County Sheriff's Department deputy he had worked with previously, failed to return to his apartment after he went out to pick up the morning paper. He was found late that afternoon, unconscious, his body badly broken, in his apartment house parking lot on Hwy 121 in Grapevine. A neighbor coming home from work found him when he came home from work and pulled into the parking lot. He didn't recognize him, and by the time anybody figured out which apartment he lived in, an ambulance had already taken him to Dallas Northeast Medical Center. He suffered injuries similar to Craig's, and his recollection of the abduction matched when he finally regained consciousness.

He remembered bending over to pick up the paper, which was lying next to the apartment dumpster when he felt the same excruciating, sharp pain at his neck then through his body. He remembered waking up in some smelly vehicle, a van he thought, and being tied up with a black hood over his head. His captors never spoke to him. He had trouble talking about the beating, but it seemed to be just about the same way Craig had reported his. He never knew when he was going to be hit again and just had to sit there waiting with no protection. He remembered hearing what he thought was a shutter banging, and there was a dog barking. But nothing else.

Andrea Ferrell was beside herself with worry when Officer Glen Harris knocked on her door.

"Oh god! Ben's dead, isn't he? Tell me! He's dead, isn't he?"

"He's not dead, but he's been hurt pretty bad," Harris told her. "May I come in?"

Andrea opened the door and let Harris into her small two-bedroom apartment. A baby cried in the background, and she ran to tend to her three-month-old son. Harris looked around briefly while she was out of the room, but everything seemed in order. There were magazines on a coffee table, women's stuff, and a couple of law-enforcement journals. The place was clean and neat. She was a good housekeeper. No postpartum depression here, he thought.

She returned almost immediately with Patrick in her arms and asked, "What happened? Where's my husband?"

"He's in surgery right now. We haven't been able to talk with him yet, but it looks like somebody beat him up pretty bad. He was tied up, and he had a black hood over his head. We think he was kidnapped and taken somewhere else then brought back here and dropped in the apartment house parking lot. That's all we know for now. Do you have someone who can watch your son? I'll take you to the hospital."

"Mom's just down the street. I'll call her. How bad is he? Is he going to make it? Where did they take him?"

"He's at Northeast. The ER doc I talked to said he thought he'd most likely be okay. He has a lot of broken bones and cuts, and he's unconscious, but so far they don't think he has any serious internal injuries or head injuries. But it's gonna take some time. And they said he was already beginning to wake up before they took him to surgery, so he's not in a coma or anything like that."

"What do they have to do in surgery?"

"My understanding is that some of his fractures had to be fixed surgically. I think he got both elbows broken, plus a leg. Nothing internal, though, so far as I know. That's really all I know."

But Andrea knew more. The rumors had hit the local law-enforcement community that there was some crazed parolee loose, probably a junkie, with a vendetta against whoever put him away, and from what Harris told her, this sounds like the same way that guy worked. Sneaks up on his victim, hits him with a stun gun, ties him up, covers his head so he can't see, hauls him somewhere to hell out in the country where nobody can see or hear him, and beats the shit out of him. Drops him off in his own front yard when he's through with him, leaves him for dead. Goes on to the next victim. Otherwise no real leads yet, she had heard.

She and Ben had been talking about it just the other day. He had told her to be sure and keep her doors locked and the alarm system on. Big deal, she had thought; it wasn't the wives he was mad at, it was the men.

Ben had told her not to worry; he was sure they'd catch him soon. He had heard about the only good lead—the Phillips boys. They were so dumb, just waiting to be caught. But what did Ben know? Cops always tell their wives not to worry while the wives keep on worrying, knowing they might never see their husbands again. Andrea never believed him when he said don't worry, and she didn't believe him this time. She always worried.

She called her mother and then her friend Jennie. She would need somebody she knew for support and someone to ride home with later. She just didn't want to ride to the hospital in the cruiser, trying to think of something to say to a cop she didn't know.

Jennie lived in the same apartment complex as Ben and Andrea. Her husband also worked for the Denton County Sheriff's Department, and the men frequently covered the same shift together. It was common for their spouses to be hours late from work and in a situation where they couldn't call home. The girls had spent many long agonizing evenings together worrying about their husbands.

They had even talked about this new scare, the guy who kidnapped the newspaper guy and the DA. They had even nicknamed him. One detective in Dallas had commented on the fact that he never spoke to his victims and had dubbed him Gabby. The name had caught on, and now the police talked about how they would just love to have a short conversation with Gabby. "Just five minutes. He'd talk to me, you damn betcha."

Andrea's mom was there within minutes to take care of the kids, and Jenny arrived just a minute later. Andrea rode in Jenny's car to Dallas Northeast Medical Center.

When they arrived at Northeast, they saw several familiar policemen standing in the lobby. The call had gone out on the air, and as always, with one of their own down, the policemen had gathered, standing quietly in the hospital hallways and congregating in the parking lot until their brother is out of danger. There was an almost prayerful silence.

The policemen seemed to be quietly saying, "Just come on and try to get him . . . Just come on! We're here, mutha' fucka'. Just come and try to get him!"

107

Detective Simonton had picked up the report and was there. When he saw his colleagues' wives enter, he walked over to meet them. "He's gonna be okay, Andrea," he said. He wanted to reassure her. "He's just coming out of surgery. They had to do some work on his elbow, but they told us he looked okay. He's even awake. I'm waiting for them to let me talk to him."

"Do you know who's doing this? I can't believe this is happening!" Andrea broke down and cried for the first time. "Oh my god!"

Simonton put his arms around her and offered his shoulder as a tissue. She sobbed a couple of minutes and then tried to compose herself. "I'll be okay. Thanks for being here, Smitty."

The nurse came out and asked Andrea if she was his wife. She said she could visit him now. Smitty asked if he could come too. "Sure, no problem. Come this way," she said.

They entered the room, and Andrea rushed over to Ben's bed. He looked so weak and vulnerable. Both arms were in long casts, suspended by wires from an orthopedic frame, and his right leg was also in a cast. His head was almost completely covered with bandages. She thought for a moment that he looked almost funny, sort of like a mummy or something. But the reality of the situation snapped her out of any thought of humor as she realized how badly he had been hurt.

"Bennie, are you all right? I was so scared. I thought you were dead! My god! I thought you were dead!"

"I'm okay. Looks like old Gabby got me." He had difficulty speaking because of the injuries to his jaw and some missing teeth. "I don't think he got me quite as bad as the other two. The good news is I'm not in a coma. The bad news is I think I remember feeling just about everything." He glanced toward Simonton.

"Good! Feel like talking to me a couple of minutes?"

"I'll try. Anything I can do to help you catch this maniac! Just go slow. My jaw is killing me."

Surely enough, Officer Ben Ferrell had remembered most of the events of the day. He remembered walking almost to the dumpster to pick up the paper. That was unusual; it was usually thrown halfway up to his front door. The dumpster was next to the entry gate to the apartment house. He figured Gabby had moved his paper so he could hide behind the dumpster to ambush him.

The only time he couldn't remember was right after the bolt of lightning from the stun baton hit his neck. But he had begun to wake up just as they were putting the black hood over his head and saw part of the van. It was old and rusty, a Ford, he thought, but couldn't be sure.

He described the same odors of gasoline and old socks that Craig had recalled. He was pulled by the ankle ropes just as Craig. It was hard to compare his memory with that of Jacobs. He had struggled and was hit with the stun baton again almost immediately. His recall didn't begin until after he was already tied into the chair. Ferrell apparently got a lighter shock; he could remember almost everything.

Ferrell was alert enough to try to remember everything he could. So he tried to memorize how many turns were made. He still couldn't tell what direction they had taken him, though. He thought the ride was about a half hour. He also remembered the dog barking and the sound of a shutter banging.

The very most vivid memory that he had was of his gradual recognition of the pattern of his abduction, and his realization that he was the third victim of the perp they called Gabby. He imagined, in abject terror, what lay ahead of him.

His memory of the beating itself was similar to that of the first two victims. He was tied upright in a chair and systematically beaten over a period of several hours. Like the others, he never knew when the next blow would fall. Like the others, his cries for explanations and mercy went unheeded, and Gabby was completely mute through the entire ordeal. The only major difference was that both his elbows were broken, and he had been hit several times in the genitals so that the right side of his scrotum was black and grapefruit sized.

He was able to say he was pulled up between eight and ten steps at the final destination. After he was pulled back into the van, he was in too much pain to remember anything helpful. All he remembered of the trip back home was the agonizing pain as the vehicle jostled his freshly broken bones.

CHAPTER 12

DR. KEN PERDUE WAS SEVERELY POST-CALL . . .

Dr. Ken Perdue was severely post-call, exhausted and hungry Sunday morning when he arrived at his home on Lake Dallas, in the Colony. He had just pulled a twelve-hour ER shift, and the "Knife and Gun Club" had been very active. In his twelve hours, he had managed three stab wounds, one gunshot wound to the chest, and the usual variety of chest pains and GI bleeders. He was happy to turn the ER over to the next crew.

His routine after a busy shift was to sit in his easy chair, read the interesting parts of the paper, sip on a cup of coffee, and have his favorite breakfast, crackers and tomato juice. The television was on for background noise, but he was barely aware of the news.

Carla, his wife of fifteen years, luckily loved to read and could spend this early time with him without bugging him. She had downloaded the newest John Grisham novel onto her Kindle and sat in her own favorite easy chair to read. Their reading room was a screened-in porch overlooking the lake. At the end of their backyard was a deck with their paddle boat docked. They weren't typical boaters but did enjoy paddling around with a picnic basket for lunch. Life was good.

Life was good for Ken too. He loved the ER and was very good at his job. He had graduated from one of the first emergency medicine residencies and never regretted his choice of specialty. This was one of the real perks, to be able to turn off the beeper after a shift and have no obligations until his next shift unless there was a civil disaster or something like that. Jokingly, he referred to himself as "just a shift-worker."

Ken had worked for several years at Richardson Medical Center's ER and still was on their medical staff. But a couple of years ago, he had gotten a slightly better offer at Memorial and had moved most of his shifts there. ER doctors can work a few shifts at one hospital and maintain a part-time load at another. Everybody in the ER at one place knows everybody at the other. Denton County was blessed in having three separate hospitals, all quality facilities, all having just a little difference in capabilities and attitudes. Ken maintained ER privileges in all three.

The recent rash of kidnappings and beatings had been bothering him. Something was wrong, and somewhere in his subconscious, he knew it. He just couldn't put his finger on it. He was sure, though, that Tom Borden's team would figure it out.

As he worked the daily Sudoku puzzle in the newspaper, he became aware of the latest "Breaking News Alert" on the TV. He didn't immediately tune his conscious mind to the television though. Everything was a breaking news alert. Probably somebody's cat got caught in the garbage barrel or something even less news breaking than that. But Carla was closer to the television and said, "Ken, look! There's been another one."

Ken routinely confided in his wife and discussed his ER experiences with her. She was a former ER nurse and could share the discussion. Ken looked up from his Sudoku just in time to see the reporter sign off.

"What was it?" he asked.

"I didn't catch all of it, but it was something about a kidnapping and beating in Allen. What little I heard makes it sound like Gabby's work again."

Thanks to modern communication technology, the Perdue household had the cable boxes that allowed you to freeze, backup, and replay the program you're watching. Ken backed up to the start of the item that was just on and pushed play on his remote control.

"Breaking news from Allen, Texas. At about 4:00 a.m. today, Jack Thompson, an assistant basketball coach at Allen Middle School, was found unconscious in his front yard. He had multiple injuries, fractures, and blood loss. He was air lifted to Parkland Hospital, and his condition, we are told, is guarded. We have no more information at this time but will keep on top of this developing story as it unfolds."

"My god! That's Gabby again, for sure," Ken said. "But what do a news guy, a DA, a deputy sheriff, and a coach have in common? This is crazy!" He couldn't relax after that, and instead, started trying to find information on the Internet about the victims. He had done that almost daily since the siege of kidnappings started but could find no common thread. He imagined that the FBI and local guys had done the same and with the same results.

But Ken felt uneasy because he knew that somewhere in his subconscious, there was a connection. He just had to think and find it.

From the look on her husband's face, Carla knew that she should let him alone with his thoughts. Theirs was a very special relationship; they could share a quiet time and enjoy it as much as a long discussion. So while he browsed, she read.

Ken knew quite a bit about Craig Jernigan through his old friend Ellie. He had never met Farley Jacobs but thought he might have heard his name someplace or another. And he had only met Ben Ferrell once, about a year ago, when he brought his wife in with a minor scalp laceration from a fall. He was pulling one of his occasional shifts at Lewisville Regional when Andrea Ferrell was brought to the ER.

"Oh my god! That's the connection," he shouted to Carla. "At least two of these guys have brought wives to the ER for injuries. One of the wives I know personally, and I know her injuries were from a scuffle with her husband. Then he was the first abduction victim. Another one is suspicious. I bet if we dug, we'd find the same thing in all four!"

Carla had already heard about Felicia Jernigan's trip to the ER. Even though doctors are supposed to keep everything confidential, most everyone knows that wives are not included in the confidentiality rules. Most physicians confide in their wives, especially about things like this. It's an almost required confidence. When bad things happen at the hospital, you feel you have to talk to somebody about it or you might explode.

Being on staff at the three hospitals in the area came in handy for Ken. From his Lewisville medical staff privileges, he could pull up any hospital in the North Texas area that belonged to the holding company that owned Lewisville Memorial. Hospitals in Lewisville and Richardson, about twenty miles away, were owned by the same company, Memorial Hospital Systems, and Allen was about halfway between the two. He could pull up any visit to either of the facilities on his personal computer. And the hospital in McKinney was under the same management as Memorial in Richardson. All he had to do was punch in a search on the names of the victims' wives.

He knew his search would be considered a violation of the HIPAA federal privacy laws. But it was worth it. He had to know. In the computer program, when it asked you what your relationship to the patient was and why should you have a right to the patient's personal medical information, he could always put in "ER Director," and he would probably get by with it.

First he opened the files from the Memorial system and put Farley Jacobs in. Nothing came up. He didn't remember Jacobs's wife's name, so he did a general Google search on Farley Jacobs. He found a profile and put the $11.95 on his credit card and found what he needed. Carmen Jacobs. They had been married for eight years and had two daughters.

Now he put the name Carmen Jacobs in the search in the Memorial database and immediately found two emergency entries in the past eighteen months. The information was only abstracted—diagnoses, procedures, medications. Things that could be used for billing. But that was enough for Ken. About eight months prior, Carmen Jacobs had come in for stitches for a facial laceration and was noted to have multiple bruises and contusions on various parts of her body. Then, about four months ago, she was in for a black eye and broken jaw. Pay dirt!

"Hot damn! It looks like I'm on to something!" he told Carla. "That's three out of four. I bet a week's pay we'll find the same thing on this coach from Allen!"

He knew that the television report had included a brief interview with Thompson's wife but couldn't remember her name. So he backed the news up again and found the report.

"Here is Sara Thompson, Jack's wife." That was all he needed.

He put that name in the search engine for Memorial and came up with twelve Sara Thompsons, but none of them fit the age profile for the coach's wife. He thought she was about mid-thirties, and these were all much older women. So he closed the Memorial Richardson program and opened the program for Metroplex Receiving, in Plano. He found four Sara Thompsons on the patient list there, and one fit the age profile, thirty-six years old.

He pulled up the record on that particular Sara Thompson and found two entries, both from the hospital in Plano. One was about a year ago for various scrapes and bruises and a laceration that needed stitches from a fall on the jogging trail. The second, only three months ago, was a facial laceration and broken nose from a trip and fall into the fender of her car. Double pay dirt!

"Where did I put that FBI agent's card?" he asked Carla. As always, she knew exactly where everything was and found it with little effort.

Ken dialed the after-hours number on the card, and Borden answered immediately. "Hello, Tom Borden," he heard.

"Mr. Borden, this is Dr. Ken Perdue. We need to talk."

CHAPTER 13

TOM BORDEN WAS ASLEEP WHEN PERDUE CALLED

Tom Borden was asleep when Perdue called him. He had been working all night after he first heard about Coach Thompson. FBI agents were on constant call, never knowing when they would be able to sleep for a full night, and so took advantage of naps whenever naps were available. He had been asleep for only about an hour when the phone rang.

Well, this must be important, he thought, or Perdue wouldn't call this time of a Sunday morning. "Meet me at Lobo's, we'll get coffee or a bite of breakfast. That's about the quietest place around." He left within ten minutes.

Borden was a serious guy. He had married Kay, his childhood sweetheart, but the marriage hadn't survived the life of an agent. Secrecy is difficult for a wife to deal with, and there are times when an agent must be gone and can't tell where he will be, who he'll be with, or for how long. For a marriage to survive, a mate must have unwavering faith. And faith can only be stretched so far before jealousies and insecurities cause a widening crack in the bonds of the marital oath. In Borden's case, his marriage had lasted through the birth of their daughter and four more years before crumbling under the stresses.

He tried to keep as closely in touch with his daughter as he could, and he was never late with child support. He went to as many of her childhood performances as possible, but after all, FBI business always came first. Kay knew she could never be more than number two in his life. He had dated once or twice since the divorce but never stayed interested for more than a couple of dates. Now, he had given up and had subconsciously taken himself off the market.

At Lobo's, a Tex-Mex restaurant just off I-45 and midway between Lewisville and Richardson, there wasn't a lot of business on an early Sunday morning. Right choice, Borden thought.

Both were nervous about what the conversation would bring. Ken, because he knew he had something big on his mind, and Tom because he had no idea what to expect. Borden arrived ten minutes before Perdue and parked in the front. He was pacing and smoking a cigarette when Perdue pulled in.

"How's it going?" he asked and shoved out a hand for the traditional male greeting. Even if you only saw each other the previous day, a new meeting required a new greeting.

"Thanks for coming. I don't think you'll be sorry. This should be worth your time," Perdue answered.

"Man, I hope so. As far as worthwhile tips go, we're in the middle of a dry spell," Borden responded. "Let's get inside out of this wind." They both went in and patiently waited while the waitress seated them. She didn't seem to be in any hurry, but like most Sunday morning waitresses, she was friendly. And this early, the pastries and coffee ought to be fresh.

Sally first showed them to a table by the window—bright, fresh, and immediately next to a family having a loud breakfast before leaving for a camping trip. Borden asked her to place them somewhere farther back, where it was dark and quiet. She found them a booth in a special dining room that wasn't being used, and they were seated while she went to get them coffee.

"It's about Gabby and his four victims. I think I've found a connection. In fact, I'm sure of it. I know the Jernigans personally. Her mom is a family doc here in Richardson, and she brought Mrs. J. in few months ago with a scalp laceration that needed stitches. Had some made-up story about bumping her head. But she was covered with bruises and welts I could swear were from an old-fashioned belt whipping! I tried to get her to talk to me about it and even brought a Women's Shelter counselor, but she wasn't ready to talk."

"So Mrs. J. tangled with somebody, sure, probably her old man. But how does that connect everybody together?" Borden said.

"Wait a minute! You haven't heard the rest of it. Something had been bothering me, and I couldn't figure out what it was until today. I knew I remembered something about Ferrell but just couldn't put my finger on it. After I heard about this fourth case, the coach in Allen, it hit me. Ferrell had brought his wife in for a laceration that was suspicious, about a year ago.

Again, had some wacky story about falling or some such thing. Nothing more than that."

"Well, I can't see how that puts them all in one pool," Borden said. "What about the others? Two out of four of our victims have lost their tempers with their wives. What does that prove?"

"Well, I had never heard of the other two. So I started looking in the hospital computers.

I'm on the medical staff, obviously, at the Memorial System hospitals in Richardson and Lewisville. I'm also on staff at a Metroplex System Emergency Center. Metroplex runs several freestanding emergency clinics—we call 'em doc-in-a-boxes.

I searched for Farley Jacobs, the assistant DA, under a bunch of web sites, and finally found an interview where he mentioned his wife by name. Then I did a search in the hospital computers, and waa . . . laa! There she was. Carmen Jacobs, wife of Farley Jacobs."

"She had been in the ER at Memorial twice in the last eighteen months, the first time with various bruises, abrasions, and laceration, and the second time about a year ago, with a black eye and a fractured jaw. I don't have the details, other than what's in the abstracted visit billing records. The diagnosis they sent to the insurance company was just 'lacerations, not otherwise specified.' You'd have to get the original records to be able to see the details of the situation. But I'll bet dollars to donuts that this she got those injuries from her DA husband."

Borden's interest was really beginning to peak now. How could this all be just an amazing coincidence? Like most detectives, he really didn't believe in coincidences unless all avenues of investigation were exhausted.

"Now for the killer final punch!" Perdue said. "I had no information at all about the Allen coach, and Jack Thompson was such a common name. I found about eleven of them in the Memorial computer. But none of them matched with the coach. Allen is a little distant from Richardson and Lewisville though. It's a little closer to McKinney. And the hospital in McKinney is owned by the same corporation as the hospital in Lewisville. You can get into medical records of any of the hospitals in that division of the corporation, from a computer connected to only one. So I got online at Lewisville and found her. Sara Thompson had been to the ER in McKinney twice in the past year and a half. The first time was for assorted abrasions and bruises and a facial laceration that she supposedly got from a fall on the jogging trail. The second time was for a facial laceration and a broken nose that she got when she tripped and fell face first into the fender of her car."

Borden was quiet, in contemplation of what this might mean. He knew that it put a completely different angle on his investigation. He agreed with Perdue; he couldn't imagine that this was all a coincidence. At least it required checking it out.

"Well, either these are the damn clumsiest four women I've ever seen, or they're married to four fucking wife beaters!" Perdue said. "All four wives have been in emergency rooms around here for injuries. I personally took care of one of them, and all three others have been in local hospital ER's in the past two years with suspicious injuries. I'll tell you, somebody is trying to get even with these guys, or teach them a lesson, and he's apparently pretty damn good at it!"

Borden realized immediately the significance of Perdue's discovery. It was exceedingly likely that he had indeed been on the wrong track with his attempts to connect the four men through common enemies because of their professions. It was easy for him to imagine a common connection among a deputy sheriff, an assistant district attorney, and finally a police reporter for the local newspaper. But there had been something wrong with that puzzle, especially after he heard about the coach. How could a coach be involved in such a conspiracy? Unless maybe he was pushing drugs or involved in some other illegal activity. And there was certainly nothing in his record that suggested that.

Borden had taken a couple of hours of computer time before he had dozed off and checked Thompson out on the FBI laptop. His record was clean, not even a speeding ticket. Church member. Goes to Lions' Club meetings. Filed his own taxes and was never late. Had a 700+ credit rating with all three agencies. Owned his own home, two cars, and a bass boat. Clean as a whistle. But there's got to be another angle. And now this was it!

Perdue left after the meeting, very satisfied with himself. His amateur sleuthing had done something to figure out what the FBI couldn't. But he still had no idea of Gabby's identity.

Borden, on the other hand, was somewhat embarrassed not to have ferreted out the common link himself. But still, he was excited to have a completely new approach to take on the investigation. He planned to take his time and not to mess up his investigation. Now that he thought he knew a potential reason why the men were singled out for these kidnappings and tortures, he was even more determined to discover who, or what group, was responsible for the vicious retribution.

First, he had to review the medical records on all four wives. He knew better than to go off half-cocked on a theory he hadn't thoroughly checked out. He'd been through that embarrassment once early in his career and wouldn't do it again.

He knew that he would be able to get much more information from the original records than what is abstracted in the computer. And he could get it, despite privacy laws. If the hospitals wouldn't cooperate with him on their own, it would only take a short trip to court to get subpoenas for all four women's records. But before that, he had to make one call. Detective Simonton had cooperated with him, and he deserved to know the latest (and really, the only) break in the case. Once he debriefed him on this new theory, being a local guy, he just might have some suggestions about how to uncover the identity of the mute vigilantes.

CHAPTER 14

VICKI STEELE WAS ALREADY IN A BAD MOOD

Vicki Steele was already in a bad mood Monday when Agent Borden walked into the medical records office at Memorial Hospital, Lewisville. She had just been reamed by an older doctor who had his privileges suspended temporarily for failing to catch up his medical records dictations. But rules were rules, and she had no options in the matter. In the modern day of lawyers chasing hospitals, medical staff regulations had developed in all hospitals, demanding that physicians keep their records current. In a battle between a medical records administrator and a senior physician at the hospital, it is no question who will win the battle. Luckily, Vicki knew that Administration would support her, and she had at least a good chance of winning the war. But because of the conflict, she was not in a mood to deal with an FBI agent looking for records.

"Good Morning, Ma'am. We're Agent Borden and Agent Schulman; we're from the FBI. We need to review a couple of medical records, if we may," Borden said.

"Agent Borden, there are basically three ways you can get access to a patient's medical records here. First, get the patient to sign an authorization. Second, if the patient won't sign, get a court order. Third, you know you can get a subpoena. But till you get one of those, I'm sorry, but you don't get the records."

Borden knew she was right, and more, he knew there was no way he could even look at the records until he followed her rules. Well, that was really not a big deal. He expected this; one of his agents was already working on a subpoena for each of the case files, for both hospital systems. They would be ready by next morning. And in an effort to be cooperative, Vicki promised that she would go ahead and get the records ready, so all an agent had to do was drop off the subpoenas and he would get the records. He gave her the names of all four wives, just in case Perdue had missed an ER visit.

He had some time to kill, so he called the victim he knew best. Craig Jernigan was still home recuperating and wouldn't go back to work for another two or three weeks. He called, and Jernigan had just gotten home from his daily physical therapy session. He was driving now, and his limp had improved. His weight bearing was improving with every session. He was through with surgery unless something went wrong. He was anxious to get back to work.

He answered the phone on the third ring. He recognized Borden's number on his caller ID and was apprehensive about the call. Having learned why he was "chosen for instruction," he continued to be concerned that Borden might somehow learn about it too.

"Hello, Mr. Jernigan. This is FBI Agent Tom Borden. How's the rehab coming?"

"Oh, pretty good, I guess. Still some pain, but it's getting better. What can I do for you?"

"I'd like to come out and talk with you today, if you have time. We may have another lead in the case, and I want to see if you have any information that'll help."

"Sure, I just got home from PT, so now is a good time. You know where we are." Although he knew that the Phillips brothers were completely innocent in the attacks, he hoped that some suspicious pattern had been discovered that would focus the investigation on their shoulders. They seemed especially vulnerable to suspicion, considering their connection to Jernigan, Ferrell, and Jacobs all three.

Borden arrived about fifteen minutes later, again with his partner Agent Schulman. This time, he let Schulman take the lead. Schulman knocked on the door to the Jernigan home. Expecting them, Craig answered the doorbell immediately.

"Good morning, agents. I hope this is good news. Have you got new evidence that we can put those Phillips psychos away with?"

"We're working that lead," Schulman answered. "But we haven't made much progress along that line lately. We haven't had any luck breaking their alibis down. We need to ask you some questions. Okay if we come in?"

"Sure." Jernigan turned and led them into the kitchen and sat them at the dinette table. "Want some coffee?" For once, Felicia was away, visiting her mother.

"Not right now," Schulman answered. "We need to ask you if you have any new information about your abduction. Have you remembered anything that you haven't told us yet? Have you had any conflicts with anyone that might have given you any idea about what happened? Maybe something you had forgotten about when we talked earlier?"

"No, not anything I can think of," Craig lied. He had no reason to open up about his e-mail from the Home Schooling Institute. Like a teenager who is two days late for her period and thinks she might be pregnant. She doesn't tell her parents of her suspicions until she's sure. Otherwise, if it's a false alarm, she has told all her secrets. Craig didn't want to tell all his secrets until there was no other way around it. "I haven't seen or heard from either Charlie Ross or the Phillips bunch since it happened."

"Well, we figured so, but we wanted to make sure," Schulman said. Have you been in contact with any of the other victims since you're getting to feel better? Called them, e-mailed them, anything like that?"

"No, nothing like that. I barely know them. I figured the less said the better. Should I have?"

"We don't think you either should or shouldn't. If you have, we just want to know if anything came up that might help."

"No. I guess I'd rather forget about it than go over the painful details with those other men."

"Something else came up, long as we're here. Do you know anything about an ER trip Mrs. J. made to Memorial in Lewisville, this past July? Looks like you weren't involved, but do you know about it? So far as we know, her mother brought her in for some stitches or something. Cuts and bruises, fell down or something."

"I don't know what that has to do with anything. It was me that got kidnapped and got the shit beat out of me, not her! I wasn't even there. I was still at work. But yeah, I heard about it."

"You didn't have anything to do with her injuries?" Schulman pressured him on the matter. "We're told that she had what looked like belt marks on her body, like somebody had whipped her with a belt. You don't know anything about that?"

"What the hell does that have to do with anything?" Craig asked. "I heard about it later. I wasn't even there!"

"How did she get her injuries?" Schulman continued.

"She told the ER doc. That should be enough!" Jernigan was beginning to sweat but managed to keep his composure.

"Looks like she said she bumped her head," Schulman said. "That sure doesn't explain belt marks. Where'd those come from?"

Now Jernigan was getting really nervous. His charade was beginning to unravel. But all was not lost, so he lied some more. "I never saw any belt marks! What are you talking about? All she got treated for was a cut on her head where she bumped into something. She's been acting like a real klutz lately. She's always got her mind on something else. I don't know anything about any belt marks. And I resent your insinuation! I'm the victim here, not her!"

Realizing he had only his suspicions, without getting more background evidence, Schulman and Borden rose to leave. First, Schulman asked, "When will your wife be back?"

This question made Craig feel even more nervous. He had to play it very cool. "She'll be back later tonight. She's just visiting her mother."

With that, Schulman and Borden made their exit to the black Ford they drove on Bureau business. In the car, Borden immediately called Detective Simonton and suggested that he go to visit Felicia Jernigan at her mom's house before Craig had a chance to talk with her. He wanted to get an uncontaminated interview before they had a chance to prepare and coordinate their stories.

Simonton was only too happy to oblige. So often the local police were squeezed out of information-sharing when the FBI was called in, and he had experienced his share of that stress and intimidation. To run across an agent who was willing to share the work, and hopefully the glory at the end of the day, was worth working for.

While Simonton and Officer Franks drove to Conlin's house, only five miles away, Borden and Schulman headed for the next victim's wife. Carmen Jacobs was home alone. Her husband was still in rehab. They arrived just as she was going out the front door, to get into her car to bring Farley some clean underwear and something to read. He was getting bored with nothing to do but a couple of hours of exercises daily.

"Hi, Mrs. Jacobs. Have you got a minute? We have just a few things we need to follow up on. It'll only take a few minutes," said Borden.

"I was just leaving. I'm taking Farley some stuff he needs. I guess I have a few minutes though. Want to go in the house?" she said as she put the key back in the lock and reopened the front door. After her husband's abduction, she had called a locksmith and ordered double-keyed deadlocks for all the doors. She opened the door and immediately the alarm sounded for the Away setting. She hurried to disarm it before the girl from the alarm service called her to see if she needed the police. They went in and sat down at the dining room table.

"What's happening? Did you catch whoever did this?" asked Carmen.

"No, nothing that good. How's your husband doing?" asked Borden.

"Well, physically he's doing okay, I guess. He still has his casts on and has trouble getting around. But I'm really more worried about how he's doing otherwise. He can't sleep, and he keeps waking up with nightmares about the ordeal. He jerks up in bed screaming stuff like, 'Who are you? Why are you doing this?' He's still on sedatives and, of course, antidepressants. I can't see that he's getting any better. Don't you have any leads yet?"

"Sure, and you can bet we're checking out every one of them. So far, nothing has opened the case up though," Borden added.

"How are the others holding up? Seems like we all ought to get together sometime . . . Maybe after this is all over. I don't even know any of the others. I've only heard of a couple of them. Why did this happen? Why these four men? I'm afraid to go out, especially by myself."

"We're sending a car by as often as we can, keeping an eye on your house," Schulman tried to reassure her. "I really don't think they are likely to bother you. It seems like the husbands are their main target."

"We wanted to ask you a couple of questions though, Mrs. Jacobs. About a year and a half ago, you went to the ER in McKinney for some cuts and bruises. You needed stitches. Can you tell us what happened? How did you get those cuts and bruises?" Borden asked. He looked carefully at her expressions. He had learned that he could tell as much from the person's face as he could by what they said and enjoyed his favorite technique of springing an open question out of the blue with no preparation or lead-ups. This time, he hit pay dirt.

Carmen straightened up immediately, looking startled, frantically trying to decide how to respond to this unexpected question. "I just tripped on a tree limb on the jogging trail, that's all. What's that got to do with anything?"

"Did you see anybody else there? Was there somebody chasing you? Were you scared?"

"No, it was just my own clumsiness."

"Were you jogging by yourself or with a friend?"

"I was by myself. I'd never had any trouble on the trails. I run at least four times a week. I'll have to admit, though, since this thing happened, I haven't been out a single time. Do you think anybody was watching me?"

"No, nothing like that. Just wondered. About a year ago, then, you went to the ER again with a black eye and a broken jaw. Can you tell us about that? What happened?" Borden knew he was getting closer. Hard to get a broken jaw most ways, except for running into somebody's fist. Again, he concentrated on her facial expression when he asked. She was looking more nervous by the minute.

She stammered, "It was raining and I was trying to get in the car without getting wet, and I slipped and hit my head on the outside rearview mirror. I broke the mirror—want me to show you the insurance receipt?" she asked sarcastically, trying to seem cool and unaffected.

"No, I don't need that. I just want to know, though, you sure that's how it happened? You sure somebody didn't help you fall? Maybe a little trip, a little shove? Maybe you ran into something else, maybe somebody's fist?" he continued. "Has your husband ever hit you?"

"Never. Why would you say such a thing? I've told you what happened. Why won't you believe me?" She began to cry. "Haven't I been through enough? I think it's time for you to leave."

The detectives accepted her invitation to leave and got back into the company car. "Well, what do you think?" Simonton asked.

"I don't believe a word of it," answered Franks. "We need to get a look at those ER records. See what the nurses said about it."

"Yeah, but first, I want to pay a visit to Northside Rehab. I'd like to see what our young assistant DA friend has to say about this."

CHAPTER 15

ELLIE CONLIN EXPECTED THEM, SO . . .

Ellie Conlin expected them, so when Simonton and Franks pulled up in her driveway, she met them on the front porch. They had called a half hour ahead, so she had time to freshen up. It was Wednesday afternoon when she typically took a half-day off for R & R, at least when she could get away from the office. This afternoon she was especially lucky: no calls, except this one from the officers.

"Hi, Dr. Conlin!" Simonton and Franks said together, almost in unison.

"Hello, officers," she responded. Can't you find anything more fun to do on such a pretty afternoon? Come in and share a cold Coke." She seemed unusually cheerful. Well, maybe she was just finally getting a little mellow after the hell she went through with her son-in-law being almost killed.

They followed her into the house and sat around the dinette table. The kitchen was recently decorated in a country motif, complete with the obligatory rooster on the countertop and the cookie jar with the hen sitting on the basket of eggs. Everything in its place and everything very neat and clean. They were impressed with the doctor's housekeeping skills, not knowing that she had a maid twenty hours a week and never lifted a hand in personal housework.

"Nice place you got here," said Smitty. Franks nodded in agreement but was more interested in getting to what they came here for. They had agreed beforehand that he would take the lead in the interview with Smitty doing backup for questions forgotten or unclear.

"Have you had any luck in the case?" Conlin asked, directing her question to neither in particular but to each in general. "Felicia's so worried and me too, wondering if anything else is going to happen."

"We're making progress," Franks gave the typical detective's evasive answer, used when you want to ask the questions, and keep control of the interview. "We just want to clear up some questions that have come up."

"Whatever I can do to help, you know, I'm glad to help," Conlin volunteered.

"We'd like to ask you about an emergency trip your daughter made to Memorial a couple of months ago. We understand that you brought her," Franks said. "Can you tell us what that was about?"

Dr. Conlin hesitated a moment, wondering what Felicia had already told them and not wanting to violate her confidence. She also didn't want to lie to the officers, so she hesitated while she gathered her thoughts. "What do you mean? I'm her mother. I would expect any mother would help out when her daughter has to come in for stitches."

"What we wonder is, how did she get the injuries, so late at night? What happened?

The tone of his question made Conlin feel that he was following the number one rule of policemen and attorneys: never ask a question if you don't already know the answer. So in a split second she decided to be honest. If she learned later that Felicia had not told them, and this was new information to the detectives, well, she had done her best.

"She called me to get me to help her to the ER to get stitches in a scalp laceration that she had gotten in a fuss with her husband," she finally answered. A sense of relief came over her. She could feel comfortable that the police had forced her into telling the truth, that she hadn't just called them and volunteered the information. At the same time, she felt relieved that the authorities would now know about Craig's meanness with his wife, and if they needed help in the future she could call them more easily.

She just hoped that Felicia wouldn't be upset. There is a balance in a parent's relationship with their grown children, when some interfering with their lives can be acceptable but too much can place a wedge between them. She hoped that this was not one of those situations.

"Well, that's what we heard," Franks said. Dr. Conlin felt relieved again. She was right; they only asked the question that they already knew the answer to. "Can you tell us anything about how long this stuff has been going on? Is this the only medical care she has needed from her husband's abusiveness?"

"I'm telling you the truth. That night was the very first I ever had even an inkling that there was hitting going on. Sure, kids all have their fusses and feuds, but I never would have thought there was anything like this. I never even thought Craig could be capable of hitting her. He seemed to be so in love with her. But truthfully, I have no idea how long it's been going on."

"Do you know if it's ever happened again since that night?" he asked.

"I really believe it hasn't," she said. "Now that it's out in the open between Felicia and me, I think she would have told me if it had happened again. We've even talked about it since that night, and she seems much closer to me, and I believe she's being honest with me."

"I sure hope so," Franks said. "You know, Texas law says a wife doesn't have to complain or even agree for cops to be able to pick up an abusive husband. We could go pick him up tonight and file charges. The law was made that way so that a husband couldn't threaten his wife into not reporting. We're supposed to file charges whether the abused wife likes it or not. But if you truly believe things have changed, we may leave him alone for the time being. We will, at some time, file charges against him. But right now, we have other things on our minds. If they come after him again, he may not be alive for charges to be filed."

"Oh! Do you think that's likely?"

"Hard to say. We have some other questions. Who besides yourself knows about this? What doctors, nurses, etc., for example, have you told about your son-in-law's abusiveness? We can figure out who was at the hospital when she was brought in, both doctor and nurse, and we will talk with each and every one of them. Maybe you can think of somebody else who knows?"

She thought for a moment. No reason to delay. So she told them, "Well, Dr. Perdue was on call. He knew what was happening. And the nurse's first name was Stacey, I think. Then she had a volunteer from the Women's Shelter, but Felicia wouldn't talk to her. And believe it or not, I haven't spoken to another single person, except Felicia."

"No friends, no other relatives, nobody at church, anybody else?"

"I'm sure I haven't. I've been very careful. If Felicia thought I had gossiped, she would probably never speak to me again."

"Okay. Well, I might as well tell you, I guess. Mrs. Jernigan probably will herself. We think our original theory was all wet. At the present time, we don't believe these abductions and beatings have anything to do with the first three victims being a newspaper police reporter and an assistant DA and a deputy sheriff. And now a junior high coach we couldn't connect along that line. We now know that all four of these victims' wives have been in emergency rooms recently, getting x-rays and stitches because of being knocked around by their husbands. Our primary theory at the present time is that somebody, or some group, has decided to be a vigilante for women. We believe these abductions are all about teaching these men and others like them a lesson."

"Oh my god! Do you have any idea who's responsible?" Dr. Conlin asked, with a look in her eye that showed a mixture of genuine concern, surprise, and fear. "What if they come back?"

"Right now we don't have any concrete leads on that. We've just begun running down leads. First on the schedule is to interview everybody who knows about this, especially anyone who might have known about more than one of the situations. Somebody from the hospital or somebody from the Shelter—someone who sees this stuff and finally got fed up with it."

"Good luck! Anything I can do, let me know," she said as Smitty and Franks arose and prepared to go out on the next leg of their investigation.

CHAPTER 16

JACOBS WAS SITTING AT A PICNIC TABLE

Jacobs was sitting at a picnic table in the commons area at Northside Rehab, getting some sun and fresh air after his morning workout. He was smoking a cigarette and drinking coffee. He had stopped smoking six months ago, but the strain of his abduction and recovery had pushed him back into the habit. Now he smoked even more than ever before.

He would be ready to go home in a couple of days and was getting more anxious every day. Maybe he could sleep better in his own bed. He just wished the nightmares would stop. It had been almost a month since his abduction and beating, but it seemed like just yesterday. He didn't notice the dark sedan pulling through the circle drive in front of the hospital until it stopped in a parking place just fifteen feet in front of him. When the agents got out, he recognized them.

Borden approached him first. "Mr. Jacobs, remember us? We're agents Borden and Schulman from the FBI. Got a minute to talk with us?"

"Anytime, any place—any news?"

"Nothing to write home about. Just need to follow up on some questions. We've had a bunch of leads but nothing has panned out yet. Nothing that tells us just who did this, anyway. How's your rehab going? Going home soon?" Borden asked.

"Supposed to go this weekend. Man, I'm ready. This place is getting to me. You can only stand this much boredom for so long."

"We wanted to ask you about something we came across. It's about a trip your wife took to the ER about a year and a half ago. Remember? She had some cuts and bruises, had to get some stitches. You remember how that happened?" Again, he watched for telltale signs of surprise and anxiety.

"Lord! That's been so long ago," Jacobs stalled. He wondered what the agents already knew and what his wife had told them. "Seems like she fell or something. I was at work, so I wasn't there. Wasn't anything much though. Just a little cut and some bruises. Why?" He had difficulty covering his nervousness, and the hand with his cigarette began to tremble just slightly.

"Well, about six or eight months later, she made another trip to the ER. She had a black eye and broken jaw that time. Know anything about that? What happened that time?"

Jacobs was visibly shaken by the series of question from Borden. He took a long draw on the cigarette, looking for even a few seconds to collect his thoughts and get his answers straight. He had talked to his wife about their stories when these things happened but not recently. *What did they already know? What had she told them? Could he trust her to keep her blab shut?*

"I really don't know what that has to do with me getting kidnapped and almost beaten to death. So far as I can remember, she told me something about falling in the rain or something like that. Again, I was at work, I wasn't there, so my recollection could be a little off. Seems like she said she fell against the car. Busted the outside mirror, I know that all right. What's this all about, anyway?"

"Just routine questions. Have you talked with any of the other victims since these abductions have happened?" Borden asked.

"No. I've met them, but as you can see, I've been a little busy, trying to get over this whole thing. The last thing I need is to go over the whole ordeal in detail with some other guys who will try to top my story with an even gorier one of their own. It didn't seem like it would be helpful. Do you think I should?"

"Oh no. Whatever you need, to get past this. Have you had any contact with anybody you didn't know? Anybody call you, anybody driving by the hospital or hanging around in the waiting room, or parking lot? Anything at all suspicious?" Borden asked, not really knowing what information he needed and not knowing whether Jacobs would tell the truth.

"No, nothing unusual. Nobody's called. Just a few friends from work, wishing me well. And they have pretty much quit coming by. At first, I couldn't get rid of the well-wishers, but I guess it got old. They aren't much coming by anymore. I guess the excitement wore off."

"Well, I guess that's about all we need for today. Hope you get to feeling better." Borden and Schulman climbed back into their car and drove away.

"Was that the picture of a relaxed and honest face?" Borden asked his partner.

"Not in my books. I think he's hiding something and afraid we'll find out. We need to get those hospital records," Schulman responded.

"Let's go by the office. Those subpoenas should be ready by now."

CHAPTER 17

VICKI SEEMED LESS STRESSED THIS TIME

Vicki seemed less stressed this time. When Borden and Schulman walked into medical records, she actually smiled at them. She felt a little sheepish about her abrupt attitude the first time they came in. "You boys bring your subpoenas with you? I've got all the records copied and ready for you."

"You're a doll, anybody ever tell you that?" Borden tried to match her cheerfulness.

"Only every day, don't you know it? Watcha got for me there?" She began to review the documents. Properly filled out and properly signed, subpoenas for any medical records from the past three years, on Felicia Jernigan, Carmen Jacobs, Andrea Ferrell, and Sara Thompson. Borden expected her to find records on Jernigan and Jacobs but was surprised to see an ER visit by Sara Thompson nine months ago. Maybe he should visit her next. There were no records on Andrea Ferrell except for a hospitalization for appendicitis about four years ago.

"Do I need to review these here, or can I take them with me?" he asked Vicki.

"Those are your copies to keep. We know better than to give an original to anybody, even the FBI," she seemed like she was going overboard to be nice this time.

"Thanks for your help," Borden said as he gathered up the approximately three hundred pages of records and left. He and Schulman drove to the office where they could devour these records in private. On the way, he called Ken Perdue and asked him to meet him the office. He might be helpful in interpreting the lingo and especially the handwriting that doctors and nurses tended to use. And he was already in the loop since he was the one who noticed the domestic violence link in the first place. He deserved a chance to participate.

They pulled into the Federal Building parking lot, flashed their ID cards at the proximity badge reader, and entered the building. On this Saturday afternoon, the parking lots were vacant and the building was quiet. The air-conditioning was turned off for the weekend, but the weather didn't demand it anyway, so they should be okay for a couple of hours. They got off at the twelfth floor and headed to the district FBI office. Proximity card again, and they were home.

At the same time they arrived in the office, Purdue pulled into the parking lot. Borden had instructed him on pushing the button, and they buzzed him into the building and then into the office suite.

Schulman had already spread the four files out on the conference table. They would take one file each. Borden reserved the coach's wife for himself. He was anxious to see if her visit to ER was the same as the others. Members of his team had visited the Metroplex Medical Records in Plano, and so they had files from both hospital systems.

First things first. They would review the charts they had access to now and later would interview the other victims and their wives (or maybe, the victims and their husbands, depending on how you look at it). As they were sitting down to work, the buzzer rang again. "Yes," Schulman answered through the office intercom.

Detective Simonton was outside. "Smitty here. I'm ready to party. Can I come up?"

"Sure, come join the fun." Schulman buzzed him into the building, and then into the office.

Smitty entered the office and sat at the table next to Perdue. Perdue had already started on Felicia Jernigan's chart, and Schulman had both visits made by Carmen Jacobs. With Borden beginning to look at Sara Thompson's record, Smitty took the file from Felicia Jernigan's first emergency room visit and began to look through it. They all went quietly through their respective chart assignments, only making occasional small talk.

Borden got up after fifteen minutes and got a cup of coffee from the automatic dispenser. Like most other offices, they had given up having actual brewed coffee with the coffee ground spills and stains and the burned carafe when it was left on Friday afternoon and sat on the heat all weekend. They instead had converted to a prepackaged coffee syrup that actually had some coffee flavor on a good day. It had the advantage of being ready, 24/7 and didn't require any waiting for brewing time. But even though the flavor left something to be desired, it did smell good, almost like real coffee.

Taking his lead, the other three filled Styrofoam cups and sweetened them. Simonton went back to the coffee machine after his first sip and got a small package of it Irish crème flavoring. He just couldn't tolerate this coffee-like drink without artificial flavoring chemicals. He sat back down at the conference table to complete his reviews, with a more satisfied look on his face. After another half hour, they had all finished and were ready to discuss what they had discovered.

"Everybody ready? Let's do this chronologically. Let's start with Felicia Jernigan. Her husband was the first one to get the treatment. Ken, what did you find?" Borden asked.

"Well, that this isn't the first time I've seen this chart," he answered. "Remember, I took care of her at the second visit, so today I'm working on the first visit. But this is the first time I've seen the nurse's notes." Doctors have to write their notes out by hand, but the nurses can put theirs into the computer and they don't get printed unless somebody asks to review them. Unless the doctor has a reason that he needs to read the nurses' notes, he never sees them.

"This first visit was on March 20 of last year, about 7:30 p.m. Doctor's note says, 'Chief complaint: scalp laceration.'" There was nothing about how it happened and certainly nothing to suggest that her husband had hit her. "That was worthless."

"Who's the doctor on that one?" Borden asked.

Perdue had to look at the record. "Says here Ron Price. I know him. He wasn't one of our regulars. A little older than most of us. I think he worked like every other weekend. Rumors are, he's got money he inherited from a rich family and doesn't have to work regular like all the other stiffs. I think he's gone now. Haven't heard from him in a while."

"But now, here's the nurse's notes. Says 'scalp laceration. Suspect battering. Tried to discuss with patient, but she adamantly denies and refuses to discuss.' That's suspicious," Perdue said.

He read on, "'Gave patient Women's Shelter card and encouraged her to call. Discussed escalation of abuse and consequences. Offered her my own private number. Not ready to discuss.'"

"Interesting," said Borden. "Who was the nurse?"

"Nadine McCarty. Good nurse. Been at the hospital over ten years. Night shift supervisor. Sure sounds like her. Doesn't take any gaff from anybody. The bigger they come, the more she likes it. A real crusader. I know she really gets into this wife abuse stuff. She has taken women over to the Shelter herself on occasion. I think she's on the board at the Shelter."

"Yeah, I've worked with her too," Simonton added. "Maybe I ought to give her a call."

"Probably right," Borden said. "But let's finish our review. There may be others we should talk with too."

"Okay, I've got the next file anyway," Simonton said. "This is the second visit Jernigan made to the ER, in December of last year. You took care of her that time," he motioned to Perdue. "Her mother, Dr. Ellie Conlin, brought her in. Says she had a laceration in her eyebrow and forehead that took seven stitches. Also says she had belt marks all over her back and legs. You all called the Women's Shelter and a volunteer counselor came out, but she refused to talk to her. Left with her mother."

"Sounds like her old man's a real piece of work," Agent Schulman offered. "Did he come in with her this time?"

"Nothing in the record about him being there. Registration was signed by the wife," Simonton answered.

"I remember that visit," Perdue said. "Nobody was with her except Dr. Conlin. We had some discussion about where she was going to go, what she was going to do. After I confronted her, she didn't make any bones about it. Didn't discuss it but sure didn't deny it either. Reason I remember that her husband wasn't with her, she was talking about what to do when he called her."

Borden asked, "What nurse was working?"

It took Simonton a minute to find the nurse's name in the paper copy of the electronic medical record. "Oh yeah, here it is. Nurse was Jill Freeman."

"Is . . . What's her name? McCarty? Is her name in there anywhere?" Borden asked.

"Nowhere," Simonton answered.

"Okay, that's one down," Borden said. "Detective, I agree, you need to talk with the nurse. Let's go to the next one. Who was next?"

"Looks like I'm up," Agent Schulman said. "Carmen Jacobs, remember, her husband was assistant DA. Started off in McKinney then moved to the Denton County DA's office. Carmen came in about eight months ago to the McKinney Memorial ER. Those records were brought up because McKinney shares management with the same corporation that owns and runs Memorial in Richardson."

"That time, she had a facial laceration and assorted bruises and contusions on her arms and back," he said. "Doc was Muhammad Alief, if I'm reading this handwriting right. Oh yeah, that's right. Here it is on the registration sheet, typed. His note says, '32-year-old woman presents with facial injuries from a fall while jogging. Injuries are compatible.' Nothing in his notes about any other cause of the injuries."

"Muhammad, huh?" Simonton snarled. "Don't those people think everybody is supposed to knock his wife around occasionally?" His racially biased comments were ignored by the others.

"Now, we get into the nurse's notes. A little more of a description of the injuries and a little more detail on how it happened on the jogging trail. But nothing about being swatted by her husband," Schulman said.

"How about the nurse?" Borden asked. He seemed to be looking into personalities of the people involved more than his partner or the others.

"Okay, looks like it was a combination of a nurse and a nursing student from North Texas Community College Nursing School. Nurse was Mollie Malone, and the student was Ester Ramirez."

"Next visit was about four months ago at Metroplex ER in Plano for a black eye and a broken jaw. Tried to claim it was another fall but got confronted by the nurse and didn't deny anything. Wouldn't accept a visit from the Shelter. Says, 'encouraged to call Women's Shelter for counseling. Shelter card given.' Not much question about that broken jaw."

"Does it say who the nurse was?" Borden again asked.

"Yeah, and pay dirt! It was McCarty again," Schulman answered. "You think we've got something here? Maybe McCarty got some of the brothers to do these little jobs for her."

"Don't jump to conclusions," Borden said. "But I'll admit there are possibilities there. That'll make that interview even more important, Detective."

"Who's got Ben Ferrell's wife? Isn't he the next one? Oh yeah," Borden caught himself. "No records found. Do we know if she might have used another name?"

"We'll have to check that out," Schulman said. "Maybe when we look at the records from Lewisville and Richardson, from the Memorial System."

"Okay, I guess that means I'm next," Borden said. "I didn't expect to see any records on Sara Thompson, considering she lives in Allen and is a lot closer to McKinney, but she had an ER visit to Lewisville in November, and guess what! She had a facial laceration that she got from a fall off her bicycle. According to Dr. Evan Stillwater, she had 'multiple bruises on arms and back, in various stages of healing,' and he talked to her about how she got the laceration."

"She wouldn't discuss it. Said no matter what, he was not to report it or to call the Shelter."

"Well, you don't fall off a bike and get blue, green, and yellow bruises," said Perdue. "She got hit on several occasions."

"You know the next question I ask," said Borden. "Who are the parties involved? And here we go. Nadine McCarty filled out the record. 'Injuries suspicious for repeated battering. Discussed with patient privately with spouse out of the room. Patient admitted privately that her husband was having some troubles but that she would be okay and that she did not want anyone to be called. Encouraged her to call Women's Shelter and gave her their card. Cautioned her about escalating abuse and its consequences. Gave her my private cell number.'"

"We may have something here," Borden said. "I say let's look at the records from Lewisville and Kingwood. Smitty, you got your work cut out for you."

They adjourned for the day. Each had his assignment. Borden and Schulman would interview the wives, and Detective Simonton would see the men. A deadline of one week was set, and they would meet again.

FBI personnel would issue subpoenas for Methodist Hospital Richardson, the only other major hospital nearby that wasn't owned by Memorial or Metroplex systems. They hoped they would find something, especially on Andrea Ferrell, and who knows, some of the others may have visited there too.

CHAPTER 18

MEDICAL RECORDS AT LEWISVILLE REGIONAL

Medical Records Department at Lewisville Regional was more accommodating than Memorial had been. The hospital at Lewisville had started off as the county hospital until it went through a series of buyouts and finally became an affiliate of HCA. As the county hospital though, it cared for more of the prison and drug clientele and was much more accustomed to police and FBI requests for medical records. The subpoenas were dropped off, and the computer had the records ready to pick up the next day.

There were records from the Lewisville hospital on a visit from Andrea Ferrell about seven months prior and one from Kingwood on Sara Thompson just three months ago. The records were left on a special shelf in the medical records office, and he was texted that they were ready for his review.

Borden picked up the records himself almost immediately after he was notified and took them to the FBI office. Since there were only two, he decided that he and Schulman could do the reviews without asking the others to participate. He also wanted to discuss another idea with Schulman, out of the presence especially of Dr. Perdue.

They entered the office, went through the ritual of small talk with the personnel, and then the ritual of getting coffee for themselves. Most of the time, they didn't even drink it but seemed to get some caffeine and alertness by osmosis, just having it sit on the desks while they worked, having forgotten that it was there. This time they both were anxious to get to the work of the reviews. They felt they had something.

Borden took the chart from Andrea Ferrell, from Lewisville Regional. Schulman took the other record, from McKinney, on Sara Thompson. Again, they sat quietly for forty-five minutes, and both seemed to finish their reviews at the same time.

"Ready?" asked Borden.

"Sure. Want me to go first?" answered Schulman.

"Suits me fine. What did you find?"

"Well, about a year ago Sara Thompson came to the ER in Lewisville with a facial laceration and, you guessed it, bruises on other parts of her body," Schulman said. "Perdue already told us that he was the ER doc. He works in Lewisville on occasion. He said it was to keep his privileges at that hospital up to date."

"What did the notes say?" Borden asked. The anxiety was obvious in his expression and the tone of his voice. He wasn't interested in a lot of small talk.

"Doc's notes say basically the same as they did in the other file. 'Multiple bruises in various stages of healing.' Do doctors memorize these descriptions in medical school? Looks like the same note," said Schulman.

"Okay, nurse's name?" asked Borden.

"This time it's a Juanita Garcia. Her notes say, 'Questioned patient about source of bruises and laceration, and she denied spousal abuse.' Nothing else in the nurses' record."

"But wait a minute. Perdue apparently has a way with these patients. His note, if I can read it, says, 'Patient admits to verbal and physical abuse by her husband but refuses to report it or to file charges.' Good for him," Schulman said.

"All right, here's the last one. Thompson, from the McKinney Hospital. There are two visits here. One about a year ago. Fell down jogging, scalp laceration that needed repair, and other bruises that could have been from a fall or from something else. Nurse was Angela Taylor, and ER doc was Jim Allison. Nothing in either the nurses' notes or the doc's scribbling that I can make out that relates to anything helpful."

"The other one, at the McKinney Hospital, just three months ago, for a facial laceration and a broken nose. Nurse was McCarty. Apparently she works at McKinney as well as Richardson. Maybe she can't get enough shifts at Richardson. Anyway, she says, "Patient with facial laceration, broken nose, and multiple other bruises, varied stages of healing. Tried to discuss with patient in private, suspect battering. She refused to discuss, refused to allow police or Women's Shelter reporting, and told me to mind my own business. Gave patient card from Women's Shelter, encouraged her to call. Gave her my own personal phone number, told her she could call me any time."

"Man, this lady is on a crusade! Wonder if Smitty has talked with her yet," Schulman said.

"Well, at least this is a start. But we've got our work cut out for us. First, is she involved in these kidnappings, or is she just a helpful nurse whose ex was a batterer or maybe her father or somebody?" Borden said.

"Yeah," Schulman said. "From my experience, most of the counselors at the Shelters are former abuse victims anyway.

"Listen, Gary. I still want your personal opinion on something," said Borden. "You know, Perdue was involved, or at least knowledgeable, in three of these four victims. Any way you can see him having a role in organizing a kidnapping team or participating in it?" he asked.

"I've thought of that too. He's kind of a little guy, so I doubt he could do more than be an organizer or a cheerleader. But I don't think we should forget him. Maybe getting us on the track of abusive husbands was a ruse," Schulman said.

"He may be a little guy, but remember," Borden said, "these guys were all snuck up on and hit with a taser. Then they were pulled up by some kind of a motor or winch. It wouldn't take big guys to do this, the way it was done."

"Yeah, I've thought about that too," Schulman came back.

"Well, let's back-burner it for now. Personally, I have more suspicion in my own mind about this big, strong RN. She's been there for three of them too and is much more direct and confrontational than Perdue. I can see her whacking some abusive husband herself if she gets mad enough," Borden said.

"Ooh, that hurts just thinking about it. Hope she's not involved. I'd sure hate to get on her wrong side," said Schulman.

"Perdue and McCarty were both involved in at least two or three of these cases. And they're both very emotionally involved in the issues. Either one of them, or both of them, I could see having a role in this. Doesn't have to be somebody personally doing the job. Maybe they hired somebody else to do the dirty work."

"Yeah, I've thought of that too," Borden said. "But in conspiracies, the wider you expand, the more people who know about it, the more chance of somebody making a mistake and tipping their hand. We need to keep these two in mind, but I'm putting my money on a single perp."

CHAPTER 19

NADINE McCARTY WAS WEEDING THE FLOWER BED

Nadine McCarty was weeding the flower bed at the side of her house when Detective Simonton called her asking permission to drop by to talk with her. She had planned her day of gardening and then a quiet relaxing evening in front of the television for several weeks. There was a special program she had looked forward to seeing. But she knew that really, after that kind of work, she would probably barely last through the evening news. The rest of the evening she would be asleep in her favorite lounge chair and wake up to go to bed at midnight. This would change her plans. She agreed that he could come by in a half hour.

Damn, she thought. *Just when I was really gettin' goin' on this blasted flower bed. Oh, well. Wonder what the police want to talk to me about.* She knew there wasn't anything she should be worried about. But she still worried. She was, after all, black in north Texas, and her life there had made her wary of the police. You just never knew.

She had time to run into her house and shower and make herself presentable before Smitty arrived. She was really already presentable but couldn't let the detective see her in her backyard clothing.

Simonton arrived shortly and parked his car on the street. He and Franks came up and rang the doorbell. McCarty was a single mother of two, but her children were grown and out of the house, so she lived alone. One daughter was a junior at Sam Houston State University in its highly regarded criminal justice program. Her plans were to become a parole officer. She was already working part time as a guard at the Hollis unit.

Her other daughter was just starting out at the University of North Texas in Denton, in the pre-nursing program. The girls were both on scholarships, and both were working part time, but mom still supplemented them. She did not want them to struggle as hard as she had to get through school, but she felt good about them contributing. Felt it was good for them.

Her house, in Wylie, was a thirty-year-old ranch style, brick with three bedrooms. She had bought it fifteen years ago when she still had a husband and thought it was a partnership. But he had flown the coop just four years later, leaving her with no child support and a mortgage. For practical purposes, she had paid for it herself. She only had three years of payments left, and it would be free and clear. She looked forward to that day.

The house was on a standard city lot, but thirty years ago, lots were bigger than they were now. Developers had figured out that you could get several more cookie cutter houses per acre, just by cutting fifty feet off each lot. The lawn was neat and trimmed. Nadine did her own yard work. There was a curved sidewalk leading to the covered front porch. Two metal chairs sat on the porch, so she could have breakfast and coffee there and listen to the birds and squirrels.

She had a favorite mockingbird that seemed to begin its daily serenade about six o'clock every morning like clockwork. *How in the world did that bird know so many tunes,* she often wondered. *God surely knew what he was doing when he made mockingbirds.*

She answered the door after the first ring. She was expecting one detective and greeted the two who showed up. "Hello, Detectives. Please come in. I have a pot of fresh coffee. Would you like a cup?"

"That sounds a lot better than that mud we're used to at the office. Thanks a lot," Simonton answered as he came in and sat down at the dinner table where he could spread his notes.

After she had served the coffee and his had been sweetened and flavored like he liked it, Simonton said, "We had some questions come up about this string of kidnappings that's been going on in the area for the last three months."

"How in the world does that affect me?" she asked, seeming honestly to know little of why he was asking a nurse such a question. "I don't even know those men unless I've seen them in the ER or something. But I wasn't working when any of them came in. Maybe you need to talk to the nurses that were working those days. I don't even think they all came to Memorial. I don't understand."

"It's not the men we want to ask you about. It's their wives."

"I still don't understand. What does that have to do with me?"

"Do you remember taking care of a Felicia Jernigan in March of last year? She had a scalp laceration and bruises, and your medical records indicated that you suspected that she wasn't telling the truth why she had to come to the ER," Smitty asked.

"The name isn't familiar. Maybe I could answer better if I could look at the chart first. I just don't understand what this is all about." She seemed genuinely confused.

"I've got parts of the medical record here with me. Your notes, at least." He slid the notes across the table to her with the name redacted for privacy purposes.

She took a full ten minutes to review her notes and then to review them again.

"Yeah, I remember this lady. Is she the wife of that first guy that got kidnapped, the police reporter guy? I read about it in the paper."

"Yes," he answered. "You couldn't get her to open up about her injuries. But your chart speaks volumes. Obviously, you were concerned that she was covering up her husband's beating her up."

"Am I in trouble for not reporting that? I didn't think I had enough to go on. Has something else happened?"

"You're not in any trouble. Was there anything else you can remember about her visit that you didn't put in your notes? Anything she said, or anything he said, that you think might be helpful?" he asked.

"I don't know what would be helpful 'cause I don't, for the life of me, know what you're trying to do," she said.

"Just anything, that's all. If you think of anything, please call me. Anything at all, any conversations, body language, anything."

"Okay, but that's been a long time ago. I don't know what I'd remember. That's why I try to put just about everything in my notes."

"There's one other thing, Ms. McCarty. Do you know someone named Carmen Jacobs? Is that a familiar name?" Simonton asked and watched her body language as she began to respond.

"It seems like a name I've heard. I don't know where. Why? Should I know her?"

"Let's let you review her medical record. She came to the ER about four months ago, and you were her nurse in the ER." Smitty gave her the record and sat back, giving her time to digest it. After only a few minutes, she glanced up at him, while continuing to review the record.

"Oh yeah! I remember this one. Man, she was bruised up. Her eye was darker than mine. And she had a hairline fracture of the lower jaw. Luckily, they didn't have to wire her jaw, or she'd still be getting her scrambled eggs through a straw."

"According to your notes, you felt very strongly that she was an abused wife. Remember that?"

"Well, after a few years in the pit, you learn to suspect the husband or the boyfriend when a woman comes in with injuries like this. And she never denied it when I asked her about it. She just wouldn't let me call anybody. Should I have? Is she ok?' McCarty seemed genuinely concerned.

"She's okay. I don't think there have been any problems since her husband's kidnapping. He's probably feeling too bad to be real mean right now," the detective said. "Do you remember anything else that you didn't document about her visit? Was her husband with her?"

"You bet he was with her, and he didn't want to leave her side for a single minute. Like he was afraid she'd say something, tell us the truth. And that's a sign we watch for, the husband who seems overprotective and won't leave her to go to registration. Took us a few minutes to get rid of him where we could talk to her privately."

"There's one final question. Do you remember a Sara Thompson, about three months ago, at McKinney? I guess you must work a few shifts a month there?" Simonton asked.

"Yes, I have to work there to get my hours. If I miss a shift at Memorial because they aren't busy, it makes it tight. Two shifts, and there goes my house payment," said McCarty. "I remember her because I saw her interviewed on TV. Isn't she that coach's wife in . . . where is it, Anna, or Allen?"

"What do you remember about her visit to the ER the night you were working?"

"I remember I really felt sorry for her. Pretty little thing, and her nose will never look the same unless she gets plastic surgery. And she had a facial laceration that'll scar too. They got the laceration sewed up okay and just taped the nose. But she'll look like an old washed-up boxer if she doesn't get that nose fixed. I talked to her but no way was she going to let me call anybody, especially the cops. I always give them a card to the Women's Outreach Shelter. Carry them around in my pocket, this happens so often."

"Do you begin to see a pattern in this? We're sure seeing a pattern. There are four guys in a thirty mile radius of us, who have been kidnapped and almost beaten to death, and you have been the nurse taking care of three of their wives when they came in after getting beat up by their husbands," Simonton finally laid his cards on the table. "Do you see why we wanted to talk to you?"

McCarty began to get a little nervous, thinking, what are they getting at. She kept her cool though and tried not to let them see her sweat.

"Have you told anybody about these women? We're thinking maybe this isn't connected to the work these guys do with the drug lords, but we're thinking some vigilante is taking these guys out behind the barn for a little Texas two-by-four justice because they're wife beaters. Maybe you told somebody, and it really made them mad, mad enough to get even. Maybe even you got so mad you decided to get even, rough them up a little."

"I know I had nothing to do with these guys kidnapping. Why, it would never even occur to me," Nadine asked, and then a concerned, fearful look slowly came over her face. She knew the answer before she asked. "Do I need a lawyer?"

"I don't know. Do you?" The usual question to answer that question and then merged into the next. "Do you own an old minivan? Maybe ford or dodge? Maybe VW? Rough, dirty, maybe has a peace sign hand painted on the back? Know anybody who does?"

"I don't think I want to answer any more questions till I talk to a lawyer," she answered. "I'm sure you can find out what kind of car I drive without my help. I believe I'd like you to leave, right now."

Simonton felt a little bad. She had been really helpful, and he really didn't suspect her. But he asked the questions that had to be asked. It wasn't a popularity contest. The detectives took her invitation and left the house. Nadine sat in her chair and began to cry. Who could she call? She had never used a lawyer since the divorce was over, and that was long ago. She just wasn't the kind of person who dealt with lawyers. Never needed to.

Not till now, anyway.

And it was north Texas after all.

And she was black . . .

CHAPTER 20

THEY MET AGAIN

They met again, this time, in a conference room at the sheriff's department. This time, they didn't invite Perdue. Only the badges: Borden, Schulman, Franks, and Simonton.

"Do we have enough to charge McCarty, or at least to search her house?" Schulman asked, getting more opinions than anything else.

"No, not yet," Borden said. "We need some more homework. We need to interview all of them, husbands and wives, and preferably as close to the same time as possible. Also, remember, Ben Ferrell's wife hasn't shown up on any of our record searches."

"Maybe she's just lucky this far. Or maybe she just went out of town or to some doc's private office. Or maybe she just hasn't had any injuries that needed an emergency room visit," Simonton said.

"Or maybe she needed it, but Ferrell just wouldn't let her go. Being a cop himself, maybe he figures to keep it away from the locals. Don't shit where you eat, I guess."

"You know, some of these bastards control their wives so completely that they wouldn't dare venture off to the ER to get some minor laceration fixed," Borden suggested. "But if it's there, we'll find it, you can bet on that."

"But let's think about this. Maybe these couples don't even know about each other, that all the abductions may have been done because they're abusing their wives," Schulman said. "Maybe they all still believe that it's because they're all heroes, and they're getting punished because they helped put some gang members behind bars. And of course, we don't really know for sure that it's related. Maybe the wife beating is just a miraculous coincidence. Maybe it really is because they're heroes."

Borden took the lead. "We have enough to pick them up for questioning. Any one of the wives could have taken part in organizing the pickups. I'd like to bring all the four wives down separately, but at the same time. Let them sit in the waiting room in the office, and see each other from across the room. Watch their expressions. If they're conspiring, we should be able to read that before we even ask them a question. Let's do this tomorrow, early afternoon, say about 1:00 p.m. We don't want them to get suspicious though. Tell them we want them to look at some mug shots. Let them sit around a conference table for a while and look at the mug books."

"Schulman, you get Jernigan. Smitty, would you bring Thompson. We can send a uniform out to get Ferrell, and then I'll get Jacobs. Plan it so you'll get back here as close to 1:00 p.m. as you can." Assignments understood, they all left for the day.

Each of them was keyed up, wondering what new revelations this strategy would bring. Realizing that even if their suspicions of a get-even conspiracy was correct, that path would necessarily fragment into a myriad of smaller, more obscure trails. Even if they could determine that the reasons for the abductions were tied to the ER trips, they still had no leads as to where that originated or who was at the root of the vigilante theory. But they were intelligent, trained and devoted men and believed in themselves. It was only a matter of time, teamwork, and pounding the pavement before they would put all the pieces of the puzzle together and determine the identity of the assailants. They would catch this guy.

Unless they didn't . . .

CHAPTER 21

THE WOMEN ARRIVED

The women arrived at the sheriff's department headquarters within fifteen minutes of each other and were led to the conference room, one at a time. None had ever met, and their expressions did not suggest anything else. But each realized why she was there and made assumptions that the other women were there for the same purpose. When Borden ushered Carmen Jacobs, the fourth and final woman, into the room, he made a round of introductions and told them that he wanted everyone to look at some mug shots. He then left the room and allowed a few minutes for the women to get acquainted. Not knowing what to expect though, the women were quiet until Schulman came in with notebooks of mug shots for them to review.

"I know that none of you saw the kidnapers, but I want you to look at these pictures and see if they bring up any memories, of anything at all," he said. "Maybe you've met one of them at the grocery store or anywhere else that you've been. You don't have to be sure, just that you may have seen someone before, even long ago."

He handed a notebook of pictures to each and asked them to pass them around when they finished each notebook. "I'll be right outside the door in this office. I can hear you if you call for me." He then walked to his office where his partner and detectives Simonton and Franks were waiting. Each had an earphone and had been listening to the conversation. Borden plugged his into his ear as well and sat down at his desk, waiting to see what would transpire.

After he left the room, the women became more animated and open, each hungry for any information that they could get about the abductions, and comparing notes about their experiences. Borden left them alone. This is what he wanted them to do. He was able to hear their conversation through a hidden microphone that was already installed in the room. It was installed in a false fire sprinkler, directly overhead. It had a fish-eye lens and would pick up the entire room.

Felicia Jernigan was the most outgoing of the group and started a conversation with Sara Thompson, seated directly across the conference table from her. Sara's head was dropped forward, looking at the edge of the faux-walnut tabletop, seeming to expect it to come alive. Felicia barely could see her eyes. She spoke very softly as if to keep her voice from the ears of the men down the hall. "Your husband is a coach, isn't he? I was so sorry to hear about him. How is he doing?"

Sara barely raised her head, seeming embarrassed or afraid. She was still in a state of seeming shock. Her husband's abduction was still painfully on her mind, her every waking moment. "Yes," she almost whispered. He coaches eighth-grade boys' basketball at Allen middle school and helps out in football and gym. I guess he's doing okay physically. He's still in rehab and has a cast on his leg and one arm."

"But he's still waking up at night with nightmares." She began to raise her head ever so slightly. She was a very pretty woman, but with the stresses she had recently faced, she looked like she hadn't slept well, and her expression was drawn.

"I don't know how long that's supposed to last," Carmen said. She seemed to be asking about the other women's experiences as if they were old pros at husband abductions even though all their experiences were the same, except that the others were just farther in the past.

"Craig did that for about two months on a regular basis. Then it started getting better," Felicia said. "He still gets real moody a lot, and I can tell it's always on his mind. The antidepressants have helped some. And Xanax is a lifesaver. The pain doesn't last forever."

"Same thing with Ben," Andrea Ferrell said. "He'd go crazy if it wasn't for his Prozac, and the Xanax too when he gets too jittery thinking about it." The women were bonding and getting into a more animated discussion.

Sometimes, just knowing that somebody else has gone through the same trauma, and survived, helps, gives you strength to keep on keeping on.

"I think Farley could get over all this a lot better if he just wasn't in pain so much," said Carmen Jacobs. At first, she didn't really seem like she wanted to talk about it. But when the others began talking about their husbands' problems since the abductions, she relaxed and began to open up with them. "What I can't figure out is, who is doing all of this and why? Has anybody got any ideas on that?"

Even though he was listening to the conversation with headphones, Borden subconsciously leaned closer to the digital panel in front of him when the women began to talk. Smitty and Schulman were also quietly listening, and they glanced at each other, so much to say, here comes the good part. It had taken almost a half hour for the women to feel comfortable enough to get even this far into the discussion. But they had all day and continued to monitor the conversation.

"They came out to the house to talk to me yesterday. Have they been out to see any of you?" Carmen Jacobs asked.

The other three women looked startled and all answered no.

"What did they want?" asked Felicia Jernigan.

"Well, first they just went over what I remembered about the day Farley was abducted, same old stuff. Talking about, maybe I'd remember something I didn't tell them the first five times they asked me about it. Then they started grilling me about a couple of visits to the ER I had made. I couldn't figure out what that was all about and finally made them leave. They really upset me," Carmen said.

"Without being nosy, what did they care about your medical history? What does that have to do with anything?" Felicia especially seemed interested in this new information.

"I have no idea. I am a real klutz and had a couple of minor lacerations that needed stitches," Carmen answered. "No major stuff. Once I was jogging and tripped and fell. Then the other time it was raining, and I slipped and fell and hit my head on the car. Got a little cut and a hairline jaw fracture. Luckily, no major injury."

"That just doesn't make sense," Felicia said although the comments did remind her of her trips to Memorial ER and the lies she had to tell to keep the real truth hidden. The snoops next door watched her face on the hidden camera and realized that she looked worried.

"How can that have anything to do with this?" Andrea Ferrell asked. "They're supposed to be trying to find some maniac on the loose, not prying into our private medical histories. Did they give you any idea why they were interested?"

"Well, they really made me mad, they acted like they didn't believe me about the injuries. They even asked me if my husband hit me. That's when I told them to pack it up and get out of my house," said Carmen.

"Oh, that's today's cops for you," said Sara Thompson. "And heaven forbid if your kid gets a bruise. You'll be hauled in for charges, and your kid will suddenly be living in foster care under Child Protective Services. You don't have a chance these days." As she realized that she was talking to at least one deputy sheriff's wife, she ducked her head again, hoping that she hadn't offended anyone.

This discussion seemed to put a damper on the conversation. Everyone became quiet and went back to looking at the mug shots. But they were no longer putting their deepest attention to the pictures. Each of the four women was thinking of her own experiences in her own troubled marriage, oblivious to the fact that the other three were thinking the same things.

Sisters in sorrow but unaware of their sisterhood and unable to gain comfort from or to give comfort to her sisters, not even knowing that they were sisters in sorrow. Unable even to ask questions, to find out if the other sisters had experienced the same pain and anguish, afraid they would think it was the sister's fault and not understanding, I'm really a good person. I didn't cause him to do these things to me. So they sat in silence with their sisters in sorrow, hoping somebody else would jump-start the conversation with just a hint of the truth.

They went back to reviewing the mug shots quietly, contemplatively. And after they had been quiet for about a half hour, they had each reviewed all the notebooks of mug shots and didn't recognize anybody. Borden returned about then and offered refreshments and bathroom breaks. Having studied their faces during their brief conversation, he was convinced that the women at least were not co-conspirators in the abductions. He thought, however, that one might have been partially involved but had no idea which one and how. He was a little frustrated. The only thing that had come out of the get-acquainted meeting was that the subject of abuse from their husbands had at least been brought up in front of all four.

Borden thanked the four women for going through the mug shots and asked if they could reconvene after lunch. He told them someone would bring up sandwiches for their lunch, but they had some questions they still needed to ask. The wives, emboldened by even their limited conversations, seemed anxious to help.

CHAPTER 22

THE MEN REGROUPED

The men regrouped at the downstairs lunch room. They each picked up sandwiches and drinks and chose a four-seater table in the corner, out of the way of traffic. Although the lunch room was a busy place, being the only convenient place for the building's office workers to take a break, it was usually quiet enough for you to hear yourself think. Maybe it was the soft Mozart that was usually playing, that made people feel like not being so boisterous as they do if it's Willie Nelson or rock and roll. They each had barely taken a mouthful when Borden, anxious to move on to the next stage, began to talk.

"Well, what do you think? Are we on the right trail, or are we wasting our time?" he asked openly, his question not directed to any one of the group.

A moment of quietness ensued then Detective Simonton spoke, "I don't think we're wasting our time at all. I think the next thing we need to do is go into another level of questioning of these women, specifically about their domestic problems, let them know that we know what's been going on. I bet dollars to donuts we'll get some worthwhile leads from some of them."

Officer Franks said, "I think you're right. This is the right trail. Then we need to do the same with the 'victims,' the husbands. We need to let them know that we aren't dummies, that we know exactly what kind of husbands they are. And if it all turns out to be a red herring, I bet we can put the fear of God in them and maybe change their behavior a little bit."

Schulman added, "Yeah, that's a good point. Let's get going. It might just work"

"Okay," Borden said. He was obviously calling the shots but had learned long ago that everybody works harder if you let them feel like they have something to say about how they get their work done. And often, like today, somebody suggests an angle you hadn't considered.

"Let's don't let the ashes cool," he added. "We'll talk to each of them separately this afternoon. We already talked to Carmen Jacobs once, so it'll only take a few minutes to tie up loose ends with her. We missed Felicia Jernigan. She and Dr. Conlin were out when we tried to talk with her. So we still have Jernigan, Ferrell, and Thompson we haven't really talked to. It's time for a come-to-Jesus meeting with every one of them. How's this? I will take Jernigan. Gary, you take clean-up on Jacobs. Smitty, if you take Ferrell, that'll leave Thompson for you, Steve. Okay with everybody?"

They all agreed, and when they went upstairs, each took his assignment to a separate interview room.

Borden led Felicia Jernigan to the first room, offered her a glass of water, and sat across the small table from her. "How are you doing, Mrs. Jernigan? Are things beginning to smooth out for you?"

"Oh, I think I'm doing okay. I went through some rough times just after it happened, scared of my own shadow, but I think I'll be okay, "she said. "I just hope you find the thugs who are doing these terrible things."

"Well, I'm going to tell you exactly what we're thinking. We're thinking we've been on the wrong track all along. At this point we don't think it has anything to do with your husband's job and his reporting on the drug trade thugs. And it definitely wasn't the Phillips boys. First place, they alibied out, and second thing, I don't think they're smart enough or organized enough to do something this elaborate without screwing it up."

"What do you mean? Who else could have done this?" She seemed genuinely shocked, and not a little scared.

"Mrs. Jernigan, we believe that we've been completely on the wrong track, trying to connect the four men through their mutual work contacts. We are going to be completely open with you, and we hope you will be completely open with us."

"What do you mean? I've been open with you!" Felicia was beginning to cry, and was getting scared of what she was hearing.

"Okay, here it is. We know for an absolute fact that you are a physically abused wife, and if you aren't aware of it yet, let me tell you that all three of the others are in the same boat," Borden said.

"What! What do you mean? What are you talking about?" Felicia began sobbing hysterically. "I'm getting out of here! I'm going home." She rose and started for the door. She had never been confronted about the situation by anyone except her mother, and this was an abrupt, unexpected attack. "We may have our problems, but doesn't everybody? Nobody's marriage is perfect!" Felicia almost screamed when she was able to control herself.

Borden stopped her at the door and pushed it shut. He was speaking very quietly now as if he wanted to console her, like he knew she had gone through a lot. "You aren't under arrest, and you aren't suspected of anything. And you know of course that you can leave at any time. But I ask you please to hear me out. I think you may be able to help us get to the bottom of this. Please," he entreated.

She paused for almost a minute at the door, considering her options. Then she began to cry softly and quietly turned back toward the table. Borden slid the box of Kleenex toward her.

He allowed her a couple of minutes, to collect her thoughts and to control her crying.

"Let's understand something. We aren't guessing or speculating," Borden said. "We know, without a doubt, and we have proof, that you have all four been hit and injured by your husbands and have had to go to the ER for medical care. Further, we believe that someone, or some group, has decided to become the vigilante for abused women. We think these abductions and beatings have specifically targeted abusive husbands, you know, to teach them a lesson or something, and to punish them for their abuse.

But at this point, we have no concrete idea and no credible leads as to who is behind the abductions."

Felicia slowly wiped her eyes and then blew her nose with the tissue he had offered. When she spoke, she sounded as if she was giving up, but reluctantly. "Sounds like you've got it all figured out. What am I supposed to do? What do I tell Craig? What am I supposed to do about him? I can't imagine what he'll do when he finds out I've talked with the police." She began to cry again softly.

"You let us handle Craig. I think we can talk him into being a good boy for a while. Somebody else may have already taught him that lesson. Do you think he has any idea about the other wives, being abused that is?"

"He sure hasn't mentioned it. But then he doesn't really think he's an abusive husband. He thinks I'm a bad wife, and I make him do it," Felicia said.

"Well, that probably isn't true. But we're gonna get all of you into counseling," he said. "The Women's Outreach Shelter has counselors who can help abused wives. But for now, let's talk about you and Craig. Do any of your friends know about your troubles with Craig?"

She laughed cynically. "Friends? What friends? I never leave the house. I have no friends. I barely see my mother, and then only once in a while."

"Do you go to church? Have you talked with your pastor? Anybody?" Borden asked.

"We haven't been to church since we moved to Lewisville," she answered. Agent Borden was beginning to understand the degree to which she had been isolated from society. He had seen it so many times before. He remembered a saying from his childhood, "Keep 'em pregnant in the summer and barefoot in the winter." He never realized the impact of that attitude until he became a cop.

"I need to know anybody you've talked to about your problems with your husband. Anybody who has seen anything, not even that you've talked to. Anybody. Relatives, friends, doctors, neighbors, anybody at all, even a very casual discussion," Borden said.

"Okay, well . . . I guess of course my mom, . . . Dr. Perdue maybe. Oh yeah, that nurse at Memorial who seemed to have it all figured out. She acted like she was really mad. I forgot her name. Seems like Nadine or something like that. I don't know her last name. She's big enough to do it too!"

Borden was taking notes, writing down names, and nodding to show approval.

"Of course, the other nurses at the hospital," she said. "I don't remember who they were. And the volunteer from the Shelter. I didn't actually meet her, but I know she knew who I was and why I was at the hospital. And I don't know who else she talked to. Prob'ly everybody she knows."

"What has Craig been like since his abduction?" Borden asked. Has he acted any differently toward you?" He wanted to know if Craig had figured out why he had been selected.

"Ever since he got home from rehab, it's like he's been a different person. Talks nice to me. Good to me in the bedroom. Just like it used to be when we first got married. But then, after a major episode, he always acts real nice for about six months. I just hope it lasts this time."

"Well, just so you'll know, we have talked to him, and we have brought up the topic of your problems with him. So he knows we're going down a different trail than we were a couple of weeks ago," Borden said.

"Oh no! What did he say?" Her face registered a new level of fear.

"Well, he got pretty mad. But they all do. They all think if they act offended and hurt, it'll make us think they're innocent. Righteous indignation, for sure."

"That's just great!" she responded.

"I guess that's all I have for right now," Borden said. Can I call you again if I have other questions?"

"Sure, I guess it doesn't matter, now that Craig knows what's going on," Felicia said.

"Next step is to get you into a counseling situation. Are you willing to do that? Will Craig go with you? You know, this is for both of you. Counseling is not just to help you put up with the abuse better. There is abuser counseling too and anger management counseling. Part of the time it's wasted effort, but in a small number of cases, the abuser can really get something out of it, they can really change."

"Really?" Felicia asked. "You really think he might change?"

"It's worth a try," Borden answered, and with that hint of encouragement, he ushered her to the door. He hoped that he wasn't giving her false hope.

CHAPTER 23

CARMEN JACOBS WAS FUMING

Carmen Jacobs was fuming, sitting and waiting in the interview room, when Agent Schulman came in. He offered her something to drink, "We have water, coffee and diet Coke," he said, purposely putting on a friendly face.

"I need something stronger than that!" she answered. "No, I guess a diet Coke is okay. I am pretty dry by now."

Schulman pushed a button on the intercom, and a few minutes later someone brought in one diet Coke and one full strength. "I'm still drinking brown sugar water, I guess," he said, a little sheepishly. Odd that a grown man has to apologize for drinking a Coke, he thought.

"Do you realize that can of Coke has seven teaspoons of sugar?" Carmen asked, seeming to relax a little.

"I guess I never thought about it that way," Schulman said. "Well, at least I don't use tobacco or alcohol. I guess everybody's got to go one way or the other. Mine will be with sugar poisoning," he tried to joke. "That diet stuff just doesn't do it for me."

"It's all in what you get used to," Carmen answered."

"Here's what we need," Agent Schulman said. "We need you to help us figure out who beat your husband to within an inch of his life. We've changed our entire approach to the case, based on new information we have."

"What new information?" asked Carmen. "I haven't heard about anything new."

"It's about all the injuries that all four of you women have had to go to the ER for over the past two years, at least so far as we know and probably even before that." He let that soak in a minute and watched the expression on her face. She turned a couple of shades of red before she regained her composure.

"What injuries?" she asked in a whisper voice.

"Well, one of you has had lacerations repaired on her first visit to the ER, and the second time she was covered with belt marks over her whole body. Another one of you had a scalp laceration that needed stitches. The third one came in for scrapes and bruises and a laceration then later returned with another laceration and a broken nose."

During this time, Carmen sat quietly glowering at the agent. She seemed to want to protect her private hell at all costs.

"Now, getting to you . . . you yourself have come in for a facial laceration and later with a black eye and a broken jaw. We know what happened, and we know it wasn't from an accident."

"Each of you has some simplistic made-up story of being clumsy, slipping on a wet spot on the floor, etc. But you can't all be that clumsy. We know, without a doubt, that you are all four victims of domestic violence. Your husbands have beaten you repeatedly to the point of requiring medical attention."

Her scowl was gradually diffusing, and a tear in the corner of her left eye replaced it. "So if you are right, what are we supposed to do about it?" she asked, then added, in a whisper, "You just don't know what it's like."

"We'll get to that," said Schulman. "But for now, we need to find out who this vigilante is and put him away before somebody else gets brutalized or maybe killed. And we need your help for that. We need you to tell us each and every person who might know about the problems you have with your husband. Whether it's a relative, your parents, a friend, a coworker, nurses, doctors, anybody you can think of."

Carmen began to cooperate albeit begrudgingly. She wiped her tears with the back of her hand and began to recount anyone she could remember who she had discussed her problem with. As in the case of many victims of domestic abuse, she had told almost nobody. Certainly not her parents or the brother she didn't really get along with that well anyway. She remembered that he had never liked Farley anyway.

Like Felicia, she rarely went out and had few friends. She had one girlfriend from college that she kept in touch with but had never confided such an embarrassing thing as a beating from her husband. Sorority sisters frequently want to let everyone think they are happy and successful beyond imagination and tend to exaggerate their positions and the happiness of their marriages. Their best friends are often the very last to know.

So at last Schulman had a few leads that would need to be tracked down. He wrote down names, and as many telephone numbers as Carmen remembered, in his notebook. He, or his team, would call everyone on the list. As often occurs in police work, nothing seems obvious. Schulman thanked her for her cooperation and asked her to call him if she thought of anything else. Then he gave her a card as she got up to leave.

CHAPTER 24

ANDREA FERRELL WAS NERVOUSLY FILING . . .

ndrea Ferrell was nervously filing on a damaged fingernail when Detective Simonton entered the interview room at 2:30 p.m. She had waited for more than thirty minutes, and there is only so long you can spend getting your e-mails off your phone before you begin to go stir crazy.

"Sorry, but I couldn't go any faster," Smitty apologized. "Is there anything I can get you?"

"Nah, I already found the rest room and the water fountain, so I'm okay," she answered. He could detect the slightest bit of sarcasm in her voice. But she was a cop's wife, so it was allowed. It was even expected.

Smitty decided to hit the ground running. "Mrs. Ferrell, we brought you here today because you share a common misery with the other three women here. You all have a husband who has been kidnapped and beaten severely. Three of you have husbands whose jobs bring them into contact with undesirable elements on a regular basis. Undesirable elements who could easily get mad and want to get even with your husbands.

"Initially we thought these abductions had to do with one of the bad guys that all three had worked on—the reporter, the deputy sheriff, and the assistant DA. But then the Allen coach came along, and he didn't fit the mold. But the bottom line is, we don't think it has anything to do with their jobs anymore.

"We know that at least three of you have been, and maybe still are, victims of domestic violence. We have seen records of multiple lacerations, bumps, bruises, broken jaw, broken nose, belt marks. But we haven't been able to find anything, at least locally, about you. You're the only one who hasn't been to the local hospital ER's. Is there anything we're missing?"

Up to this point, Andrea had been putting on her very best poker face and doing a pretty good job of it. Good thing Simonton hadn't gone fishing at Methodist Hospital in Dallas. She had succeeded in covering up her single ER trip by going to the Methodist Hospital, on the far side of Dallas, almost fifty miles from home. He had bruised her several times and caused lacerations twice, but she had been able to take care of them herself with pressure and Steri-Strips from Wal-Mart. But the last time he had twisted her little finger until it came out of socket, and she had to go to the emergency room to get it fixed.

She knew it was inevitable that the police would find out about her trip to Methodist ER. She didn't realize, though, that the hospital in Plano shared computer records with all Methodist Hospital branches, including the hospital in Oak Cliff. But she felt that Simonton was too good. He would eventually find the Methodist records. Andrea decided that continuing her charade was futile and declared to herself that she was going to come clean and be honest.

"No," she said with a defeated look on her face and her head bowed toward the table. "You were right the first time. We're all the same. We've all needed stitches. I've managed to take care of most of mine myself, with pressure and Band-aids, but I've been to the ER too. I went to Methodist Hospital ER in South Dallas. But tell me, what does this have to do with anything?"

Smitty was surprised at her candor. She had gone out of her way to keep her dark secret just that, and now she was giving it up the first time he asked her.

"Well, we believe someone, or some group, has appointed themselves as vigilantes for women, and they're trying to teach your husbands a lesson. Right now, we're focusing most of our man hours on that idea. I hope you can help me."

"Whatever I can do. If this keeps up, somebody's going to get killed," Andrea said. She had rapidly compartmentalized her own personal problems into the larger picture and was willing to forgo her privacy for the sake of helping the bigger problem. And also, she realized, Smitty would find out, whether she cooperated or not. There was nothing she could do about it. Might as well cooperate.

"You got that right," Smitty agreed.

"So what do you need from me?" she asked.

At the same time, Detective Steve Franks had taken Sara Thompson into a separate interview room, two doors down from Smitty and Ferrell. He went through the same questions as Smitty had done with Ferrell with the same goal in mind to make her comfortable so she would be freer with her answers. Do you want a drink, did you find the bathroom, sorry about the delays, thanks for coming down, etc.

"I understand your husband is a coach," Steve started with an icebreaker, commenting on a benign topic that they both knew was just that, an icebreaker. "Where are you all from, before you came here?"

"Yes. He coaches the eighth-grade boys' basketball. At Allen. We've only been here less than a year. We're both from McAllen, originally. We both taught a couple of years in the valley to help pay back some student loans. We moved here because this is where Jack found a job. I haven't been able to find a job yet, except for some substitute teaching."

"Yeah, I know they've laid off some teachers. Well, good luck," he said. "Let's get into why we asked you to come here. I guess you've gotten acquainted with the other three women?"

"Yes. They seem very nice. I had never met any of them before," she said.

"All of you have some things in common. First, all of you are married to men who have been systematically abducted, driven out to God only knows where, and beaten to within an inch of their lives. At first, we thought this was related to some criminals that the other three had all worked to put in prison and now was out, getting even. You know, the police reporter, the deputy sheriff, and the assistant DA. We were tracking down leads right and left and figured it was only a matter of time before we put it together.

But then you and Jack came along. We thought, 'what does a fairly new junior high coach have to do with busting criminals? What's the connection? It blew our theories out of the water."

"I've kept up pretty well with the investigation, at least between the newspaper and the TV news. Then when Jack was kidnapped, I was completely confused. I don't see any connection," Sara said.

"Well, we're working on a new theory now. I need to ask you about a trip you made to the emergency room at the hospital in McKinney back in November. Do you remember that?" Franks asked.

"Yes, I remember," she answered softly, but a tear came into the corner of her eye, and she began to look nervous. "I ran into a problem with my bike. I ride it almost every day, and this time there was a rock on the trail, that I didn't see. I fell and split my forehead. Had to get some stitches."

"Mrs. Thompson, I'm going to ask you to be honest with me on this. We know that's not true. We don't blame you for trying to keep that secret. But we know what happened to you, and we know it wasn't from falling off your bike. We know that your husband has hit you, on several occasions. In fact, all four of you women have been beaten by your husbands. We aren't guessing. We know." Sara was beginning to cry, very quietly, but was not protesting.

"And we believe that may be connected to why all four of your husbands have been abducted and then beaten so badly. We believe that someone is trying to send a message to these four men, and possibly others. We believe your husbands have been beaten by someone who has decided to be a vigilante for abused women. We also think there may be more of the same. This psycho has tasted revenge and won't stop with these four men."

Sara looked frightened and worried but seemed to invite a chance to discuss this problem. "So that's why the others were talking in circles in the conference room," she said.

"Now . . . we believe that somewhere deep inside, one of you has information that can help us get to the bottom of this. And we want you all to come clean with us and help us put a stop to this before it gets worse," Franks said.

"You mean you think they might be back again? Oh my god! Another episode like the first, and they'll kill him," Sara began to cry more loudly. Franks slid his ever-present box of tissues toward her. She took several.

"No, we don't really think that your husbands are likely to be visited again. We believe that each only gets one episode and then they'll either quit or move on to someone else. But we need to go over some questions with you," he said.

"I'm sorry I lied. I'll be honest, I promise. But you can't let my husband know I've talked to you. You don't know what it's like, trying to keep it a secret . . . such shame . . . such guilt," she continued to sob and whispered through her snubbing. But she was beginning to gain control a little at a time.

Franks gave her a couple more minutes to gain her composure and asked, "I need a list of everybody you have told about this or everybody you think has figured out your secret. Your family, your friends, doctors, nurses, counselors . . . anybody. Have you told your parents?"

"I think they suspect something. I rarely visit them anymore. I used to be over there all the time. But we've never discussed it. Truthfully, the only person I've talked to is the nurse at the ER in Kingwood. Even the doctor didn't seem interested, and when I told him I fell off my bike, that was enough for him. But the nurse was really nice. She asked me all about it. I didn't tell her, but I think she figured it out. She even gave me a card to the Women's Shelter."

"Did you call them?" Franks asked.

"No, I was afraid that would just make it worse when Jack found out," she answered. Franks expected that answer. His experience had taught him that abused women usually keep it all to themselves until it becomes so obvious that they give up and tell.

"Are you talking about Nadine McCarty?" he asked. "Big, strong black woman?"

"I didn't remember her name, but that sounds like her. She told me I could call her if I ever wanted to talk about it. Even gave me her private cell phone number. I'm sure that's her."

"Have you seen her or heard from her since that ER trip? Has she called you?" Franks asked, hoping for more. "Anybody else? Big brother, friend, anybody? Has anybody asked you about it, to make you think they might have figured it out?" he asked.

"Nobody else. I've been extremely careful not to let on. I do have a big brother. I can just imagine what Eric would do if he found out. He'd prob'ly kill him. I stay home when I have bruises somebody might see. And it doesn't happen all the time, just when he's been drinking too much," she said.

"How often is that?" Franks asked, not really expecting an answer. Once he had determined that she was an abuse victim like the other three, he was less interested in the details of the abuse than he was in figuring out Gabby. He didn't really expect an answer to his last question.

"Has anything changed in your relationship since he was abducted?" Franks asked. "Has he said anything to make you think he knows about the other three being abused wives?"

"No, nothing at all. He has mentioned several times that he doesn't see what he has to do with the others. He's never met them, and he's not in their line of work. Why would the drug lords do this to him, he has said several times." She looked out the window for a minute, focusing on everything and nothing.

"I would say, though, that he sure has been nice to me since his abduction. Doesn't seem to want to cross me or offend me. And he's almost quit drinking since this happened."

"That's a good sign. Have there been any times he was more worried than others? Has he said anything to make you think whoever did this has contacted him?" he asked.

"Not that I can think of." She continued to look out the window, this time at a single oak branch directly outside the window and swaying in the breeze. After a minute's pause, she said, "Well, there was that . . . Oh, that probably didn't mean anything."

"Tell me what you started to say," Franks said. "What may mean nothing to you might mean something else to me. What were you saying?"

"I wasn't snooping!" she exclaimed. "But the other day, I was bringing him a sandwich, and he was sitting with his laptop on his lap in front of him, looking at e-mail. When I brought it around to set the dinner tray in front of him, he was trying to shut down whatever he had on the screen, like he didn't want me to see it."

"Really! What did you see?" Franks's interest was suddenly piqued. "Could you see anything before he closed it?"

"All I could see was the word Congratulations in great big red letters. Then there was some other wording, looking like a certificate for something, and I remember the word Home Schooling in the middle of it. But he got it shut down before I could figure out what it was about. I even asked him what he was getting congratulations for, and he said, 'It was just spam!' But that didn't seem right. It seemed odd to me, and it seemed to bother him a lot. Then, the rest of the day, he was on edge, and wouldn't even talk to me."

"You didn't ever see that e-mail again?" Franks asked.

"No, never."

"Does that mean anything to you, the "home schooling" part?" Franks asked, nervously hoping he could link it to what they already knew it might mean.

"No, I have no idea what it means. We never home schooled our children or anything like that."

"Is the laptop still at home?" Franks asked. "Do you know his passwords?"

"It's still there, but I don't know any of his passwords. I have my own computer," she said. "What do you think it means?"

"I don't really know. Would you be willing to let us take the computer downtown for a day or two?" he asked, knowing that Texas is a community property state and anything a married person owns is also the property of the other. She had the legal right to let him see the computer without telling her husband. He also knew that he could easily get a search warrant for the computer if she wasn't able to help him.

"I'd like to, but I'm afraid of what Jack would say if he came home from rehab and found it missing. Isn't there some way you can download stuff from it and work on it without him knowing it?"

"We can try," Franks said. "I'm not exactly a computer pro, but I have people in the office that are. I'll talk to the pros about it. I'll be in touch with you. Thanks for coming in. And thanks for being honest with me. I'll get an officer to take you home."

With that, Sara Thompson gathered up her purse and what was left of her diet Coke and left the interview room. Detective Franks went to the debriefing room where Borden, Simonton, and Schulman were waiting for him, each ready to see if someone else had been more successful in getting useful information from their respective assignment, but each realized that his own attempt had come up dry.

"Well, Steve, how did you do?" Borden asked. "We all seem to be shooting blanks so far. All we've gotten is that everybody finally admitted the abuse from their husbands. But about Gabby, we don't have a clue."

"I'm in the same boat," Steve Franks said.

Borden said, "Looks like our best suspect is the nurse, Nadine McCarty. "She was there, every time you turn around. And militant about abused women, she is."

"I may have come up with something, but I don't understand it yet," Franks said. "Sara Thompson said she had stumbled on an e-mail that her husband was scrambling to get rid of, that he obviously didn't want her to see while she was bringing him lunch. She noticed it before he had a chance to get if off the screen, but she could only read a part of it. Said he seemed upset and barely spoke to her the rest of the day."

"What did it say?" asked Borden.

Franks pulled out his black pocket notebook that he had kept his notes in ever since he started with the department. "Let me see, exactly what did she say . . . Oh, here it is. She didn't have time to read the whole thing before he got it shut down, just saw highlighted words. It was in big red letters, "CONGRATULATIONS", at the top, and she noticed, also in highlighted letters, the word "home schooling". Any idea what that means? She had no clue. Said he wasn't up for any awards she knew of unless someone is giving him some kind of honor because of what he's been through. His football team isn't doing so well, so there sure aren't any kudos due on that front."

Borden asked, "Can we get that computer? I mean, without a search warrant?"

"She seems willing to cooperate," said Franks. Wants her husband to be kept out of the loop, of course. I'll take one of the IT guys by tomorrow while he's at rehab. He should be able to download the stuff and bring it back here."

"You know, I'm thinking I've heard something about home schooling," Simonton mused. "I remember a case about ten years ago where the husband, before he knocked the shit out of his wife, he would tell her something like, he was going to give her some old-fashioned home schooling or something like that."

Borden answered, "Yeah, I've heard something like that too. We may have a connection. We'll see, from the e-mail. Franks, you got your work cut out for you."

CHAPTER 25

ANDY TRAYLOR THOUGHT . . .

ndy Traylor thought it would be simple to get the needed e-mail files from Thompson's laptop. "This is kids' play, breaking somebody's e-mail password. The best these passwords do is to slow a guy's wife down, from finding his porn stash," he told Franks. "Any tenth-grade computer geek can do this."

Steve Franks called Sara Thompson to be sure it was still okay to come by for the computer download. She seemed not only willing but anxious, hoping they would be able to find something that would help uncover Gabby.

Franks and Traylor got into a black and white from the sheriff's department, that the detectives often used on assignment. Andy drove. The trip to the Thompson house in Allen was a thirty-minute drive, and during the drive, Steve briefed Andy on what specific e-mail they were wanting. The car carried a strong odor of cigarette smoke, mixed with a slight odor of the last guy who had vomited in the back floorboard. You just really can't completely get rid of that even with what the maintenance guys did to clean the cars up. It's what a cop just has to get used to. Windows down was helpful.

"So wattaya think?" the younger Traylor asked. He had his left arm resting on the window frame, his cigarette blowing in the breeze and controlled the steering wheel with a two-finger grip. The way a real man drives.

"About what?" Franks answered. Sometimes he felt Traylor asked stupid questions, and it got on his nerves.

"Well, the case, the e-mail, the wives, the husbands, what do you think?" Traylor retorted.

"Well, if ya really wanta know, I'll tell you. I don't believe in coincidences, and having four random women whose equally random husbands just happen to be fuckin' wife beaters is way too much of a coincidence. I believe this may be a very interesting e-mail, if we can get it."

They pulled in front of the Thompson house. It was a thirty-year-old wood frame single-story house with an attractive flower bed skirting the house. There was a single large white oak in the center of the yard and acorns were scattered over the yard and the driveway. There was new white paint on the house, with contrasting hunter green shutters. The venetian blinds were all closed. There was a ten-year-old black Ford pickup in the driveway. In front of the pickup was a small pink child's bicycle kept upright with training wheels. A basketball goal was attached to the edge of the garage roof. The basketball lay in the grass a few feet away.

Detective Franks rang the doorbell, and Sara opened the front door almost immediately as if she had been waiting for them. She ushered them into the dining room which Jack had been using for his office. The television was tuned to the Disney channel, and the Mickey Mouse Club was babysitting the toddler sitting in the floor less than eighteen inches from the screen, entranced by the characters. An eleven-year-old boy sat on the couch, still in his pajamas. His six-year-old sister stood next to her mother, not sure what to think of the visitors. They almost nearly never had visitors so this was really an occasion.

The dining room was occupied by a wooden table, too old to be new and too new to be an antique, and a small china cabinet. Three of the chairs around the table matched, and the third was similar but not the same. There was a flower arrangement on the table, straight from the local craft store, and there was no dust on the table. Sara collected decorative salt and pepper shakers and stored her collection on the shelves of a curio cabinet in the corner. A six-foot artificial ficus tree gave the room a pleasant impression of outdoors. The overall impression was of a growing family who didn't have a lot of extra money but had some taste. And a wife who took pains with keeping a neat, clean house. Sara opened the blinds behind the ficus. With the blinds closed, the room was just a little dark and dreary.

Sara directed Andy to Jack's E-Machine desktop computer on a small computer desk in the corner of the combination dining room and office. Andy sat at the computer and connected his external hard drive to it. It was short work, downloading the data from the computer, making sure to include the e-mail files. In fifteen minutes, he stood up and said, "Okay, that's that. I've got the files."

"Please, keep in mind that I really don't want Jack to know about this. If nothing comes of it, there is no reason for him to know I gave you his files," Sara said.

"We fully understand, but you must also understand that we may have to disclose some of this, to be able to use it properly, depending on what the files reveal," said Franks. "We really appreciate your remembering this e-mail. It may be very important. Of course, we won't know until the IT guys take it apart. It may mean absolutely nothing, in which case your husband will never be told that we were here."

Franks and Traylor then got back into the car and backed out of the driveway, being careful to avoid the several children who were playing Super Hero in the street.

When they arrived at the sheriff's department, Franks went to his office while Traylor went to the computer center at the other end of the long building to begin dismantling the files. It was 4:00 p.m., and Franks knew better than to expect any results for a day or two. He needed to update himself on another case that was pending, and his caffeine level was getting dangerously low.

Franks stopped at the coffee machine. The one good thing about the new coffee syrup machines was that there was no such thing as stale coffee anymore. But that was a laugh. The coffee was only a mix of coffee syrup and hot water and tasted that way. It was advertised as freshly "brewed" on demand. But he believed what his wife had told him, that if you put enough chocolate in coffee, you can't taste the stale.

He met Detective Simonton on the way to the coffee room and briefed him on his trip to see Sara Thompson. In the meantime, Smitty had called and questioned Felicia Jernigan, Andrea Ferrell, and Carmen Jacobs about any unusual e-mails they might have noticed since their husbands' abductions. None of them could talk openly at the time, but Felicia Jernigan had called him back an hour and a half later and said maybe she had noticed something unusual in her husband's e-mail and offered to come back to the office to discuss it. Obviously, she didn't feel safe talking about it at home, possibly getting overheard by Craig. But she could be at the office in fifteen minutes.

Franks and Simonton went to the interview room and drank their coffee while they waited for Felicia to arrive. They were too keyed up to start another fifteen-minute project and knew it wouldn't be productive anyway.

CHAPTER 26

FELICIA JERNIGAN ARRIVED

Felicia Jernigan arrived on time and was ushered immediately to the interview room where Detectives Franks and Simonton awaited her. Smitty's ostrich skin boots were resting casually on the table, and he took them down when she entered. She sat at the interview table across from the detectives. There was no recording this time, but both men had pen and paper at the ready, for notes.

"Thanks for coming down," said Smitty. "Can we get you anything? A drink—coffee, water—we even have diet Coke." He had learned over the years that you can't really interview most females without keeping diet coke handy.

"Thanks, I'm ok," she answered as she sat at the small conference table in the interview room. She was still a little sensitive, from the prior day's revelations. She laid several eight-and-a-half-by-eleven pages of computer paper on the table.

"I was able to get into Craig's e-mail and printed the one I told you about. This is the one that caught my eye. I left it on his computer and was careful not to change it at all. I don't think he is computer-savvy enough to be able to tell that I've opened his e-mail. At least I hope not."

With that, she dealt copies of the e-mail to Smitty and Simonton and kept one copy for herself.

The first page only said,

≈ *Congratulations* ≈

The second page of the e-mail continued:

This certifies that **Craig Jernigan** has just successfully completed:

Homeschooling 1.01,
A Tutorial for the Instructor

Home Schooling 1:01 is a tuition-free one-day course, offered only to the most qualified and advanced students. You were chosen because of your long history and experience in the field of home schooling.

Home Schooling 2:01, a more advanced one-day course, will be offered to students who continue to demonstrate a need for instruction. The Home Schooling Institute will monitor your progress, and, if it becomes obvious that you need the additional class time, you will again be transported to the Learning Center for this additional one-day tuition-free course. Again, of course, no registration will be required. The first eight hours of HS 2:01 will consist of a review of HS 1:01, with even more extensive laboratory demonstrations. The remainder of the course will be tailored to the student's specific needs.

Please note that the Home Schooling Institute will not divulge this information to any person or agency. It is for the student to use as he sees fit, for guidance in future relationship issues as they present themselves.

Again, congratulations on your success, from the
The Institute for Home Schooling!

Keep in mind that no additional training past HS 2:01 is planned, *as we do not anticipate that any student will survive HS 2:01!*

"Oh my god!" Smitty exclaimed when he read the e-mail. "Does this mean what I think it means? They plan to kill him if he doesn't straighten up."

"That's how I interpreted it," Felicia joined. "Sometimes he uses the term *home schooling* when he's really angry or drunker than usual."

"Yeah! We're familiar with that use of the term," Franks said. "Were you able to go through his e-mails to see if there are others like this?"

"Yes, except the computer self-purges periodically when it decides you have too many spam messages saved up," Felicia said. "I was able to go back at least six weeks, so I think this must be the only one. That is, unless he has deleted some others."

"Our computer guys can track down deleted e-mails if we need for them to," Franks said. "We'll cross that bridge when we get to it. Right now, let's see who else has this kind of message on his laptop." He and Simonton arose to leave.

Smitty said, "Thanks for your help. I guess that's all for now. You can leave anytime you like. We'll be in touch."

As Felicia left, Franks quietly whispered to Smitty, "Well, this is two out of four so far. I'll betcha a dime that every one of them has gotten the same e-mail. But for now, we've gotta see if IT can figure out where these are coming from."

CHAPTER 27

ANDY TRAYLOR WAS RIGHTFULLY . . .

Andy Traylor was rightfully high on his success in cracking both the passwords and the origin of the e-mails sent to Craig Jernigan and Jack Thompson by the Home Schooling Institute. He came into the detective work room with a smile on his face, saying, "Got it!"

"Come on in, let's see what you got," Borden responded. "I hope to hell you got something because we sure don't got nothing, and I mean nothing, nada, nil, zip, zero," he said as he waved his hand across his desk to indicate a clean surface.

"First off, I opened the entire e-mail files not only the active files but the deleted files as well. And these two e-mails were definitely isolated messages. There weren't any more like them on either hard drive. But I found out where they came from and the date and time they were sent. They were both sent from a rental computer at a Kinko's in North Dallas. But that doesn't help identify the sender. To do that you'll have to go through Kinko's charge files for the two days they were sent, and see if a sender is mutual for those date and time slots. And you better hope they weren't cash transactions."

"Okay, that puts us a definite step ahead of where we were before," Borden said. "Let's get the computer drives from the other two victims and see if they got the messages too. If they aren't willing, we can get subpoenas for them. Getting their computer data will help narrow the search down."

"Let's split up like we did before," Franks volunteered. "Me and Smitty can take Ben Ferrell, if you two can do Farley Jacobs. Can we get started this afternoon?"

Everyone seemed anxious to get to the next phase of the investigation and felt they were on the verge of learning Gabby's identity.

Franks dialed Ben Ferrell's number, and it was picked up on the second ring. "Hello, Ferrell here."

"Hey, Ben. Steve Franks here. We got some more questions that came up, we need to come out and visit for a few minutes. Is this just as good a time as any?"

"Sure, Steve. Seems like I've told you all I know, but what the heck. Come on out. I'm not exactly tied up with anything important recently. I'll put a pot of coffee on. Andrea's visiting her sister, if you need to talk with her too. I'll see you in a few minutes."

Smitty drove, and Steve took shotgun. It was quicker for him to get a vehicle from the motor pool than to wait for the Agency to get one. It was only a twenty-minute drive to the Ferrells's home. En route, they had time to plan the interview strategy. Steve seemed to have a better rapport with Ferrell, so he would take the lead. The detectives both had a sense of adventure as well as a sense of urgency. They both had a feeling that this could be a productive mission.

Andrea and Ben Ferrell had a one-story home in Denton, where you could get a fair-sized lot without wasting the family fortune. The home had adequate but not extravagant landscaping, but the day-to-day mowing and trimming was somewhat behind. Probably because Ben did his own lawn work and had not been up to the task lately. Looks like he would have to hire it done if he wasn't able to get back to it fairly soon.

They parked on the street and walked up the driveway past Ben's blue Mazda 3, which was beginning to bear the signs of three weeks of idleness. The yellow pollen so common in north Texas that time of the year had coated much of the car's blue paint and given it a green hue. Driving a car seems to blow the pollen off the paint, and idleness allows it to accumulate. But once through the car wash, when Ben was able to drive again, and it would become its old shiny self.

Ben could be seen in his dining room/office through the front window. He got up to let them in and opened the door before they rang the doorbell. "Hey, come on in out of the sun."

Franks and Simonton both came in and shook Ben's hand. "How are you getting along, Ben?" asked Franks.

"I've seen better times," Ferrell answered. "But I really think I can see some progress, especially in the past week to ten days. I'm not hurting nearly as much as I was, and I'm feeling like I should be able to get back to work pretty soon. Come on in and have a seat."

Franks had decided to hit the topic head-on. He didn't think Ferrell had heard about the recent realization that all four victims were abusive husbands and wouldn't have time to mount a defense.

"There are a few things we need to ask that have come up. Do you recall an emergency room visit your wife took about a year ago, for some kind of laceration?"

Ferrell was stunned. This was not what he expected. "Yeah, I guess . . . barely. What does that have to do with this anyway?"

"We understand she had a laceration that needed stitches. We need to know how she got that laceration. We need you to be honest with us."

"I don't like your tone of voice. Am I on trial here? I thought I was the victim. I think she fell off her bike, or something like that," Ferrell was obviously nervous.

"We really just wanted to give you a chance to come clean. We know that isn't true. We know that the laceration was from your fist. This isn't a guess. We know it for a fact. Now, can you help us out?" Franks laid it out.

Ferrell hesitated. Perspiration was beginning to appear on his forehead. "I still don't see what this has to do with my problems. I thought ya'll were supposed to be working on finding out who took me out, not some year-old fuss I had with my wife."

Franks decided to come clean and to quit asking questions like this as he had asked Ferrell to do. "Here's where we are, Ben. We know, for a fact, that the wives of all four of you *victims* have been in emergency rooms in the past year or year and a half, with injuries that they got from their husbands. So what does that make you? It makes you a fuckin' wife beater. These facts are established. And these facts will be dealt with in proper time.

"But that's not what we're working on right now. Why it's important, and what we're working on, is that we have reason to believe that a self-appointed vigilante has decided to get even or to teach you guys a lesson. We think Gabby is somebody who's mad at you all and has done this in revenge. Now, does any of this ring a bell?"

Ferrell sat there for a minute, dumbfounded. Like most abusive spouses, he didn't really think of himself as a wife beater. Really, his situation was different. It really was his wife's fault, and he only responded like any normal man would. But confronted by another policeman like this, it sounded different. "Are you sure about this Gabby guy, trying to get even with random husbands?"

"We're absolutely sure," Franks said. "Now, the main question we want to know is, have you had any communications, letters, e-mails, or anything else, that seemed to be coming from someone about your abduction and beating? Anything that used the words *home schooling* or H*ome Schooling Institute*? Something that congratulated you for finishing a course in home schooling?"

Ferrell was still reluctant to discuss his situation openly. But he was beginning to think that he had no choice. After another period of hesitation, he said, "Yes, I got an e-mail like that. I didn't pay any attention to it."

"Sure you didn't! Well, I'll need to take your hard drive in for our IT guys to work on. We need to try to figure out where the e-mails are coming from."

"You mean somebody else has got e-mails like mine?" Ferrell asked, incredulously. "Oh! Lord!"

"Yeah, at least two other victims have received identical e-mails like this. We would prefer to just take the laptop rather than the hard drive. Would that be okay?" Smitty asked.

"Sure, I guess I can use my wife's laptop for a few days. Mine is over here." Ferrell went to retrieve his own laptop. Smitty gave him a receipt for it.

"What does this mean for me?" Ferrell asked. He seemed to have accepted that he had no other way out of this than just to be as honest as possible. He knew it would be harder on him, the more he lied. He would have time to put a better spin on it later on. "Are you able to keep this quiet, or am I gonna be pulled through the ringer about this?"

"Ben, you know as well as I do that some small-town cops turn a deaf ear to family squabbles. But Texas law doesn't like wife beaters," Franks answered. His disgust prevented him from being tactful. "This is sure not my priority at the moment, but I have no way that I can protect you from this. Charges will be filed against you for this, and soon. But right now we're working on finding Gabby before one of you fuckers gets his ass killed."

"How much time can I have? Am I going to be arrested?" Ferrell nervously asked.

"You know the drill. What happens from now is that I file a report tomorrow morning, real early, and in the next forty-eight hours a warrant will be issued for your arrest. That's about as far as I can go with it for now."

"By the way," Smitty mentioned. "We need your passwords."

Smitty wrote down the passwords then took Ferrell's laptop, and the detectives left. They were anxious to get the computer to Traylor to see if the e-mail came from the same site as the others. If they could determine that Gabby sent e-mails to all four victims from the same computer at Kinko's, it would be much easier to break this down when they visited the Kinko's.

CHAPTER 28

KINKO~S, LIBRARIES, AND . . .

Kinko's, libraries, and other computer sources open to the public are great if you want to sneak around and send anonymous e-mails that could get you in trouble if your victims know your identity. But that is only if you are pretty sharp on the computer. You can check in, pay with cash, send your threatening or libelous e-mails, bounce around from one store to the other, and you're essentially undetectable unless the store manager has the memory of an elephant. However, if you are only moderately computer literate, like most of us are, you are likely to slip up and get caught by nerds who know a lot more than you do.

Agents Tom Borden and Gary Schulman met Farley Jacobs at his home the same afternoon. Schulman took the lead in the questioning and had decided to take a more circuitous route than Franks had taken with Ferrell. It took a little longer, but he finally got Jacobs to admit that he had hit his wife (maybe once or twice, but you know, not real hard, and 'sometimes ya just get so fed up ya gotta do something') and that he had received the same e-mail as the others. He turned over his laptop with only a minor fuss. He too thought there was no way to deny his difficulties with his marriage and his wife, and at least this way he would have some time to think it over and to perfect his story.

The men all arrived back at the sheriff's department about the same time and went in to give Andy the additional computers.

"Hey, Andy, we got some more work for you," Smitty said. He handed the two computers to Andy.

"Gee, thanks a lot! Nice to know you're thinking of me," Traylor said. While they waited, the agents were able to discuss the interviews with Jacobs and Ferrell.

Schulman asked, "Now the men know at least that their wives have talked about their husbands with us. What do you think are the chances they're gonna get the hell slapped out of them tonight?"

Borden had thought that out. "I think between slim and none. First, they know that we know, and if their wives come in with black eyes, they know they won't go twelve hours without being hauled in. And remember, the wives don't have to file charges. The police can do it even without their permission.

Second, did you read those e-mails? That was basically a death threat, and nobody knows who Gabby is yet. I bet they're scared shitless. No, I think they'll all be on their best behavior today."

Less than an hour later, Traylor came back to the detectives' office, again with a bright smile of accomplishment on his face. Sure was nice to be able to do something nobody else in the office could do. "Nothin' to it!" he said, his exuberance contagious to the detectives and agents. "All four came from the same computer at the same Kinko's. With the electronic time and date stamps, all you gotta do is pull the sign-ins at Kinko's and find out who was there all four times. Now, what else can I do for you, gentlemen?" His ego was smeared all over his face.

"Man, I owe you a big one," Smitty said as the four took the information into the interview room, sat down, and planned the next phase.

"Okay, guys, let's get this creep!" Borden exclaimed. "Anything we need to do before we go out to Kinko's and go through the credit cards?"

The others were all in agreement that a trip to Kinko's was next on their agenda. Since Franks and Simonton's jurisdiction was limited to Denton County, Borden and Schulman took this assignment and piled into an agency car for the thirty-minute trip to North Dallas.

CHAPTER 29

KINKO'S COMPUTER GEEK

Kinko's computer geek was more than willing to help when he realized he had two FBI agents looking for information. He wanted to get into the mix and tried to find out what they were looking for. Most exciting thing he had encountered in his six months at the job.

"I'm Agent Borden, and this is Agent Schulman, FBI," Borden introduced themselves.

"I'm Jerry Finnigan," the computer guy countered. "How can I help you?"

"We've got four e-mails that were sent from your shop on four different days. We need to match those dates and times with your sign-in log and see who was here all four days. What's the best way to do that?" Borden asked. He had isolated the times and dates from the body of the e-mails and arranged it in table form on a single sheet of paper.

Finnigan was nervous and figured he better let the boss in on the request or risk getting canned. So he left for five minutes and made a call from a private room. He explained what the agents had requested and, to his surprise, was given the go-ahead to cooperate fully.

It wasn't so difficult. Finnigan was able, in a matter of minutes, to pull up the names, times, and credit card numbers of every person who had rented computer time those four days. He even had it categorized according to which computer each person rented. This was great, Borden thought. Thanks again to modern technology.

"Come on, you guys, I've cooperated. Tell me what you're looking for. Terrorists?" Finnigan asked. He had a pitiful look on his face, and Borden decided to toss him a bone.

"We're looking for Gabby," he said. "Know who Gabby is?"

"I've heard the name. Isn't he the guy who's kidnapping people and beating the shit out of them?" Finnigan asked. "I don't know much, but I'm not brain dead. I live over on the west side, and it's a small town type of place. I'd have to be in a coma to never hear about Gabby. You think he may have come in here? Wow . . ."

"Ya never know," Borden said. He always enjoyed the look of ecstasy on civilians' faces when they get anywhere near an FBI investigation, especially when they think they are actually contributing to it. He'll have something to tell his grandkids someday, Borden thought, how he helped the dumb FBI catch Gabby. Borden and Schulman left, driving back in Friday afternoon traffic toward Lewisville.

Sometimes it took more than an hour to navigate the twenty miles north on I-45, with Friday afternoon traffic. Today they made it in forty-five minutes, passing one wreck and two traffic stops. But they had learned to take it in stride. You make the same money for an hour sitting in slow traffic, sipping a coke, as you make for an hour sweating over chasing bad guys. So why not enjoy the cool air?

They arrived back at the Denton County Sheriff's Office at 2:45 p.m., leaving enough time to digest the organized report of a real computer geek. They called Smitty and Franks in to let them know they had the critical information. They had four sheets of reports, one for each day in question. One also for each of the investigators. They sat around the interview table and compared notes.

There were about two hundred customers on each of the four days. That's eight hundred entries to go through. The names came out alphabetized, so they couldn't just go to the correct time. It was painstaking to go over each entry, to check the time. They highlighted each entry that occurred within an hour either way, of the time of each e-mail, to cut down on the number of possibilities. Then Borden took the lead and read each name, one at a time, allowing each of the others to go through the entire sheet looking for duplicates.

"Man, I wonder if Mr. Computer Man couldn't have arranged this by time of entry! This is gonna take awhile," Schulman complained.

"Well, I didn't think to ask him. Just bear with us. We'll get it. This is no more boring than an all-night stakeout. We've all done that jillions of times," Schulman responded.

After two hours of coordinated searching, they found the information they were looking for. They found three names which appeared more than one time. One was at Kinko's on two of the dates and time frames in question, and one was on three. The last on their list was at the shop on all four dates. Two out of four would seem odd. Three even more so. But for one individual to be channel surfing at Kinko's on the same days and times as the "Congratulations!" e-mails seemed to be too much to be coincidence.

The sign-in sheet wasn't too helpful. The signature was so illegible it would take a psychic to interpret it. But the name on the credit card slip was unmistakable. Ellie Conlin, with identical signatures to match on all four slips.

"Oh my god!" said Detective Franks. "Is Dr. Conlin mixed up in all this?"

"Maybe she bankrolled the abductions or arranged them in some way," said Agent Schulman. "But she just doesn't seem the violent type. You know, these abductions weren't planned or done by a wuss. Do you really think she could be involved?"

Smitty responded cynically, "Well, if she wasn't, it's an absolutely amazing coincidence, and you know how I feel about coincidences."

"She also has a lot to lose if we prove she was involved in a conspiracy to kidnap or the actual abductions themselves," said Borden. "She can lose her medical license, to say nothing of going to prison herself."

"So where do we go from here?" asked Smitty.

"First thing we do is bring her in for questioning," Borden said. "Now is as good a time as any. Gary, you ready to go?"

"Man, am I ready!" Schulman answered. "This time of day, she should be home from work. Let's go."

"Let's call Smitty. He can work on a search warrant so we can have it available if we need it. You might even be able to execute a search of her home while she's here in questioning," Borden said.

"No problem," Simonton agreed. "I got a judge owes me a favor."

CHAPTER 30

WHILE SMITTY VISITED JUDGE

While Smitty visited Judge Harry Levine to try to get a search warrant, Borden and Schulman went to Ellie Conlin's house unannounced to bring her to the station for questioning. They were unusually quiet on the short drive out. There didn't seem to be anything to say. Finally, about ten minutes from destination, Schulman had to break the silence.

"This feels really weird."

"What do you mean, Gary?" Borden responded.

"I can't put my finger on it, but I've been thinking, what if little old Dr. Conlin did arrange these hits. Are we gonna have to lock her up? It just feels weird," Schulman didn't have the right words. Weird was the best he could come up with.

"We'll have to treat her like any other suspected perp," Borden said as he rounded the corner and pulled up in front of her house. The lights were on, as expected. It was only 9:30 p.m. We have to do this right—Miranda rights and all. We have enough information to arrest her if she doesn't cooperate.

Borden rang the doorbell tentatively. He almost hoped she wasn't home. He dreaded this encounter more than any he had in a long time. After just over a minute, when he was about to ring the bell again, a figure wearing a bathrobe and slippers appeared at the door. She asked through the intercom, "Who is it?"

Borden answered, "Dr. Conlin, it's Agent Borden and Agent Schulman. We need to ask you some questions."

There was a seemingly long delay. The robed figure turned on the porch light and looked through her peephole to confirm the agents' identities. Finally satisfied, she slowly turned a key in the door and opened it. "What can I do for you, officers?"

"We've made some progress in the investigation. Can we come in? Some questions have come up that we need your help with," Borden said. Schulman kept quiet during this time.

Dr. Conlin had almost a smile of relief on her face. "Sure, come on in," she said. "I've been expecting you."

They sat in the living room, Borden and Schulman on a long love seat and Dr. Conlin in a wingback mauve Queen Anne chair. The chair was made for her small body and prim and proper posture. A narrow dark wood coffee table with beveled glass sections sat between them. There were several current women's magazines, all neatly arranged, on the table.

"Well, what do you need?" she asked. "Do I need a lawyer?"

"You sound like you almost know what we need. Have you missed any credit cards lately? Any break-ins, any lost purses at the hospital? Any charges you couldn't reconcile?" Borden asked.

Dr. Conlin had thought through this scenario many times in the past few weeks. She knew that the likelihood of getting caught in her games was very high, and after considering all her options, she had decided to come clean. Once the FBI agents got on the right trail, she knew that it would be impossible to lie her way out of it.

"Come on, fellas," she said. "We all know why you're here. Can't you just cut to the chase and quit beating around the bush. No, I haven't lost any credit cards, and nobody has broken into my house or stolen my purse at work. Now, where is this leading?"

"Okay, fine with me," Borden said. With a nod, Schulman chimed in his agreement. Borden nodded back to him, their unspoken signal that he was turning a bit of the questioning over to his partner.

"We have found several credit charges for computer time at Kinko's, which have what we think is your original signature. Do you personally use Kinko's for their Wi-Fi or use their computers?"

"Yes, I occasionally stop by there. Why?" she answered.

"Well, what we've discovered is that e-mails were received on different days by the four abduction victims. We have found that the four e-mails were all sent from rental computers at a Kinko's in North Dallas. Then, lo and behold, we discovered that you did business on a computer at that very Kinko's on each of the four days that the e-mails were sent. Can you respond to that?

"How can I respond? Amazing coincidence, wouldn't you say?" Ellie answered. She knew she was cooked.

"Dr. Conlin," Schulman started over. "Is it possible that you loaned a credit card to someone who might have used it on those days at Kinko's?"

"I never lend my credit card to anyone except my daughter, and it's been years since she needed it, so in answer to your question, no I'm afraid I didn't lend a credit card to anyone."

Schulman wanted so badly for Dr. Conlin to give him an answer that would explain the "coincidence" of the e-mails and Kinko's. But he couldn't think of any more indirect, beating-around-the-bush questions. He studied a scratch on the toe of his left shoe for a long moment before finally raising his head.

"Ahem . . . Dr. Conlin, did you send those four e-mails?"

She waited, seeming to weigh her options. She decided to go through with her earlier decision. "Yes, I sent the e-mails."

After another long pause, Schulman finally said, "I think you need to go to the station with us. Right now, I need to advise you that anything you say can and will be used against you in a court of law. You have a right to remain silent. You have a right to an attorney. If you cannot afford an attorney, one will be appointed for you. Do you understand these rights?"

"Yes, I understand the Miranda," she answered. "Am I under arrest?"

"Not at this time. Do you mind coming with us?"

"Thanks for giving me a choice. No, I don't mind. I've been expecting this," she said in a quiet, almost defeated voice. Can I take a minute to put on some real clothes?"

"Of course. We'll wait in here. Take your time," Borden said. Conlin left the room.

"Damn, man! This isn't what I expected. She almost admitted she was involved in whoever kidnapped these guys and tortured them," Schulman said.

"I haven't figured this out yet. Hopefully, she'll fill us in on the details. We need to get everything we can out of her before she changes her mind."

"I haven't got the foggiest notion of what to expect out of her. She just doesn't seem like that kind of person," Schulman said. "Man, this is unreal.

No matter what she ends up telling us, she has to be implicated in a conspiracy with somebody to kidnap and torture these victims. Wow! I bet she paid the bills!"

"I think she's just a mother bear who'll do what it takes to protect her kid," Borden answered as the doctor returned, dressed in jeans, sneakers and a sweatshirt.

"I'm ready, let's go," she said.

CHAPTER 31

IT WAS ALMOST MIDNIGHT

It was almost midnight when Schulman pulled the black FBI sedan into the sheriff's department parking lot with Dr. Ellie Conlin. She was not arrested, so she didn't have to wear handcuffs. In fact, both Borden and Schulman spent a major part of the trip in wondering what kind of charge they could find for her. Deep inside, they both still hoped that she would be able to offer an explanation that would be acceptable. But for the life of them, neither could think of a suitable explanation.

They went in and ushered her into an interview room. They offered her the obligatory coffee or diet Coke and brought her the drink and a napkin. They both got themselves coffee, seeming to want to postpone the inevitable questions that they would have to ask.

Finally, Schulman broke the silence. "Dr. Conlin, we have to let you know, this is all being recorded. But what say, let's give you some free rein. Can you just make it easier for all of us and just explain all this to us? From where we're sitting, you have a lot of explaining to do. Like, what in the world prompted you to send those cryptic and threatening e-mails to those men? And what did you have to do with the kidnap and torture of your son-in-law and three other sons of bitches who like to treat their wives like punching bags?"

Ellie had gone over this scenario in her mind and had prepared her responses. She had decided long ago that she would simply be honest and take whatever came. "You know, in a suburban medical practice, especially family practice, you see a lot. And I've seen a lot of battered wives in my twenty years of practice. But they don't tell you they're battered wives. They just come in with black eyes and odd stories about lacerations that don't make sense. And you know, there's not a damn thing you can do about it. Even when they admit what's happening, you can't get them to leave or get away from the situation. They 'love' the bastard. The most I've been able to do is to take care of them when I can, or when the Women's Shelter refers them to me, and make an occasional donation to the Shelter.

"But when I realized my daughter was being hurt, I couldn't stand it any longer. I had to do something about it. I decided I had to teach my, pardon the disgust, son-in-law a lesson he wouldn't forget. Unfortunately, I'm not a six-foot two-hundred pound brute, or it would be an easy solution. I'm smaller and weaker than most any man."

"So you hired some thugs to do this?" Schulman asked.

After hesitating for a long moment, Conlin answered, "No, I didn't hire any thugs. I am the only one involved."

"My god!" Borden exclaimed. "I can't believe this! How did you do it?" It was obvious that partly he was asking how a small middle-aged woman could overpower these strong young men with no help.

"I didn't want anybody to get killed, but I didn't mind them shedding some blood. So I went to an army surplus store and bought myself a stun baton. Then I took my old VW bus that I've had in storage for over twenty-five years, rigged it up with a winch and ropes so I could transport him far enough out so nobody could hear him cry and beg."

She continued to talk. Borden and Schulman didn't have to ask any questions. There was none of the back-and-forth banter that usually went with an interrogation.

"Finally, I rented myself an old abandoned house way out in the woods and rigged another winch there so I could encourage him to follow me into the 'training facility.'

"I wanted him to hurt, and I wanted him to go through something that would take time to heal. I thought about maybe a baseball bat, but I'd probably kill somebody with that. So I bought a T-ball bat. Big enough and hard enough to hurt real bad but probably not likely to kill anybody.

"The rest is history."

The agents sat stunned. They never thought that this might not be a conspiracy at all. For a conspiracy, you have to have somebody to conspire with. You can't conspire all by yourself. They never imagined that this small, petite, subdued physician was capable of so macabre a plan and able to carry it out with no assistance.

Schulman asked, "You're trying to tell us you did all this by yourself? I don't believe it! Who are you protecting? Somebody must have helped you!"

"I'm afraid I have to take all the blame or all the glory, whichever your bent," Conlin answered.

"Where's the VW?" asked Borden.

"It's in the barn at the 'learning center,'" she responded. "There's a dry barn that you can't see from the road."

"And I suppose, the T-ball bats and the stun batons are all there?" Borden said.

"Yes, that isn't exactly something that fits the decor of a medical office very well," Conlin tried to add some levity. She had decided to come clean, so she might as well enjoy it. However, she tried not to be smug.

"You know the stuff you did is as illegal as shit, don't you?" asked Schulman. "How did you think you'd get away with it? You haven't even tried to lie to us. At least I guess you haven't, although I'll admit, your story is so unbelievable, it might be a lie! But I have to say, if you're lying, you're a pretty good liar!"

"Check it out," Conlin said. "Every word I've said is true. Nobody helped me. In fact, nobody but you even suspects me."

"That's right . . . 'Gabby' never spoke to his . . . I mean her . . . victims, did she?" Borden recalled. "Damnation! I never expected this!"

"Do you realize you'll probably go to prison and lose your license to practice medicine?" Schulman asked. "Is it worth all that, just to get even?"

"Well, we'll see about that," Ellie countered. "Maybe I will, maybe I won't. But yes, it's worth all that, definitely. If I go to prison, I'll remember every day that if it helps keep my daughter from a life of abuse, or even worse, becoming just another statistic, another DOA at the ER, it's worth every minute I spend locked up. And what's my medical practice worth to me if I lose my daughter? I've thought this out and consciously decided to do it and to come clean about it when you guys catch me!"

"My god!" Borden exclaimed. "But what about the other three? How did you even know about them?"

With an almost mischievous twinkle in her eye, Dr. Conlin said, "Well, you know, doctors and nurses talk. Once my ER friends found out about my daughter, everybody and their dog tried to console me by telling me about another well-heeled couple in the same situation. If you ever want to find out about what's going on in the bedrooms and kitchens across town, your friends in the hospital are a good resource. But I really don't remember specifically who told me. It's just hospital gossip. Incidentally, if anybody ever asks, it is definitely not comforting to hear about other families with the same problems yours has."

"Dr. Conlin, you know we're gonna have to arrest you, don't you?" Agent Borden asked. By this time, Detective Simonton had arrived, having been called earlier by Schulman. The arrest would be handled by Simonton and the local guys.

"Sure, I know that. And thanks for the no-handcuff ride in," Ellie seemed almost relieved, like it didn't feel as bad as she had thought it would. Once the detectives arrived and the decision had been made to arrest and book her, she again received the standard Miranda advice from Simonton.

And she did come dressed for the occasion. She would fare better with the others in lockup in her jeans and sweater than she would in her usual out-of-the-house attire of professional clothes or scrubs, which she wore most of the time. Scrubs were just easier than regular clothes, especially since someone had finally designed some with a semblance of style and femininity. But she felt she was too old to wear the scrubs with Hello! Kitty on the front, like so many hospital nurses did. Just colored scrubs with a little ribbon or lace here and there. And nobody expected you to iron your scrubs either, so they were much lower maintenance than real clothes. Tonight, though, she just wanted to blend in, incognito, just one of the lost souls in lockup, not a physician who looked like she was on her way to the office and the rest of her life. Now, though, she found that her clothes didn't matter; she would wear the orange jumpsuit of the county for a while.

She was fingerprinted and booked for kidnapping and assault and battery. They left off the more serious charge of attempted murder because it was obvious that she hadn't planned on anybody dying. The detectives still didn't completely believe her although they couldn't come up with a legitimate reason not to.

CHAPTER 32

THE LADIES IN LOCKUP

The ladies in lockup barely looked up when Ellie was first ushered in. But after a minute or two, the twenty or so ladies already there looked up at her in what seemed a concerted sweep of eyes, like a ballet of lost, disheveled faces, and forgotten souls as she came into the large holding room. Some sat on the floor, some on the few benches lining the walls, and some standing but none looking happy or content. There were a couple of hookers in their usual sensual garb, looking anything but attractive. Several were obviously still on the downhill side of a drug/alcohol binge. They were any age—teens to women in their late middle age.

They all had their own particular demons. One in particular caught Ellie's attention. A woman who looked to be in her late forties (or fifties, or thirties, who could tell), sitting in a corner, apathetic expression, resigned to whatever fate held for her. Her face bore the scars of years of abuse, and the bridge of her nose was sunken, having been broken dozens of times. *How many women had suffered like this*, Ellie thought.

She wasn't particularly scared. She thought female inmates were somewhat less likely to get violent than their male counterparts. At least for her first encounter, she was right. Nobody spoke to her at first, but they could tell that she was different, and one teenager scooted over on her bench to give her a place to sit down. She graciously accepted.

She spent most of the night there. One by one, the other women were called out and ushered to a cell, which at least had a cot. Some had already been fingerprinted and booked; others went through the process now. Finally, about 4:00 a.m., her name was called.

When she got to her cell, she immediately took advantage of the cot and lay down. During her years of being on call, she had learned to go to sleep quickly. A physician quickly learns that if you don't figure this out, you'll lose precious minutes of rest. She was asleep within minutes. She didn't stay awake worrying about what lay ahead. She had thought this through and made decisions on how she would handle the questions which she knew must be coming. And she was at peace with her decisions.

After what seemed only a couple of hours of sleep, she was awakened and brought to an interrogation room. She was left there for almost an hour. She thought, this must be how they keep you on edge, and off guard, not knowing who was coming in and what they were going to say. It worked, she thought. For the first time, she wondered what she had gotten herself into. Her only previous encounter with the law was many years ago, as a teen, when she was brought in on suspicion of shoplifting. It was all proven to be a mistake, and the officers were polite to her, but she had at least been to the station and questioned. But this time would be different. This time it wasn't a mistake.

Finally, detective Simonton entered the room, carrying his coffee and an extra cup for Ellie. The FBI agents had turned the rest of the procedures back to the local boys, and he needed to get his own story of the events. "Dr. Conlin, how are you? Want some java?"

"I'm okay, but a little stressed and more than a little embarrassed," she answered. "This is very unfamiliar ground to me. And yeah, I could sure use the caffeine."

The detective sat down across the table from her and looked in her eyes for what seemed to be the longest moment. The room had only a steel table, bolted to the floor, and two metal chairs, also bolted down. The dark window, Ellie knew, was a one-way mirror. She wondered who, if anybody, was on the other side, monitoring the interview.

Simonton blew into his coffee cup and sipped it carefully like he wasn't sure just how hot it was and didn't want to burn his lips. Finally, he spoke.

"Dr. Conlin, what in the world have you gotten yourself into? I never in my wildest imagination expected to be looking at you in an orange monkey suit, questioning you about a felony."

"Well, you know, detective, sometimes a girl's gotta do what a girl's gotta do," she answered, almost smugly. "A mother can only put up with her children being hurt so much, then you better get out of the way!"

"I need to know all about it, your involvement, who helped you, how it all went down, everything."

"I'll tell you what you want to know," she calmly stated. "I've been through all this in my mind and am ready for what comes."

"You've done this, fully knowing you were going to get caught and going ahead anyway?" Simonton seemed stunned. He couldn't remember the last felony perp he had ever dealt with who, on first interview, had come clean. He didn't seem to know how to proceed.

The interview lasted until mid-afternoon, except for bathroom breaks and a half hour for a deli sandwich from the jailhouse cafeteria. They reviewed everything. Permission to search her home, her car, the "learning center," the barn, the VW minibus. No need to get a search warrant if the owner gives you permission.

The questions didn't have to involve the usual tricks to discover information and guilt. She was openly confessing everything that had happened. But Simonton seemed to need more and more information before he really believed what he was hearing. He asked where she had gotten the stun baton, the black disguise and mask, the ropes, the winches.

"Who installed the winch in the minibus?" he asked.

"I've been a single mother for a long time. I've learned over the years to do everything for myself. I don't need a man to help. The winch wasn't so hard really. All you need is a good drill and some bolts. At first I didn't expect to use it but once, so I didn't have to make it where it would last. Just bolted it in and wired it to the battery. Same for the one in the house too. They did the job. If it wasn't for the stun baton and the winches, I couldn't have got the job done by myself. And I sure wasn't going to ask for help. This way, it was easy."

"I guess it would have been hard to explain why you wanted somebody to install a winch inside a minibus," Simonton said.

"Oh, probably not," she answered. "Coulda' told them you wanted it for hauling deer. But this way, nobody else was involved. Just little old me."

After the interview, Conlin was led back to her cell. She was arraigned the following morning, and bail was set. She had called the attorney who worked for the Women's Shelter, asking for a reference for a defense attorney who might have some insight into her case and had gotten the name of Mandy Jensen. She called the office and was told that Jensen was in a hearing that would last several more hours, but a junior associate, Edie Davis, would come out and get started.

Jensen was a late Texas transplant. She grew up in California, and got her law degree from the University of Chicago, just about as far away from her home as she could get. She had written her senior law school research paper on the self-defense plea in spousal murder cases.

During her last year in law school she had volunteered at the Legal Aid Center, a pro bono organization for people who couldn't afford a lawyer's fee. For the first two years after graduation, she had worked for the Chicago area women's shelter, getting protective orders and divorces for abused women.

She had moved to Dallas seven years ago. For the first five years there, she had been an associate at Murray & Shepard, a criminal defense firm, before opening her own firm two years ago. Now she was an experienced attorney, and at age 36, she was considered to be Dallas' expert in the area of domestic violence.

Edie Davis was Jensen's only associate. She joined the Jensen firm directly out of law school, and was making a name in her own right. She was a hard worker, and smart. And she had the right attitude for working in the area of women's issues such as domestic abuse.

She was unmarried, but lived with her boyfriend, an architectural engineer designing small office buildings in the Dallas suburbs. She came to the jail promptly, to do the initial intake interview with Conley. She wore "lawyer casual," neat, dark woolen slacks, a pale green blouse, a dark blazer and medium heels. She carried the obligatory thin quilted briefcase for her notes and phone.

Davis came to the interview room where Ellie sat with her left wrist handcuffed to a steel ring in the center of the table. There was a stark contrast between the "lawyer casual" and the orange jump suit of the jail inmate.

"Dr. Conlin, I assume?" asked Davis, extending her right hand toward Conlin.

Ellie took her hand. Women respond to a firm handshake the same as men do, somehow disdaining a jello grip. Davis' grip was firm. Ellie felt better.

"Hello," Conlin responded. "Thanks for coming on such short notice. Please sit down."

Conlin and Davis spent two hours in the initial conference, catching up on necessary information as well as reviewing Conlin's reasoning behind what she had done and how she expected to get out of a prison sentence.

Davis was inexperienced, but Jensen had previously defended two separate women who had finally murdered their abusers. In one case, she had been able to convince the jury that the woman was indeed in fear of her life and get an innocent decision. In the other, she was unsuccessful, and the woman was in prison while she worked on the appeal. At least she wasn't new to the field of defending victims of abuse.

But this was different. There was no way she could use self-defense, and even if she was able to get the judge convinced that she feared for her daughter's life, it was hard to argue against this simply being a planned, premeditated attack.

And for her 2nd, 3rd, and 4th home schooling "students," there wasn't even a question of protecting her family. She was simply filling the roles of police, judge, and jury. And she had punished the abusers (alleged abusers, that is; no trial had been held) in a way that even the judge and jury would never be allowed to do. This was uncharted territory. It could go either way. It would require a lot of work, and the result would be unpredictable.

Davis took her time in the initial interview, knowing that Jensen would go over it all later in the day. After the initial interview, she left, to think it over and to begin the tedious job of legal research, to find the cases most nearly on point. But she doubted if she would find a lot. She thought that most likely there would not be many decisions anywhere near on point with this case.

CHAPTER 33

THIS TIME IT WAS ELLIE

This time it was Ellie calling her daughter to let her know she was in trouble. She had to do it now while Jensen worked on her bail. It wasn't something she could tell her over the phone, and it was the only thing she had not been able to plan. Exactly how could she tell her daughter that she had almost killed her husband. And now Craig would learn the identity of the Home Schooling Institute's headmaster. But it had to be done.

There was no answer at the home phone, so she called her daughter's cell. Felicia was in the grocery store checkout line. Her phone rang four times before she could get it out of her purse and pick up the call. She frequently missed calls because she couldn't find her phone in time in her oversized purse. Thank goodness for caller ID.

"Hello," she answered. She didn't recognize the telephone number from jai, but realized it was a number from Lewisville.

"Lisha, this is Mom," Conlin started but was cut off before she could get any farther.

"Hi, Mom! What's going on? Where are you calling from?"

"Lisha, I need your help. I'm in jail at the Denton County Sheriff's Department. I need you to help me get out."

"What? What happened? What did you say? You're in jail? What's going on? Are you hurt?" Her head was full of questions, but she was too stunned to ask and too confused to wait for answers.

"I can't talk to you over the phone, just please come over here," said Ellie. "I'll tell you when you get here. But I'm okay. I just need to get out of this place."

"Do I need to bring anything with me?" Felicia asked, still confused. Her mother, who never passed the speed limit, came to a complete stop before turning right on red, filed her taxes at least a week early every year, and went to church most Sundays, was in jail!

"Just your checkbook, I guess. I'll probably need some bail," Ellie said. "I've never been in this situation before. I don't really know how all this works."

Felicia apologized to the checkout girl, told her there was an emergency, and left her groceries in the cart. She came immediately and arrived a half hour later. She was shocked by the call and had no idea what it might mean. She tried to imagine what her mother might have done or how she might have gotten herself in such a fix. She imagined such things as drugs, maybe she was growing marijuana, she had heard of crazy things coming from people you never imagined it from. But her mother! She was about as straight-laced as anybody she knew. She simply couldn't imagine.

Felicia had never felt quite as restrained by speeding laws as her mother and hit 85 on I-45 on the way to Lewisville. Luckily, she didn't see any patrol cars, and traffic was light. She parked in a no-parking zone and rushed into the Denton County Jail. She told the intake officer that she wanted to see Dr. Ellie Conlin, her mother. She signed the visitors' register and sat down to wait while her mother was brought out to the visiting/interview room. She felt like she was going crazy, wondering what this was all about.

She was finally led into a visiting area and sat waiting while her mother was brought in. The room was about twenty-by-forty feet with two rows of three tables each. It was large enough that you could talk privately without everybody hearing your conversation unless you get carried away. At that time, there were three other families visiting their relatives. The picture of her mother, wearing jailhouse orange, startled her and she began to cry quietly.

Ellie came over and hugged her daughter and began to cry as well.

"Mom, what happened? What's this all about?" Felicia asked. Her mother had not given her any information at all, simply told her to come to the jail.

"Oh, Lisha, I've done something you may hate me for." She began to cry more openly and was unable to speak for another two or three minutes. Felicia was getting more scared all the time. She couldn't imagine what had happened. She had tried to guess what might have happened. Maybe a DUI accident, but her mother never drank to the point of drunk and refused to drive if she had even one beer. She just couldn't imagine what might have happened.

She looked into her mother's eyes and, for the first time, saw the terror that Ellie was finally feeling. "Mom, what have you done?"

"I was scared you would get really hurt. I couldn't stand to see you being beaten. I had to do something," Ellie cried.

Felicia was confused. What was she talking about? "Mom, tell me! What did you do?"

"Lisha, I am Gabby. It was me that beat Craig up. I'm so sorry! But I just couldn't stand by and see you brought to the ER dead someday. It was me!"

Felicia, hearing this out of the cold, was stunned. At first, she couldn't believe or even understand what she was hearing. "No, no, I don't understand. What do you mean? You did what? You couldn't have! How?"

"Yes, it was me!" Ellie tried to pull Felicia closer to her, but at the same time, her daughter pulled away from her and turned her back to her mother.

Felicia was still in shock, not knowing what to say, not knowing what to think. Maybe this was a dream. This couldn't be happening. With both hands in fists, and pressing against the sides of her head, she screamed, "What have you done?"

An officer came to their table and said politely, "Ma'am, you'll have to be quiet, or you'll have to leave." This seemed to pull Felicia back into reality, and she sat at the table and leaned over and buried her face in her crossed arms.

She took a full five minutes to regain her composure. Finally, she looked up at her mother, who had sat down on the opposite side of the table, with her hands loosely holding Felicia's elbows. She felt she had to touch her. How she handled this may make or break her relationship with her daughter forever. There was no right thing to say.

"Lisha, you have to understand, I couldn't let that happen to you anymore, I just . . ."

"Are you telling me that you are the person who kidnapped Craig? Are you the one who hauled him somewhere and beat him, almost killed him?" Felicia seemed in a daze, like she could not assimilate this horrible information. Tears continued to pour down her face.

"Yes, I'm afraid so, but it was for you. You gotta understand."

"For me?! For me?! You didn't ask what I thought about it, did you? What about me? Why didn't I have any say in this?"

"It wasn't something we were even able to talk about, once you decided to stay with him," Ellie said. She was unable to explain in a way that her distraught daughter could understand and accept.

"I've gotta go! I've gotta go! I don't know what to do! My own mother!" Felicia got up abruptly and ran to the exit, pounding on the glass door until an officer opened it and let her out. She ran to her car and rapidly pulled out, almost hitting a patrol car that was turning into the parking lot.

On the freeway, she slowly began to cool off and think a little more rationally about what she had just been told. At first she was heading toward home but then realized that she couldn't face Craig right now. Not until she had thought this through. Instead, after driving randomly, with no destination, for a half hour, she pulled into a favorite retreat, a neighborhood bookstore, where there was a coffee shop in the store and nobody would bother you for a while. She got a large latte and a magazine and sat down at a corner booth out of the traffic. She opened the magazine but didn't read it. It was time for some serious thinking.

CHAPTER 34

FELICIA DIDN'T COME HOME

Felicia didn't come home that night, or the next. Craig had only been back to work for two weeks, and so far, since the e-mail from Gabby, he had been the perfect husband. She left a message on the home telephone, knowing that the first thing Craig did when he got home was to throw his coat on a chair and push the button that let him review his voice mail for the day.

"Craig, I need some private time. I'll either be staying at Mom's house or a hotel. Please don't try to call me for a couple of days. I won't answer my phone. I am okay. I just need to be alone for a while."

Craig honored her wishes for two days then began calling her cell phone and Ellie Conlin's house. Felicia's cell phone went immediately to voice mail, and Ellie's phone did the same after five rings, the way she had set it up. On the third day, he called Ellie's office and was told that she would be out of the office for an unknown period of time and wasn't making any appointments at the present time. The receptionist had not been told what the emergency was, so she wasn't lying when she said that a family emergency had come up but she didn't know any details.

Knowing that Felicia was not abducted, Craig hadn't reported her as missing but instead had called Detective Simonton, just to see if he knew anything.

"Smitty," the detective answered.

"Hey, Detective Simonton, this is Craig Jernigan. I've got a problem. I wondered if you had heard from my wife. She hasn't been home in several days. She left me a message, so I know she's safe, but I don't know what's going on. Thought she might have contacted you."

"Well, I don't really know exactly where she is, but I know something about what's going on. Why don't you come on down to the office, we'll talk about it," Simonton would rather have this discussion in person rather than over a telephone.

"Why, what's going on?" Craig asked.

"Let's just say there are some new developments in the abduction case. We think we may have figured out Gabby. Come on down. I'm pretty free in about a half hour. See you then."

Craig didn't know what to think. Why would Felicia leave for a few days? What did that have to do with Gabby's identity? He knew that Simonton had reason to suspect something, that his abduction had something to do with his wife. He was worried too because if they had found Gabby, they would also know, and not just suspect, that his abduction and beating had nothing to do with his work but only with his wife. He knew there was no way he could avoid this confrontation, so he might as well get it over with.

He drove the fifteen-minute route to the sheriff's department. He arrived just after 6:00 p.m. He went directly to Simonton's office and knocked. Smitty immediately opened the door and ushered him to a seat. "Thanks for coming in. Still no word from your wife?"

"Not yet. Listen, I'm out of my mind here. What's going on?" Craig asked, not really knowing if he was ready for the answer.

"Okay, give me a minute. Don't get ahead of yourself. Want some coffee or anything?" Smitty asked.

"No, I just want to know where my wife is," Craig countered, having difficulty putting up with the detective's taking his own sweet time to tell him what's going on. But he gritted his teeth and kept quiet. He just wanted some information.

"I really don't know where she is. But I'll tell you what I do know. I planned to call you anyway. You know, we discovered that each of you four 'victims' had wives who had been to local ER's with injuries that we believe were inflicted by their husbands or the kidnapping 'victims.'"

"I told you how Felicia's cut happened!" Craig argued. "I don't know about those other jerks, but as far as my house is concerned, there's no goddamn wife beating going on!"

"Mr. Jernigan, I don't intend to argue with you about that. We have proof, and we know exactly what's been going on behind your closed doors and the other three too. And I assure you, we'll talk about that later, and you will undoubtedly face charges. But for now, let's get back to the matter at hand. We don't have all the details, but at this point, we do know who was responsible for the abductions and the beatings. As of now, we have Gabby in custody."

This information put Jernigan on his butt. He leaned back on his chair and sat for a minute, assimilating the new information and thinking about what to say next. "Well, tell me. Who is he?"

"We don't know if anybody else is involved. We still think there was someone else helping, or coordinating or something, but we have both evidence and a confession that Gabby is none other than your mother-in-law, Dr. Ellie Conlin."

CHAPTER 35

FELICIA DROVE SOUTH

Felicia drove south into Dallas to hide out while she did some very private thinking. She turned right onto Loop 12 and pulled into the first hotel she passed, a new high-rise Embassy Suites. She could stay there a few days. They would feed her and let her veg out for a while. She gave no concern to the possibility that someone could track her credit cards and find her. *If they wanted her that bad, let them come,* she thought.

She had not had time to give this trip any planning and so brought nothing with her. But the hotel had room service all night, and there was a K-Mart a block away, where she could pick up the bare necessities for a couple of days' hideaway. But first, she needed to pick up some cash, so she drove through the outside drive-through ATM and withdrew $500, the daily limit for her account. She could get more tomorrow. She thought she may even decide to clean out the account but had to think about it. That was an extreme step, and once she did that, it would be hard to change her mind.

She registered under her own name and decided to go ahead and pay with a credit card. She asked the clerk not to put any calls through and not to tell anyone she was registered but to let her know if anyone called. She told her that she was trying to get away from an old boyfriend and needed some privacy. The clerk was very understanding as if she had experienced the same kind of breakup herself. Felicia felt as if she had found a friend.

Instead of going to her room, she went to the K-Mart and did some shopping. She bought a supply of all the personal items she could think of and then a couple of pants and blouse combos that really looked pretty good. She didn't take time for her usual shopping pickiness. Sometimes she would spend a full day without buying a single article, not finding exactly what she wanted. Today it was jeans and blouse, underwear, and a bathing suit. May as well relax by the pool so long as she was there anyway.

Then she picked up a magazine, the Dallas Morning News, and a book. She was a John Grisham fan, and his latest volume had just come out. For some reason, she thought she might even be able to get some reading in. She really had no idea how long she would be there. But she knew one thing for sure. Things were going to be different, no matter what decisions she made. She never opened the book.

She didn't think anyone official, like the sheriff's department, would be looking for her very soon. It would seem obvious to everybody that she had simply gone off on her own, and police don't look for runaway wives. So it would be Craig and her mother wondering where she was. And she knew they would probably just sit back and wait at least for a couple of days, figuring she would finally make contact.

She was partially right. She had run out of the jail so fast that she had completely forgotten about her mother's bail. Well, she could just cool her heels in jail for a day or two. She's a big girl, and she can get her lawyer to do the bail.

"Get her lawyer," she said out loud. She never imagined she would be saying those words about her mother.

In the meantime, Ellie had in fact gotten a visit from her lawyer. Mandy Jensen, of Jensen and Associates, came to see her three hours after she called. She was in a hearing, so couldn't make it any quicker. She came into the interview room, introduced herself, and asked what she could do to help.

"I got your name from the Women's Shelter," Ellie said. "I'm Dr. Ellie Conlin. Call me Ellie. I've gotten myself into a jam and really need help."

"Good to know you. I've heard your name. Aren't you in practice in Richardson?"

"Yes, I've been there ever since I finished my residency."

Jensen was a very attractive, neatly dressed woman. She came directly from the hearing, wearing her courtroom uniform, a pinstriped charcoal grey suit, white blouse, and contrasting red scarf. Her hair was pulled up into a loose French braid, beginning to suffer the wear of almost ten hours of activity. She wore comfortable but still proper three-inch black heels. Her only jewelry was a watch and diamond stud earrings. She looked at her notes as she began the interview.

"So why are you here?" Jensen asked, already knowing the answer to the question, having reviewed the police reports while she waited for Ellie to be brought out.

"I understand they think you had something to do with the four abductions that I've heard so much about the past few weeks. Wasn't there a reporter, and a cop? I don't remember the others. Tell me about it."

"Yes, that's what they think." Ellie liked her straightforward, no-beating around the bush approach to the interview, and felt like she had made a correct choice in calling her firm. She also appreciated that Jensen made no assumptions of innocence or guilt, she simply want to hear Ellie's story.

"Goodness, where do I start? I recently learned that my daughter, Felicia, has been in an abusive relationship, especially when her husband has been drinking. I took her in for stitches once, and apparently it's been going on for a good while. I just couldn't stand to see her hurt."

"So what happened? What did you do?"

"Well, I've decided to say it straight. I'm the Gabby that you've been reading about in the papers. I took my son-in-law out and beat him up. Of course, he's bigger than me—isn't everybody? So I snuck up on him and used a stun baton to subdue him. I tied him up and hooded him so he wouldn't know who I was, and I never spoke to him, he would recognize my voice. Then I pulled him into my old VW bus, with a winch, and took him out to a house way away from civilization, and beat the hell out of him. Later on, I sent him an anonymous e-mail from Kinko's, to explain why he had been beaten up."

Jensen was as stunned as everybody else had been at this news. When she received the call, she half-expected to hear about some type of problems that harried physicians tend to get into, like IRS problems, fraud, drugs, alcohol, or something similar. She was blown over at what she heard.

"First thing we have to do is get you out of here. They've only charged you with felony assault and battery, so the bond is only $5,000. These kind of charges usually go to scumbags who don't have any money, so the bond isn't usually too bad. They don't expect to file these charges on practicing physicians. They started to charge you with attempted murder, but it's pretty obvious you had no intent to kill him, so they left that off. That would have jacked up the bond quite a bit. Can you pay that bond, or do we need a bonding agent?"

"Oh! I can pay that. They have my checkbook, in my purse," Ellie answered.

After the bonding, she got her belongings back, changed into her own clothes, and left in Jensen's car. She was anxious to get home, shower, and change clothes to something clean. She wasn't accustomed to wearing clothes for two days, much less three.

"Let's go to my office," Jensen said. "One question came to me though. There were four guys who got abducted, weren't there? I know the assistant DA, and there were a couple more. Where do you fit in with that? Your charges said four counts of assault and battery. Do they think you did all four of the 'victims?'"

"Well, I saw how easy it was and heard about some other wives in the same boat as my daughter. My friends in the ER's told me about some guys you would never imagine, who were battering their wives. So I guess I just decided to give them a taste of the same medicine I gave Craig. Then they all got the same e-mail, telling them why they were chosen for their own 'home schooling.' And it's worked, so far. None of the men have touched their wives since they got the e-mails"

"You know that for a fact?" Jensen asked. "What did that e-mail exactly say, anyway?"

"It told them why they were abducted and told them we would be watching and that their treatment would be repeated if they ever hit their wives again, and the second time would be worse than the first."

"Well, anything worse would be fatal, wouldn't it?" Jensen commented.

"That was the plan. Scare them into being good little boys or indeed think they might not survive the second course of study."

"Okay, terroristic threat, maybe. That might not have been such a good idea, depending on how it's worded." Jensen said. "But maybe not. Did you say the e-mails were sent anonymously?"

"Yes, but I've already confessed. They know it was me," Ellie answered.

"So you've confessed already? To everything?" Jensen asked. "My god! Why didn't you wait till you talked to me?"

"I thought this out and decided to confess and to let the judge or whoever decide what to do with me. I decided if I went to jail, that would be better than seeing Felicia come in DOA, when it's too late to do anything. I've given them permission to search my home, office, car. I've told them where my old VW bus is, and all the equipment I used."

"I still wish you had called me first. But spilled milk, you know. Our approach—we have to convince the jury and the judge that you only did what any reasonable mother would do in the same situation. The problem there is that of all the reasonable mothers in the world, who have abused daughters, none of them have done this, so that may be a rough point to argue."

"How does a trial go when you've already confessed?" Ellie asked.

"In such a case, there's no trial on the issue of guilt because that is already established," Jensen explained. "The only thing you need a trial for then is to decide punishment. And it might help us to make a point of comparing your assault and battery with the assault and battery that the wives were all subjected to by their husbands. And repeatedly, I might add. It will also help somewhat that you've been completely cooperative with the police."

They sat quietly for a few minutes while Jensen drove to her office on Preston Road, about forty-five minutes from the jail in Lewisville.

"Lord, have mercy on my soul!" Jensen said, almost under her breath, as she turned into the parking lot at her office. It was a high-rise modern building seemingly covered by glass. Conlin didn't respond to her comment.

CHAPTER 36

ELLIE'S ARRAIGNMENT . . .

Ellie's arraignment was a week later. Judge Jason Thompson read the charges, aggravated assault and battery, four counts, and asked for her plea.

"Guilty, your honor," Conlin answered. She was dressed in a dark blue-grey pinstriped pantsuit with an open white collar and a pale blue scarf. She wore three-inch heels. She wanted to look professional and feminine but not exotic. She didn't want or need to look like a bully. In fact, she looked like just another lawyer in the court.

"Well, this was pretty easy, I must say," said Judge Thompson. He set trial for three months later. For Jensen, the trial would simply be to argue the mitigating circumstances and to try to get as low a punishment as possible.

By then, word had gotten out that Gabby was arrested. The news had also publicized her identification. It was difficult for Craig's paper to publish this information without maligning one of its own. When his editor learned who Gabby was and why Craig had been abducted, he suggested Craig be transferred to a sister newspaper in another area. But he had difficulty getting the sister editor to agree, so he placed him on paid administrative leave.

At the time of her mother's trial, Felicia had not returned home yet. But even though she was still angry at her mother for what she did, she had at least decided that she did it out of love for her daughter. A very confusing conundrum, to say the least.

Craig tried to contact Felicia several times, but she was unable to accept his calls. Finally, after several sessions of counseling, she decided to give him one more chance. At her counselor's suggestion, she agreed to talk to him if he stopped drinking, became active in AA, and underwent abuser counseling. And she refused to get into any more of a relationship than simply talking, in public places, until he had proven he was serious. To her, that meant one year of sobriety and counseling. He agreed.

Gabby became the talk of the town for the communities of Lewisville and Richardson. Two very different attitudes seemed to predominate. Some felt that Conlin had done wrong, taking the law into her own hands and to those she became known as the "Vigilante Doc." As expected, most of those were men, and it was suspected that some of them may have had attitudes toward women that were similar to the "victims."

But the majority of people thought of her as a hero, a mama grizzly who had only protected her cub. Posters were displayed: "Gabby Getcha' Gun." "Don't Mess with Texas Mamas." A group developed who called themselves the Barn Contingent, advocating the old technique of "take him out behind the barn" to teach him a lesson. The gay and lesbian community got behind Ellie with a march to protest her charges. With no action on Ellie's part, legal fund contributions started coming in. A bank account was set up, and by the time of her trial, a quarter of a million dollars had accumulated. Ellie was grateful and promised that any money left over after her defense fees would be donated to the Women's Outreach Shelter.

There was a surge, at least locally, in the sale of stun guns and personal firearms. Classes for self-protection, especially involving instruction in the use of firearms, increased substantially, primarily for women. Applications for concealed gun licenses tripled.

There was also a surge in applications for protection, both in women's shelters in north Texas as well as in the courts. There were several groups who asked Dr. Conlin to speak to their memberships, but Jensen refused to allow that until after the punishment had been decided. She did not want anyone to suggest that Conlin had planned to get famous from what she did.

Conlin was not at all interested in publicity or fame from her activities. What she really wanted was just to go back to her home and her practice. But the practice was impossible for now. She had to concentrate on working with her attorney and getting through this mess. She did what she did to protect her daughter and because it needed to be done, she thought. For no other reason.

She never in her wildest imagination suspected that she would become some form of folk hero. She just wanted her daughter to be safe.

The Texas Medical Board became aware of Conlin's charges but did nothing about her license until a final judgment was made. In Texas, a physician who is convicted of a felony loses her license to practice medicine. But the board wisely waits until the final judgment is in, to avoid damaging a physician who is finally judged innocent. Dr. Conrad Murray, for example, had an unrestricted license to practice medicine in Texas until his final conviction in Michael Jackson's death.

CHAPTER 37

CONLIN'S TRIAL

Conlin's trial, to decide only the punishment issue, lasted just two days. Jensen recommended a jury trial but had to explain to Ellie that she could waive that if she wanted to and leave her fate up to the judge alone. Ellie insisted on a bench trial where only the judge made the decisions. It would probably have been difficult to find an unbiased jury panel anyway. And the district attorney's office would probably suffer untold reputational damage from prosecuting someone who beat up one of their assistant DAs. Especially when it was known to everyone by that time that the reason he was beaten was that he was a wife beater. In all, it seemed better for everyone, and everyone breathed a sigh of relief when it was realized that there wouldn't be a jury trial.

In his previous legal life before becoming a district judge, Thompson had been a defense attorney and had defended several wife beaters. It had always left him with a bad taste in his mouth, and he never really felt good about it. But a lawyer has to protect bad guys as well as good guys, so he did his job competently, freeing men who really should not be freed.

One case caused him to change his approach to domestic violence. Seven years ago he had defended a local man for wife abuse and had been successful, taking the approach that the wife instigated the beatings and getting him a probated sentence. Six months later, that wife had been brought to the ER comatose and had died after a touch-and-go week in intensive care. He had never gotten over that, and never defended another man in a domestic violence case. That, in fact, was probably the single most important factor in his deciding to get out of the criminal defense business and run for judge.

Since becoming a judge, he had subconsciously tried to right that by meting out reasonable punishment for abusers. But he was also fair—he encouraged abuser counseling and many times had seen men who really did change their stripes, respond to counseling, and become good husbands.

But this was different. This was uncharted territory, and Jensen couldn't predict how Judge Thompson would feel toward someone who in fact was a vigilante. Even though he was sympathetic toward abused women, he still had to deal with the reality of the case. Self-defense didn't seem to apply. Nobody had ever threatened Dr. Conlin. And defense of a family member didn't work. Felicia had not been in immediate peril. They hadn't even reported it to the police.

And certainly the other three men were no danger to either Conlin or her daughter, so there was no place there for a self defense plea. No, these were planned abductions resulting in serious bodily injury. The area newspapers were having a field day.

Even nationally, talking heads were split into two groups, those who think it's about time somebody did something to punish abusers and to protect their mates. And the other group, which was smaller, who seemed to want to lock Dr. Conlin up and throw away the key.

"We have to show 'these people' that there are legal remedies. They can't just have their own way with the law. Where are the controls? These 'poor men' almost died at the vigilante's hands. Why, what she did was much worse than anything that any of her 'victims' did."

Yes, in the minds of the antivigilante side, the victims were no longer the wives who had suffered for years at the hands of their abusive husbands but the abusive husbands themselves. The wives' injuries and brutality became only background, and there were few cries for justice for them, only justice for the second-level victims, the abusers.

Jensen tried to keep the judge focused on the abuse that had gone on for such a long time. She asked each of the wives to testify, hoping to keep the judge mindful of who the real victims were in the first place. But the district attorney brought each of the men up for the same purpose on the opposite side. Each one described in detail the horrible experience of being subjected to Dr. Conlin's "Home Schooling Institute."

The testimony went smoothly; there was none of the usual trick questions involved in determining guilt. That was established. All that was left was to decide how many years Dr. Conlin would be locked away. Without the jury, Judge Thompson could streamline the trial to his whim.

After only two days of testimony, the judge closed for the day and promised his decision in the morning. He had researched the question of vigilante justice already and, that afternoon, consulted an old buddy who was an appellate judge. He knew that he couldn't be overturned on the guilt aspect but wanted to avoid criticism if his punishment was not in line with what the appellate court would feel. Then he went home, poured himself a stiff drink, and went his library. He had an opinion to write.

CHAPTER 38

THE JUDGE WAS LATE

The judge was late for the sentencing. But who's going to criticize a judge for being a few minutes late when he holds their future in his hands?

He was actually in the courthouse, in his study, finalizing some wording that he had been having difficulty with. When he came in and the bailiff went through the "all rise!" ritual, he began.

"This is not a simple decision. On the one hand, it seems fairly simple. There is no question of guilt. The defendant has openly confessed her role in the abduction, kidnapping and ritualistic, brutal torture of four men. She was not in fear of her life or safety, and there was nobody she was protecting who was in immediate fear of life or safety. So it would seem that all I have to do is decide the penalty for this degree of assault and battery.

"There is no question of the severity of her victims' injuries. Texas defines "serious bodily injury" as that which leaves permanent disability, loss of a body part, or loss of the function of a body part and injuries which subject a victim to a serious risk of death. There can be no argument that these were serious bodily injuries.

"There was no attempt on the part of the defendant to work within the legal and judicial systems to obtain justice. She never reported any of the alleged abuse to the police. She never advised any of the alleged victims of abuse, except her own daughter, to seek assistance and protection in a Women's Shelter. She never even discussed the alleged abuse with any of the alleged victims except for her own daughter. Instead, the first steps, in fact the only steps, that she took to obtain justice were to make preparations for the kidnapping and torture of the alleged abusers.

"The reason that the state doesn't allow vigilante justice is part of a larger system, to prevent excessive punishments for menial crimes and to determine as accurately as humanly possible where guilt lies in questionable cases. Here, the defendant had good reason to believe who was the abuser of her daughter. However, after that, she acted on the basis only of gossip and third-party rumor. She had no basis but her own unverified belief that the other three of her victims were indeed guilty of any crime at all.

"In our judicial system, we also have balances to help us to avoid making a punishment too harsh for the crime. Here, even if she were correct in her belief that her victims were responsible for physical assaults on their own spouses, she responded with much more vigorous and damaging punishment than any that her victims may have accomplished. Did her punishments fit her victims' alleged crimes? I dare say not.

"On the other hand, are there circumstances which might mitigate the ferocity of her attacks on her victims? We are told that the defendant was overwrought over seeing her daughter in a repeatedly abusive relationship and that she could do nothing about it. In fact, we have been told that she worried that if she confronted victim #1, she risked losing the relationship with her daughter, one of the most prized relationships that can exist. A mother's protection of her child is a strong incentive for action indeed.

"But where is the incentive for her treatment of victims # 2, 3, and 4? She had no dogs in those fights. She simply made the conscious decision to become the sheriff, judge, jury, and executor all in one. So she cold-bloodedly planned her second, third, and fourth kidnappings and horrendous beatings of her next three victims, not really knowing if she was even correct in her assumptions of their guilt. Our judicial system does not allow that type of vigilante justice.

"So how do we make this right? Do we imprison the defendant, who up to now has unarguably been a leader in her community and in her profession? And at the same time let the alleged abusers, who are accused of crimes against their wives and against the State of Texas, run loose without punishment, possibly to continue abusing their wives or to bring the abuse to their next relationships? Do we tell abusers that it's okay to hit their wives and that if anybody tries to strike back, we will protect them and send the person to prison? Or do we pat the defendant on the back and say, 'Good job! You gave them what they deserved.' Neither seems reasonable.

"Once proven guilty or once a guilty plea is entered, the kidnapping and beatings in this case constitute aggravated assault and battery, a second degree felony. In Texas, a second degree felony is punishable by a fine of up to $10,000 and imprisonment for not less than two and not more than twenty years.

"After giving full consideration to all the factors at play in this case, I have to make a decision regarding the defendant's punishment. She has a clear record up to now. She has a responsible position in the community, although once she is convicted of this felony, she will likely lose the license necessary to continue in her chosen field. She was obviously under severe duress, at least regarding the first victim of alleged spousal abuse, her daughter, in that there really was nothing that she could do to protect her. And she has worked with victims of spousal abuse and observed that rarely is any corrective action taken against their alleged abusers.

"On the other hand, it cannot be argued that this was not a premeditated, planned assault and brutal torture of four victims, alleged abusers of their wives. She had no proof of their guilt. She did not enlist the assistance of the police whose job it is to bring justice for such transgressions. She simply appointed herself as a one-woman vigilante force and took out after them alone.

"There was a time in Texas when vigilante justice was more accepted. But in those times, there were not adequate numbers of sheriffs, police officers, and courthouses to satisfy the community's need. So the only solution seemed to be for the community to rise up and protect its people even if it required a lynch mob. But there was a problem. Many innocent men and women paid the ultimate penalty for crimes they did not commit. And many others paid penalties much more severe than their crimes warranted, whether guilty or not. This is one of the hazards of letting the wronged person handle the punishment herself.

"My decision, then, takes all these things into account and will likely still be severely criticized by persons on both sides of the controversy.

"Would the defendant please stand?"

Slowly, Dr. Conlin stood up, with Jensen standing by her side. Conlin was sweating and began to shiver. She had thought she could take this calmly but now that the moment was here, she found herself scared. Felicia was in a seat in the front of the courtroom, directly behind her mother. She reached out and touched her shoulder, wanting to give her some support. The courtroom was very quiet, except for the murmur of pens on paper from many reporters who realized the impact this decision would have.

The courtroom was overflowing and about fifty people watched in the jury prep room on closed-circuit television. The four abduction victims were there with their wives. It was too early to tell exactly what the revelations of abuse would do to their relationships, but today at least, the relationships were as strained as they had ever been. But none of the four men had raised a hand to his wife since he received the e-mail from the Home Schooling Institute. Each man sat with his wife, but the couples were scattered, not sitting together. They had not communicated with each other since Gabby's identity had been determined. Now each cast an occasional sheepish glance toward each of the others, wondering.

Representatives of area women's shelters were there. Lesbian leaders strained to hear the punishment verdict, hoping for compassion in the judge's decision. Dr. Ken Perdue was there. He had always supported Ellie, both because of their long friendship as well as his own attitude toward abusive husbands. Nadine McCarty and several other nurses sat together, praying that the judge would be lenient.

Carol and Jeremy sat at the back of the courtroom. Jeremy was one of the closet abusers, who in his day was active but in later years had stopped drinking and mellowed, and now they finally were able to coexist peacefully. Somewhere in their relationship there was some love, but a lot of it had been burned out by years of maltreatment.

As the judge neared his pronouncement of Dr. Conlin's fate, the people in the jury prep room got even quieter. A cell phone rang, and fifty heads angrily turned at once, glaring at the offender, as if to say, "Take the battery out of that damn thing. Don't let it go off again."

CHAPTER 39

THE JUDGE STOPPED

The judge stopped and cleared his throat and then took a sip of water from the pitcher that was always placed on his desk.

"Ellie Conlin, you have pled guilty to four counts of kidnapping and aggravated assault and battery. You are hereby sentenced to a fine of $8,000 and to two years in the state prison. You will be given credit for time served. Court is dismissed."

He immediately got up and walked to his chambers to avoid the clamor which undoubtedly would follow. He avoided the reporters.

Felicia ran to her mother, trying to put her arms around her. Both were crying. They were not allowed such touching however. Correction officers stepped forward and placed handcuffs on her hands and led her out of the courtroom.

Craig made his way slowly to Felicia's side. In the recent months, awaiting trial, he had been doing his best to regain his life. He had tried to comply with her requests, and had started attending AA. He had been sober for two months. He tried to put his arm around Felicia, but she wasn't ready for that. Not from him anyway. She drew back, turned toward the exit, crying, and ran out of the courthouse to her car.

EPILOGUE

THE JERNIGANS

Craig and Felicia Jernigan separated and later divorced. Craig was able to keep his job, on six months probation. He continued with his AA group, at the encouragement of his employer, and entered an abusers' counseling program, sponsored by the Women's Outreach Shelter. Three years after his abduction and with eighteen months of sobriety under his belt, Felicia allowed him back into her life. He worked the twelve-step program even to the point of step #9, apologizing to all those he had hurt.

First on his list of amends was Felicia. She was reluctant but agreed to reconsider after he had proved himself by being clean and dry for six months. Second was Dr. Conlin. He visited her in prison, asked for her forgiveness, and was relieved when she granted it.

Third was Charlie Ross, Chicken-shit Charlie. It was hard to find him and even harder to talk with him. But Craig finally convinced him that he was sincere, was able to get him into his AA program, and agreed to be his sponsor. He went with him personally to his boss, told the truth about his encounter with Ross, and helped him get his old job back. Since then, Craig and Charlie became good friends and attended meetings together regularly.

Felicia became a counselor at the Women's Outreach Shelter. Craig has maintained his abstinence.

Craig finally proved to Felicia that he was sincere in his abstinence, remaining sober for more than two years. They started over, dated for a year, and finally remarried. At last report, their relationship was succeeding.

He never hit Felicia again.

THE JACOBS

Carmen and Farley Jacobs weren't so lucky. In the aftermath of his rehabilitation from his injuries, it was discovered that he had two prior girlfriends and one ex-wife whom he had also abused. The publicity destroyed his self-image and threw him into a depression. After a short time of coming to work drunk, he lost his job, and his wife divorced him. At last report, he was selling used cars for Landmark Chevrolet. Carmen went on and, at last report, had begun cautiously to date an old high school friend.

However, Farley never hit Carmen again.

THE FERRELLS

Andrea and Ben Ferrell decided to tough it out alone. Neither went into counseling but rather settled back into a life of trying to cope. Two years following the trial, they divorced. Ben kept his job on the police force, and Andrea enrolled in Lone Star College, seeking training as a paralegal.

However, he never hit Andrea again.

THE THOMPSONS

Jack and Sara tried to improve their marriage and entered into counseling. However, Jack felt he would lose his coaching job, so he resigned before his record could be completely destroyed by his being fired. They moved to Borger, Oklahoma, near Sara's parents and tried to start over. However, the stress proved too much. In the next six months, Sara was in the ER several times for injuries of various sorts. Eighteen months after arriving at Borger, she was brought in unresponsive with a severe head injury. Despite competent attempts at the ER, she died without regaining consciousness after a week in a coma.

Jack was convicted of second degree murder and sentenced to ten years in prison. In his sixth year in prison, he was killed by members of a prison gang. He would have been up for parole in just six months.

DR. ELLIE CONLIN

Dr. Conlin was an exemplary inmate. She worked in the prison infirmary and took care of many women who were victims of abuse themselves. She wrote a book while there. The Texas Medical Board suspended her medical license with a proviso that she could reapply after completion of all obligations under her sentence but was not guaranteed that she would ever practice medicine again. She was paroled after eighteen months behind bars. Felicia visited her regularly, and when she and Craig reestablished their relationship, they visited her together.

After she completed probation, she reapplied to the board. She was initially denied her license but told that she could be reconsidered after she completed a year of postgraduate education and twenty hours of ethics education successfully. She applied to residency programs in the area and was accepted. She essentially did another year of internship. She reapplied and this time was granted her license. She returned to her same home in Richardson and to the same medical office. She developed an office-based practice and never applied for hospital privileges.

She became a fairly popular speaker, being requested to discuss women's issues and especially victimized women. She was a frequent guest on local and even national talk shows, especially those starring women.

She never married or even dated.

THE "VICTIMS"

After their "education" by the Home Schooling Institute, other than Jack Thompson, none of the remaining three kidnapping victims ever again raised their hands to their wives or to any other woman.

THE AFTERMATH

The news of Dr. Conlin's sentencing and imprisonment hit the national news with a vengeance. Her trial and sentence were broadcast on all four major news networks and UPI. She was discussed on each of the news talk shows and even became a folk hero for the nighttime comics. Jay Leno and David Letterman each talked about what she had done, making jokes about a Texas woman's method of teaching a good old boy a lesson he won't forget.

Felicia was invited to appear on *Good Morning, America*. She made a decision to decline all such publicity until her mother was out of prison.

Ellie began to receive letters of support from women's groups and well-wishers across the country. She also received a few letters from people who wished she had been given the ten-year limit or even more.

Nine months after her sentencing, a report came from Omaha, Nebraska. A man there was knocked out, taken to a distant area, and beaten. It was later discovered that his wife had been in the University of Nebraska ER several times that year with injuries that she wouldn't discuss but that looked suspicious for repeated assaults. His assailant was never caught. The man never struck his wife again.

Three months later, reports came almost simultaneously from the Seattle, Washington area and from Lone Grove, Oklahoma, of men who were kidnapped and beaten. The Washington man left the area immediately after being released from the hospital, never to return. The Oklahoma man went back home to his wife. She never returned to the ER.

During the following year, there was virtually an explosion of reports from various states and cities in the United States of men being kidnapped and beaten. A few had histories of abuse already known. Most of the men's abuse, however, was unknown to the public and even to their families.

But apparently someone did know. The women knew. Friends can tell when something is wrong. Best girl friends tell best girl friends. And best girl friends go home and tell their own boyfriends or husbands. A web of stories is woven. Most stories were simply hashed and rehashed, and like so many times before, nothing was done. Everybody only hoped the abusers would quit. But every once in a while, somebody just gets fed up, watching a loved one harassed and beaten by a good-for-nothing man.

The reports were remarkably similar, seemingly copied from the UPS reports of Dr. Conlin. The men were stunned or restrained by some similar device—a stun gun, a two-by-four, a club. Then, while they were unconscious, they were tied up and hooded and taken to a remote location. There they were subjected to varying levels of Home Schooling 1.01. Their captors were all completely quiet, just like Gabby. They all stopped just short of irreversible injury or death.

That is, until the case outside Laramie, Wyoming. A service station manager was abducted and beaten. He suffered not only broken bones but a skull fracture and head injury. He was left in his yard in February and wasn't discovered for almost six hours. The combination of his injuries and his exposure to the Wyoming winter cold was too much. He died two days after he arrived at the hospital, a combination of head injury and exposure to cold. His assailant was never discovered.

At last report, not one of the kidnapers was caught.

THE TRUE STORY OF BRENDA (NOT HER TRUE NAME)

I had been out of the air force for about four years and was practicing in the North Texas area in my home town, Denison. Brenda came in as an acute problem visit with heavy vaginal bleeding. She was a sixteen-year-old runaway from out of state. She was having a miscarriage. She was brought in by a thirty-six-year-old man, whom she described as her rescuer.

We took care of the miscarriage, but her story didn't pass the smell test. I was able to get her away from her escort and asked her about her situation. She was unwilling to talk about her problems at home that made her run away but adamantly denied that her rescuer had gotten her pregnant. In fact, she proclaimed that he had rescued her from a life on the streets.

I was suspicious and told her so. But without her willingness to talk, what could I do?

I told her as I always do in such a situation that I believed her but didn't really believe her and gave her a card to the Women's Shelter. I promised her that anytime in the future if she needed help, just call me and say, "This is Brenda." I promised her that I would always remember her, and my door would always be open.

About two or three years later, without calling me personally, Brenda made an appointment in my office for a well woman/birth control visit. She was about eighteen years old then and had a small baby. She seemed to be dressed like a little girl playing mommy and dressing in mommy's clothes. She had on a pair of aging red high heels and a dress that sort of matched but was a size or two too tight. She had on a little too much makeup, but it was neatly applied.

She told me that she had married the man who originally brought her to my office. She just couldn't give him too much praise, saying he was the best thing that ever happened to her. He had found her when she was in trouble and had protected her from all the bad things in the world.

Again, I told her I believed her but didn't *really* believe her. And again, I reaffirmed that she could call me any time whenever she needed help or whenever she needed to talk. I wished her luck and told her that I hoped that her life was as good as she said.

About a year later, I received a call at home, on a Friday evening. The caller said, "This is Brenda." I knew immediately what was going on.

I greeted her, "Hi, Brenda! How are you?"

"Oh, fine," she initially claimed.

We chatted a minute or two, and I asked her what she was calling about.

"Well, I've been having these headaches," she answered, and I asked the usual doctorly questions, how long, how severe, what home remedies has she tried, any relationship to her periods.

"That's the other thing. I've been bleeding."

"Brenda," I said. "You didn't call me to tell me about headaches or funny periods. What's going on?"

She didn't answer my question. I heard a TV in the background.

"Are you able to talk, Brenda?" I asked.

"Not really," she almost whispered.

"Then let me ask you some yes or no questions. Is that okay?"

"Yes," she said.

"Are you safe right now?"

"Yes, I'm pretty sure."

"Is your husband there with you?"

"Yes."

"Is your head hurting because of something he did?"

"Yes."

"Are you bleeding right now?"

"No, I got it stopped."

"Can we set up a time to talk tomorrow? Does he go to work?"

I learned that he did go to work every day, but the times were not completely predictable. But we arranged for her to call my private line when she had a few minutes of privacy.

She called again Saturday afternoon, the next day. She told me that she lived in a nice three-bedroom brick house, fairly new, with all the modern conveniences a young wife and mother needs. But it was directly behind her husband's filling station. He had installed a large glass window in the back of the building so that he could watch the front of her house. He had a shotgun aimed at the circle driveway of the house at all times.

She was essentially imprisoned in the house. She was allowed to leave only to visit her husband's parents. He did the grocery shopping and all other trips away from the house. She had not been in touch with her own parents since she ran away at age fifteen.

Denison, Texas, is about four miles from the Red River and Oklahoma and is the town where Dwight Eisenhower was born. During high school, I threw the paper route that passed his birth home, which by then had been turned into a museum.

Brenda lived just across the river in Oklahoma. I asked her if she knew someone who lived nearby that she could trust. As I expected, she had met no one. I asked her about a minister, and she told me that she had gone to a church a few times but didn't know if the minister knew her or not.

So I called the minister at the church she had attended. He didn't recognize her name but agreed to help if he could. So I worked with the local Women's Shelter to set up a rapid drive-by to pick her up. We synchronized our watches and agreed that the minister would pass through her circle driveway at a predetermined time Sunday afternoon. At that time, Brenda was to have her child ready and to throw everything that she could pack into a garbage bag (she didn't have any luggage; you don't need luggage if you don't go anywhere). She was to run out to the minister's car, throw the garbage bag and the baby into the backseat, jump in, and ride with him over the Lake Texoma bridge to Denison. There, we had volunteers from the Women's Shelter waiting, ready to place her in a motel under an assumed name until we could get her out of town.

The rescue went without a hitch. Although I helped set it up, I wasn't involved with the actual rescue.

Once we determined that she was safe, though, we had an opportunity to talk privately. She told me something about the extent of her imprisonment. She was regularly punished for any infraction of her husband's rules. He frequently grabbed her hair and threw her into whatever was handy. In the most recent attack, her husband pulled her by the hair onto the driveway and banged her head into the front fender of his car. That was what she was talking about when she said she was bleeding but had gotten it to stop. She had packed her eyebrow laceration with talc to make it stop bleeding. He wouldn't allow her to go to a doctor or emergency room. Not with that kind of injury, at least.

She also told me that it wasn't her periods that were irregular but that he was poking toys into her, things that didn't belong there, and that was making her bleed. I knew we were doing the right thing to help her.

The Women's Shelter at that time didn't have an actual shelter building but had funds for temporary motel bills and for bus fare. They paid for Brenda's room until she could figure out what to do. She made calls to distant relatives that she hadn't seen for years and found an aunt and uncle in the Midwest who agreed to make her welcome. So the Shelter bought her a one-way ticket, and after a couple of days of rest, she and her baby were put on the bus.

As she was leaving, I told her I would like to hear from her. I wanted to know if she was safe.

Five years later I received a card from her, stating that she was safe, he had never found her. It was signed simply, "Thanks. Brenda."

That was twenty-five years ago. I have not heard from her since.

If she reads this book, I would love to hear from her again.

THE TRUE STORY OF JANET (NOT HER REAL NAME)

Janet was a young woman with pelvic pain due to endometriosis who had been seeing me for several years for attempts to control her pain. She was a typical endometriosis patient. She had severely debilitating pain with her periods as well as pain with intercourse. She was not interested in having any more than the two girls that she already had. But her husband, Bill, had always wanted a boy.

Finally, after trying to relieve her pain with all the conservative methods at my disposal, I offered her a hysterectomy as a last resort method, hoping to cure the pain.

The difficulty with sex was the final blow for an already-troubled marriage. The combination of alcohol and sexual frustration led to progressively worsening brutality. After hearing about the problem for more than two years, and her husband persistently refusing counseling, I encouraged Janet to divorce him. She reluctantly agreed. But the surgery must come first, she felt.

At the hospital, Bill presented the image of the concerned husband. But as Janet was wheeled to the operating room, he leaned over the bed and whispered into her ear, "I know you are having this operation just so you won't have to have any more babies with me."

The operation was a success, and the pain was gone. I didn't hear from her for two or three more years. Then she came in for her annual checkup. Remembering her previous problems with Bill, I asked her how it was going.

"I took your advice," she said. "I got the divorce—it was final about six months ago. I just couldn't put up with it anymore."

"Are you safe? Has he bothered you anymore?" I asked.

"I think I'm safe," she answered. "I have a restraining order on him. But I guess that doesn't do too much good in the long run. He doesn't seem to pay much attention to it. A couple of weeks ago, I ran across him in a parking lot, and he hit me in front of a policeman. They took him to jail but didn't really do anything about it. He was out in a few hours."

Janet revealed to me that Bill had said the seven most dangerous words that an abusive husband can tell his wife. In a fit of anger, when she had mentioned leaving him, he told her, "If I can't have you, nobody can!"

I was somewhat uneasy about her answers to my questions but didn't feel there was anything else that could be done that hadn't already been done.

Two weeks after her appointment at my office, Janet was pulling into her apartment parking lot after getting off work at 3:00 a.m. The lot was well lighted but did not have controlled access. As she pulled into the lot, a car facing her started up and began pulling out. As they passed each other, driver's window to driver's window, Bill rolled his window down, pointed a pistol at her, and shot her in the left temple. She died instantly. An hour later, he called her mother and told her, "Well, I killed the bitch."

To show support for Janet's family, I attended part of the trial. Bill was convicted and sentenced to forty-five years in prison.

I felt confused and frustrated that we hadn't done more to protect Janet. But if a man decides to kill somebody, there is not much anybody can do about it. Or is there . . .

Edwards Brothers Malloy
Oxnard, CA USA
December 11, 2013